PRAISE FOR *SACRED CHOICES*

Sacred Choices was a really great story. The characters are confronted with important life-changing choices that the average person hears about all the time. Anyone can relate to the conflict that each character is facing. But each one makes their choice with the knowledge they have at the time. The characters and their stories have stayed with me and I look forward to hearing more about them in future work.

The story brings in a study of history and culture, which can be relevant at any time and is certainly relevant today. Along with that is the differences in viewpoint from one generation to another. But ultimately it shows that in many ways, we are all alike and are only different because of the choices we make.

~DIANE MUELLER, MSLIS

The author kept me interested from the beginning to the end. I am an avid reader and if the plot line is too simplistic I get bored. This did not happen with *Sacred Choices*. I identified with all the female characters especially Judith. The setting of the story mainly takes place in a small town in Mexico near the site of the apparition of Our Lady of Guadalupe. The way the author incorporated the spiritual into the story was my favorite part. I am looking forward to a second book with the same characters and a few new ones. I would highly recommend it to anyone.

~SUSANNE L. LOE

Sacred Choices is a heart-warming, well-written story with a difference. Smart and career-minded Ceren, an adjunct Professor in Art History, still falls for her boss, the Dean of the Humanities Department. Pregnant and feeling betrayed by the man she loves, she is adeptly transferred by him to Mexico where she is assigned to work as assistant to Dr. Judith Truman. Bitter and twisted since having an abortion in her twenties, Judith does not intend to make life easy for Ceren.

Sacred Choices centers around the book they are writing on Our Lady of Guadalupe and Ceren's inner turmoil as she tries to decide whether to have an abortion or to keep the baby she is carrying. A giggling girl in a white dress will captivate you as she teases both Ceren and Judith. The author combines history, religion, culture and the supernatural into a very enjoyable novel.

~RITA LEE CHAPMANON

This is a very compelling and interesting story about a woman and a difficult choice. Her inner struggle is framed by her family, colleagues, and her research into pre-Columbian Mexico. There is Tlaciaualtepetl, a pyramid that became overgrown with weeds, hiding its true identity. There is also Tepeyac, where the goddess Tonatzin was worshiped. Is this the origin of our Lady of Guadalupe? Find out in this poignant book about a young woman who is at a crossroad in life.

~Douglas W. Tallant

Bartell's book is one that takes a courageous look at an issue of profound importance today, with compassion and understanding, but nonetheless unafraid to face the fundamental questions begging for answers, and too often ignored because they are difficult even to discuss.

The story itself is engaging, at times putting the reader on the edge of his/her seat. Very early on, you begin to care about the heroines and what happens to them. The characters are well-drawn, particularly Judith and even the creepily evasive Jarek (many could swear they've met someone like him before). The basic situation is all-too-common.

But here the story departs from taking the easy way out and plunges headlong into the meat of the matter. Some might be tempted to dismiss the moral framework depicted here as mere personal opinion, but the questions raised are so fundamental and universal that they cannot be dismissed so easily, and the reader owes it to himself/herself to consider them. This divisive issue will never be resolved until everyone can look it squarely in the face as the author has done.

A heavy subject indeed, but still lightened by the hopefulness of the characters, their willingness to look at the big picture, and their desire to provide lasting help rather than a quick, temporary fix. The background story of the religious and cultural traditions of Mexico is interesting and lends relief from the tension of the central problem. All in all, a very enjoyable and worthwhile read that I would recommend to anyone. Looking forward to the sequel!

~PLB on Amazon

Sacred Choices

Other books by Karen Hulene Bartell:

The Sacred Journey Series:
Sacred Gift
Sacred Choices

Belize Navidad
Sovereignty of the Dragons

Coming soon . . .
Peshtigo: River of the Wild Goose
Christmas at the Alamo
Holy Water: Rule of Capture

Sacred Choices

by Karen Hulene Bartell

𝓟
Pen-L Publishing
Fayetteville, Arkansas
Pen-L.com

First Edition Printed and bound in USA
ISBN: 978-1-940222-31-8

Cover design by Peter Bartell
Formatting by Kimberly Pennell

with love and special thanks to Peter

for Justi

Contents

Love Puts the Hope in Tomorrow

"Fairy tales are more than true; not because they tell us that dragons exist, but because they tell us that dragons can be beaten."

~ G.K. Chesterton

September 3: Ceren woke up grinning, knowing. Her chocolate-brown eyes smiled mischievously at her reflection in the dresser's mirror. Her complexion, creamy in the morning light, contrasted against her lustrous, coffee-brown hair.

With a gleeful squeal, she hugged herself, squeezing her knees. Then she reached for the phone to call Jarek.

Mid-air, she paused. With a moan, she pressed her lips into a hard, white line.

No, not yet. He'll want proof. Something 'quantifiable.'

Instead, she set the receiver back in its cradle, closed her eyes, and replayed the dream still fresh in her mind.

She had been chasing a numinous, white snake until it disappeared

1

around a corner. When she rounded the bend, the serpent was gone. All she saw was a beautiful girl, no more than two years old, with long, silky, black hair.

The little stranger had looked up through dark, dancing eyes and said, "Hi." With that one word, she expressed volumes, as if telepathically.

The greeting had resounded, echoing, until it woke Ceren. With a wistful sigh, she wished the encounter had lasted longer.

Was that just a dream or a message? Then the feeling in the pit of her stomach returned, answering her question. Nodding to herself, she smiled.

But proof, I need proof.

ॐ

Ceren took the steps two at a time, her brunette ponytail bouncing against her neck and battered, leather briefcase knocking against the railing. She burst into the Humanities office as a draft caught and slammed the door behind her.

Startled, the office assistant looked up from her paperwork.

"I . . . I ran all the way." Ceren stopped to catch her breath. "Didn't want to be . . . late." Hearing herself, she chuckled at her unintended joke.

From behind thick bi-focals, a mirthless stare greeted her.

Ceren felt her smile droop. *Does she think I'm a student, too?* Her lips instantly curved into a self-conscious smile as she composed herself. Fresh from grad school, she looked to the older woman, to everyone, for acceptance as a university lecturer. Cheeks flushing, she smoothed the wisps of wind-blown tendrils escaping from her tightly pulled-back hair.

"I have a meeting with Dr. Witunski."

"The dean's busy. You need an appointment."

Ceren straightened her shoulders. "I have an appointment. I'm Professor Hernandez." She glanced at the clock above the dean's door, adding, "At three." She watched as the minute hand ticked past the hour.

"You're late." The assistant shuffled a stack of papers, smirking as she thumped them with the stapler.

Its echo told Ceren she was being dismissed, but, taking a deep breath, she stood her ground.

Another cold stare met her. Behind her glasses, the woman rolled her eyes. "Dr. Witunski's in a meeting."

Ceren settled onto the nearest chair. "I'll wait."

"Suit yourself." The assistant gave an indifferent sniff and feigned returning to her paperwork.

Ceren felt the assistant's eyes on her. She took a textbook from her briefcase and pretended to read but instead watched the clock, chafing until she could tell Jarek the news.

The assistant peeked over her bi-focals, appraising her. Eyes narrowed to slits, the assistant sucked her teeth as her lip curled.

Twenty minutes later, the dean's door opened. Anticipation shot through Ceren as she raised her eyes.

Out walked a thirty-something, angular woman dressed in sensible black shoes and a conservative gray suit, its austerity relieved only by a scarf's muted colors.

"We're due at the Pearson's at five," said the woman over her shoulder.

As she crossed in front of Ceren, the assistant said, "Welcome back. How was your stay at the clinic?"

The woman acknowledged her greeting with a smirk. "Lost eight pounds."

"Congratulations!"

What am I, invisible?

When she reached the outer office door, the woman turned back, arched an eyebrow at the dean, and said, "Don't be late."

Even after she closed the door, Ceren stared, her jaw slack. Was that his ex-wife? She knew about her husband's first wife. Jarek had told her what a cold, loveless union it had been. A marriage of convenience, nothing more, he had said.

Besides, that's in the past. I'm Mrs. Jarek Witunski now. She breathed deeply, centering herself on that knowledge. *But what's she doing here?*

The assistant's steely glare drew her attention, causing a flush to start at the base of her neck. Ceren snapped her mouth shut but straightened her shoulders, refusing to cower before the woman's calculating expression.

"No more calls or appointments, Peg." Ceren looked up expectantly at Jarek's voice. He stood in the doorway of the office, his silver-gray hair glinting in the overhead light. "I have to prepare for the inter-departmental meeting."

Ceren's heart quickened, while the phrase 'silver fox' popped into her head. A wide, silver streak in his light-brown, wavy hair added a distinguished elegance to his otherwise boyish appearance. His tanned face sported a few freckles on prominent cheekbones. His cerulean blue eyes caught and held hers as she studied him, trying to read him.

"But I . . . that is, we have . . . had an appointment, remember?" Ceren stood up, never dropping her gaze from his. Only when the book slipped from her lap and clattered to the floor did she break eye contact. She stooped to retrieve the textbook, her cheeks burning a brighter shade than when she had entered.

"Ah, Professor Hernandez." He smiled with a father's indulgent tolerance. "That's right. You'd called earlier, hadn't you?"

"There's no record of it in your appointment book," snapped the assistant, eyes narrowing, observing him over her bifocals.

"Hold all calls please." He gestured Ceren inside and closed the door on the assistant's scowl.

His full lips curled into a half smile. "We wouldn't want to be disturbed now, would we?"

He held out his arms, and she ran to him. Throwing her arms around him, she kissed him as if it had been months, not hours, since she had last seen him. Though reluctant to break the mood, she had to ask.

"Who was that woman that just—"

"So," he interjected, holding her at arm's length as if to see her better, his gaze piercing. "What's so important that you called my cell?"

His shower of attention changed her focus instantly. Remembering her news, she chewed her lower lip and took a deep breath. She felt like a child with a secret: could not wait to share it, yet was unsure how to announce it.

He eyed her expectantly. "Yes . . . ?"

"It's positive!"

Shrugging, he shook his head. "What's positive?" he asked with a quizzical, half laugh.

"I'm . . . we're pregnant!"

"Pregnant!?" Glancing at the closed door, he brought his voice to a hoarse whisper. "What do you mean, we're pregnant?"

Ceren flinched. This was not the reaction she had expected. "The test was positive."

"You're sure?!" he asked, visibly paling beneath his freckles.

"It's confirmed." Proud she had taken the initiative, she added, "It wasn't a home pregnancy test. I just came from the gynecologist, and I'm . . . I mean, we're preg—"

"You're sure it's mine?" he interrupted, his voice gruff.

"Of . . . of course, I'm sure it's yours . . . . What are you implying?"

"Nothing, nothing at all," he said, hugging her close, stroking her back. "I'm just surpr . . . so incredibly happy."

"You doubt it's your baby?" Her joy stolen, she felt suddenly empty, barren. She pulled back, watching his expression.

"Of course not, how could I? Nothing could be farther from my thoughts." As his eyes roamed the room, his arms grasped her, enfolding her. "You're an elixir to me, Ceren. With you, I'm ten years younger. Anything's possible."

"Do you mean that, Doc . . . Jarek?" In private, he was Jarek, but, on campus, he preferred that she call him Dr. Witunski. To be alone with him at the university was a first, blurring the distinction between private and public. She shook her head as if to settle her thoughts. Why be shy about using his first name? We're certainly on a first-name basis . . . especially now. She raised her eyes to watch his response.

While his lips smiled, his eyes remained aloof, distant, as if his thoughts were elsewhere. "Of course, I mean that. The world's ours . . .

which reminds me. I have news of my own that I hope you'll find just as exciting as I do."

"What? Tell me!" Delicious thoughts swirled through her mind as her heart leapt. Tell everyone? End the secrecy of their marriage? Take that honeymoon he had promised?

He paused as his eyes shifted from bookcase to file cabinet to desk, but his prolonged delay only increased her anticipation.

"Don't keep me in suspense. Is this a game? You want me to guess?" She watched his eyes settle on a stack of paperwork. All she could make out was the word 'Mexico.' "I know! You're taking me on our hon—"

"It wasn't easy," he began slowly, as if searching for his words, "but I secured you a place on the Writing-Across-the-Curriculum, inter-departmental grant." Responding to her blank stare, he added, "How do you like that?!"

She opened her mouth to answer, but no words came out. Except for a small gasp, she remained silent.

He began speaking faster as his eyes drilled into hers. "It was a challenge convincing the review board to add a new adjunct professor to Dr. Truman's project. But I persuaded the foundation that, with your Hispanic background, excellent Spanish, and most importantly, expertise in Religious Art History, you have all the necessary credentials. In fact, you're the only woman for this job." He held her at arm's length, looking at her. "What do you think?"

"But—"

"Just think," he said. "This faculty-exchange program with Mexico will give you the opportunity to lecture and conduct your research at a foreign university. What a once-in-a-lifetime experience for you. Plus, you'll come back a published author."

"But that would mean being apart. I don't—"

"Only long enough for the gossip to settle down." His eyes met hers.

"I still don't see why we have to keep our marriage a secret," she said, unable to keep the disappointment from tingeing her tone. Glancing at the door, she grimaced. "I'm your wife, yet even your office assistant thinks I'm a student. Why this charade?"

"There are some in the academic world who wouldn't understand us marrying so soon after my divorce."

"I want to tell the world—"

"You can when you come back from Mexico. We'll be together, a prestigious academic team."

"But you'd said—"

"We'll start fresh, no encumbrances." He held her closer, and she gazed into his azure blue eyes, unable to see past them to his thoughts. "Think of it. You'll be on your way to becoming a full professor at this university with this feather in your cap."

"We'll have a baby to consider—"

"That's right," he said, working his jaw. "We'll be raising a family."

His lips curling in a smile, he bent his head to kiss her. His long kiss left her weak-kneed, yearning for more, yet the pause gave her time to think. The baby would be showing in two, three months.

"How long," she cleared her throat, "how long would this faculty-exchange program last?"

"Only until the end of the semester, maybe less, just long enough for the paperwork to be finalized."

"What paperwork?"

"For the annulment," he said.

"But you said—"

"And . . . just for the interim . . . it might be best if we kept the news of this between us." He winked as his hand gently gripped her belly.

"What do you mean? I'll be showing soon. Whether or not we announce it, everyone will see for themselves. Why can't we share our news now?"

"How do you think that would look to my wife's lawyers?"

His choice of words irked her, and she pulled away. "Why did you say *my wife's* lawyers?" An exasperated sigh escaped her lips. "I'm your wife. Why not *the lawyers*, or at least your ex-wife's lawyers?"

"Habit, nothing more, but, whatever I call them, they'd jump on any opportunity to delay court proceedings."

"But you said the divorce was final when we met months ago, that it was 'just a technicality' holding up the paperwork."

"It's the annulment that could drag on for months," he said. "You wouldn't want our baby born before we're married in church, would you?"

"When the Justice of the Peace married us, you said that—"

"This is just a minor technicality, some legal mumbo-jumbo." His blue eyes looked into hers. "We don't want to give them any reason to slow down the due process of law, obstruct justice by raising questions about a correspondent, do we?" Not waiting for an answer, he continued, "Now, if you're out of town—"

"You mean, out of sight." Shoulders drooping, her heart sank.

"Never! How could you think I'd want you out of my sight, out of my reach?" He drew her to him tightly, caressing her. "I simply mean if you're out of town—"

She stiffened. "Out of the country—"

"Exactly," he said, not missing a beat, "that would remove any suspicion on the part of my . . . the lawyers. We could be married in church by the end of November, by Thanksgiving."

"But you said by October . . . at the latest. By the end of the semester, I'll be entering my second trimester."

"Plus," he said, pausing, "maybe I can arrange to join you in Mexico for part of this assignment, possibly next month. We could make it a romantic getaway, that honeymoon you want. Wouldn't you like that?"

"I still don't see how—"

"Believe me. You'll thank me later for giving you this opportunity. Besides, when you're busy with this assignment, the time will zip by until we're together again."

She breathed deeply, trying to catch her breath after having the wind knocked out of her. *No!* shouted her instincts. *This isn't right.* She looked into his face, recalling their recent vows. Love defeated instinct, and she tried to view the scenario from his perspective.

"I don't feel now is a good time to leave, but if—"

As if sensing his advantage, he put her on the defensive. "Don't throw away this opportunity for yourself just because you're unsure of us."

"I'm not unsure of us." She rushed to vindicate herself. "I love you.

I've never been surer of anything than my love for you. I'm just uncertain that you—"

"Nonsense, I adore you. You should know that by now." When she didn't answer, he pressed her closer to him, kissed her tenderly, and then tipped up her chin to look at him. "Shouldn't you?"

She stared into his eyes for answers or, if not answers, at least clues: *nada*, zero disclosure. Still his nearness was irresistible. With a sigh, she nodded.

"Good, then we're agreed." Abruptly letting her go, he pressed the intercom. Caught off-guard, she had to take a step back to regain her balance. "Peg, ask Dr. Truman to come to my office."

PhD –> Push Here, Dummy

"Without education, we are in a horrible and deadly danger of taking educated people seriously."

~ G.K. Chesterton

"Have you two been introduced?" asked Dr. Witunski. Not waiting for an answer, he continued, "Dr. Truman, I'd like you to meet your colleague in this inter-disciplinary grant project, Ms. Hernandez. Judith, meet Ceren."

"*Ms.* Hernandez?" she asked, emphasis on the title. The trim, blond, sixty-something professor sneered. Her eyes narrowed as she stared down her nose. "Not Doctor Hernandez?"

"I'm an adjunct professor," said Ceren.

"You do have your doctorate, don't you?"

Ceren winced. "Not exactly."

"What do you mean, 'not exactly'?"

"She's an ABD doctoral candidate," said Jarek.

"You're joking, right?" Judith rolled her eyes as her chest moved in a silent sigh.

"Not in the least," he countered. "Ms. Hernandez will be an invaluable assistant in your research . . . and writing. Her Master's thesis was titled *Sixteenth Century Marian Imagery.*"

Her head tilted back, the tenured professor seemed to weigh the information as Jarek pressed on.

"And she completed her MA in Religious Art History at Rutgers University while acting as the Curatorial Assistant at the Museum of Biblical Art in Manhattan." Before Judith could respond, he said, "You may have the anthropological expertise, Dr. Truman, but Ms. Hernandez can round that out with her knowledge of sixteenth-century art."

"I worked at MoBIA for two years before graduating and being accepted here," Ceren offered. "If there's one thing I know, it's art history, especially from the sixteenth and seventeenth centuries." She could not help the tinge of pride in her voice.

Judith parted her tight lips into a grimace that almost passed for a smile. Then, riveting her eyes on Ceren, she folded her arms across her chest.

"Regarding the ABD, when will you defend your dissertation?"

"I'm scheduled for this spring . . . but . . . ."

"Next semester," Judith asked, picking up on the hesitation, eyes narrowing, "or do I sense . . . an obstacle?"

"With the news today," Ceren blurted out, "I may need to delay—"

"This assignment may well postpone her defense," Jarek interrupted. "However, Ms. Hernandez is willing to accept this risk in view of the opportunity she'll gain by collaborating with you in this prestigious, inter-departmental grant."

Judith addressed her question to Jarek. "I had understood that Roger was accompanying me."

"Dr. Lauber was one of the front contenders," Jarek said. "However, Ms. Hernandez is the best-suited collaborator for this grant."

"And what panel, board, or foundation has selected her as 'best-suited?'" Judith's hostile eyes challenged him.

"As Interim Dean, the final decision is up to my discretion."

"'Discretion' . . . is that spelled 'favoritism?'" Judith smirked.

Ceren instinctively moved closer to Jarek, while he nimbly sidestepped.

"Ms. Hernandez is the Art History Department's best-qualified woman for this assignment."

"You mean the Art History Department's only female instructor. I don't need her or anyone else. I can research it myself." Judith turned to walk away.

"Leave now and you're walking away from the biggest grant this university has received in decades." When she didn't answer, he added, "It's not too late to replace you . . . ."

Judith stopped in her tracks. She spun around, her chest heaving. Ceren could see her struggle to control her tongue. It was common knowledge that Judith needed this grant to maintain her position in the academic community. She needed both the publication and publicity that would come from it. Publish or perish, they all knew the drill. A tenured professor was expected to publish annually, and it had been several years since her previous book.

With a thinly concealed smile, Jarek said, "If you want to participate in this grant, you'll collaborate with Ms. Hernandez."

Me, Myself, and I

"The way to love anything is to realize that it may be lost."
~ G.K. Chesterton

Ceren read on the flight to Mexico City, trying to finish Judith's book about Teotihuacán, *When Goddesses Walked*. She felt the more familiar she was with Judith's research, the better she could work with her.

"Excuse me?" She looked up from the page, toward the direction of the voice.

"Would you like something to drink?" the flight attendant repeated, bag of peanuts and napkin in hand. "Wine, beer, or a soft beverage?"

"Just water, please," Ceren said, her thoughts sending a smile to her lips as she refocused on the baby. How quickly life could change.

As her hand rested on her belly, she shook her head. *It's still hard to believe. I'm going to be a mom. Me.* Filled with wonder, she tried to imagine how she'd feel holding the baby for the first time.

Then Jarek came to mind. Her smile drooping, she crossed her arms over her tummy, hugging the baby in his proxy, gently rocking. *I miss him already.* Then she took a deep breath, bracing herself.

This, too, will pass. I've got to look at this separation the way he does: an opportunity. Once it's over, we'll have the rest of our lives together.

On that thought, she returned to reading Judith's description of how the Aztecs had adopted the former Toltec gods into their religion, and how the Toltecs had incorporated the previous Teotihuacán gods into theirs while embracing the ancient Olmec gods. According to Judith's book, reincarnations of the Mesoamerican gods had descended from each other in a disjointed line, reaching back thousands of years.

Ceren bookmarked her place. Glancing out the window, she saw a ribbon winding through the landscape. *Is that the Rio Grande? Are we crossing over into Mexico?* Surveying the land that would be her home for the semester, Ceren's mind returned to the issue at hand: Judith.

How am I going to collaborate with her when she clearly doesn't want my help? With a frustrated sigh, she looked out the window again, staring but no longer seeing.

I've tried being friendly, polite, but the harder I try, the less she seems to respect me. She sighed. *I should probably just do my work, not examine it. Just do it, like tearing off a band-aid. Just grin and bear it. What's the phrase? Depersonalize the relationship. I should just grit my teeth, endure her, and somehow muddle through this semester.*

But I can't. She's impossible to talk to, let alone work with. I'm wasting so much time stressing over this situation, I can't focus. I'm not doing what needs to be done, like now.

She thumped the book. *I can't even concentrate on reading her last book, something I'll not only learn from, but something that will flatter Judith when the subject comes up.*

Try though I do . . . She sighed. *I don't like her. I can't. She's unlikeable.*

Ceren grimaced. *She'll probably sense how I feel, which will only make things worse, a vicious circle. Working with her when I don't like her is one thing, but working with her when she doesn't like me would be quite another.*

She rolled her eyes. *So what do I do?*

I've read enough pop psychology to know that people only collaborate when they like you. The more people like you, the more they'll help you. The more they cooperate, the more you'll all accomplish.

Settling into a scowl, she shook her head. *Grinning and bearing it's a recipe for disaster.*

Okay, so why don't I like Judith? What is it about her? Ceren thought back to their meeting in Jarek's office. *She's so pretentious about her doctorate degree, trying to belittle me for being ABD.* Ceren looked off in space, staring sightlessly at the clouds.

Suddenly, seeing a parallel in their lives, she inhaled sharply. *Ever since I became a doctoral candidate, I've felt a cut above instructors with Masters Degrees. And when I received my MA, I was ... a tad ... condescending toward undergrads. Okay, it's possible there's a small resemblance.*

But she's so over-ambitious, so pushy. Judith's assertive to the point of being downright aggressive. I can't stand that in her, and there's no comparison there. I'm certainly not pushy.

Ceren grunted as the realization struck home. Not many people are doctoral candidates lecturing at a university at twenty-six. She felt the pride well up at her achievement. *Maybe I'm not hostile, but over-ambitious? All right, maybe we have that in common, too.*

Now that I look, I'm seeing more similarities than differences. So what is it about her I don't like?

Idiot! Ceren jammed her fingertips into her forehead. *I don't like the darker side of what I see in me, but it's so much easier to dislike her annoying traits than see my own.*

Ceren chuckled at herself. *Okay. Maybe getting to know Judith better, recognize the things I can't stand about her, will help me learn more about myself, help me overcome what I don't like in me.*

In the meantime, I have to focus on her book. She closed the window shade, opened Judith's book, and did not look up until she heard the announcement that they would be landing in fifteen minutes.

Ceren raised the shade and saw a smoking mountaintop. A volcano? A column of smoke rose through an invisible chimney and then flattened out as it reached the stratosphere. Ceren groaned. *I feel like that smoke, always aspiring, working, climbing until I collide with some unseen force, some glass ceiling, that holds me down, keeps me from reaching my goal.*

ॐ

Judith dozed on the smooth flight to Mexico City. No air turbulence, and with her seat in 26A and Ceren's in 29F, she found no need for irritating chit-chat. However, Judith's privacy was short-lived. As she struggled to lift her trunk off the revolving carrousel at the Benito Juárez International Airport, Ceren grabbed the other end.

"Let me help."

"I can do it myself, *thank you*." Both lips and knuckles white, Judith wrenched it away. In the process, the handle tore off in her hand, and the trunk fell to the floor. Judith looked at the girl in disgust.

"I was just trying to help."

"Help . . . is this how you intend to help me with the grant?" Judith tried to shove her out of her way, hoping to scare off the newbie.

To her surprise, Ceren regained her balance and stood her ground.

"Look, Judith, like it or not, I'm here for the duration. We'll be working together very closely for the next few months."

Judith did not respond, thinking Ceren was through.

"We don't have to be friends," said Ceren, without a smile, her eyes never wavering. "But can't we at least be civil?"

Judith paused, head slanted back, reappraising her. "Maybe you're not the complete bimbo I'd thought."

"The hotel has a café," said Ceren. "After we're settled, why don't we meet over a cup of coffee?"

ॐ

Ignoring the café's aqua and harvest-gold walls painted with rustic murals of Mexican scenes, Judith scrutinized Ceren while the waiter took their order.

Preferring beer to coffee, she got to the point. "Why are you here?"

"Jarek . . . ."

"You mean, Jerk." She eyed Ceren closely, watching the reaction to her thrown gauntlet.

Ceren continued as if she had not heard. "Jarek thought it would be a good career move."

Sipping her *cerveza*, Judith asked, "What career? Counting the summer semester, this is your second as a lecturer."

"I lectured at Rutgers University." She glanced down at her coffee.

"Lectured . . . don't you mean, student taught? I read your curriculum vita."

"Semantics," Ceren countered, her cheeks reddening.

Judith shook her head. "I'm not your mother superior. I don't care how much or how little you embroider on your CV. I just want to know why you're here instead of Roger Lauber . . . and why you were substituted at the last minute."

"Jarek—"

"Jerk!"

"Why do you insist on calling him that?" Ceren's voice rose. Judith watched the struggle reflected in her large, brown eyes. Taking a moment to control her voice, Ceren finally continued. "Jarek's a fine, honorable educator."

"Are you that naïve?" Wrinkling her nose, Judith blew out a contemptuous snort. "The man's a joke."

"He's the Dean of the Humanities Department."

"Interim dean . . . and only by default. Nobody else wanted the job. It's all paperwork and pretense . . . no prestige, no promotion."

"It's a stepping stone, a rung in the academic ladder."

"Grow up." Judith scoffed. "He has a one-year appointment as interim dean, and then he goes back to lecturing . . . amidst hard feelings from his peers." She finished her beer and, holding up the bottle, motioned for the waiter. "*Señor, cerveza, por favor.*" Turning back to Ceren, she asked, "You want anything?"

"No, thanks. I'm fine." Her eyes riveted on her coffee, she shook her head.

Judith motioned one to the waiter. Then, tilting back in her chair, she crossed her arms, studying Ceren. "You don't drink?"

"Sometimes." She squirmed. "At least, I used to."

"Did you give it up for Lent?" Judith sneered, pursing her lips into a moue, her joke intended to irritate more than amuse.

"Something like that," said Ceren, lifting her eyes and staring into space.

"I'll drink to that," said Judith with a wry laugh as the waiter brought another. Raising her bottle in a salute, she took a long draft, paused, and said, "I used to be like you, a teetotaler."

Ceren shook her head. "I don't think so."

"Don't think what? That I was a teetotaler?"

"No, that you used to be like me." Their eyes met.

"What are you trying to say?" Judith hardened her jaw and narrowed her eyes, challenging Ceren.

"I'm not insinuating anything." She gave an exasperated sigh, paused, and met Judith's stare. "I'm just saying, I doubt you were ever . . . in my shoes."

"Go on . . . ."

"Can I share . . . ?" Her eyes sparkled and then dimmed. "Never mind," she muttered, "you couldn't appreciate it."

"Don't start something if you can't finish it. We'll be working together this semester, so, if you've got something to say, spit it out."

"That's true," she said slowly, as if considering her words. "Besides, you'd notice in a few weeks, anyway."

"Is that why you're not drinking?" Squinting, Judith took a long look, sizing her up. "Are you trying to tell me you're pregnant?"

Ceren nodded with a sudden, gleeful smile.

Judith leaned forward and jabbed the rustic, wooden table with her finger.

"Then kiss any academic aspirations goodbye!" She curled her upper lip in disgust. "Why are you throwing away this opportunity?" Then, not waiting for an answer, she demanded, "How far along are you?"

Ceren mumbled, her shock not affecting Judith.

"Speak up."

"Five weeks," Ceren said.

Judith scoffed. "Get an abortion." She drained the bottle and motioned to the waiter for another.

"How can you say that?" The blood drained from Ceren's face. "How can you even think that?"

"What's the matter with you? Nobody even needs to know. Your secret's safe with me. Just do it . . . and the sooner, the better."

"You obviously don't know what you're talking about."

"Oh, puh-lease . . . ." Acknowledging the waiter as he brought her another beer, she winked. "*Gracias*, and keep 'em coming." Turning back to Ceren, she parodied her words in a high, falsetto voice. "You don't know nuthin' about birthing babies, Miss Scarlett." Leaning close to Ceren, she whispered hoarsely, "I know quite a bit about pregnancy and abortion."

Nostrils flaring, Ceren backed away. Judith grunted in disdain.

"Let me give you some advice, and take it from one who knows, chippie. Lose it. Get rid of it. It's a missed period, a worm, a clump of cells . . . nothing more. Don't ruin your career, your life, because of some stupid mistake. Take care of it!"

"You're so wrong." She shook her head. "I tried to share . . . . I don't know what your problem is, Dr. Truman, but you've got some warped world view." She rose to leave, the heavy wooden chair grating across the Saltillo tile floor. "What's my share of the bill?"

"Oh, sit down. No need for any Roe versus Wade drama." Judith sighed and took a long swig from her bottle. When Ceren remained standing, she hissed through clenched teeth. "Sit down!"

Still glaring, Ceren sat.

"You remind me of my sister, *the Sister*." She scoffed. "How old are you?"

"Twenty-six."

"Twenty- six," Judith repeated in a whisper, shaking her head. She drained the bottle, and the waiter brought her another, even before she could motion. "You, *Señor*, are getting a very big tip. *Gracias*."

"Were you ever pregnant?" Ceren asked.

Judith paused, recalling the waves of sheer terror and thrill and amazement that hammered her soul when she first learned the news. "Once, the winter I defended my dissertation," she mumbled, shuddering as she tried to shake off the uninvited memories. Then noting Ceren's expression, she added, "That was a few years back, in '72, when I was your age." She took a long draft from the bottle, blocking the memories that surged through her mind like streaming video.

"So did you have a boy or a girl?"

She scoffed. "If the fetus weren't incinerated that day, it's long since decomposed."

Ceren swallowed hard as her delicate, pink-gold complexion paled to a ghostly white. Then her eyes widened. "You had an abortion?"

"It was one of the first legalized abortions in the US." Noting her interest, Judith continued. "I took a bus to Manhattan . . . alone."

"The father . . . ."

"The father was a jerk. Like I said, I took a bus to Manhattan . . . alone."

Ceren lifted her smoldering eyes to look at her and then quickly lowered them, as if avoiding any contest of wills.

Sneering, Judith tilted her head away. She had made her point, but it was an empty victory. It wasn't enough. She needed Ceren to understand. "I've always done what I had to do . . . always . . . never needed anyone . . . nobody, no how . . . always take care of myself, that's my motto . . . just me, myself, and I."

Ceren nodded in acknowledgement but did not make eye contact. "Weren't you afraid?"

Judith took a deep breath and then a long draft from the bottle before answering. "If I hadn't been so determined, so filled with loathing, I doubt I'd have been able to go through with it. I wanted to be rid of it . . . free from any connection with the father. Free to pursue my dreams, my goals."

"Wow." Grimacing, her left eyebrow raised, Ceren clasped her hands almost in a prayerful pose. "That's . . . so . . . ."

"Heavy, as we used to say in the Seventies." Staring into space, Judith snorted, reliving the past.

If I'd kept the baby, he—I'm sure it was a he—would be nearing his fortieth birthday. I'd probably be a grandmother by now . . . . The waiter interrupted her reverie with a chilled bottle of beer.

Startled, she looked up. "*Gracias.*"

As she raised the bottle to her lips, she glanced at Ceren. *That could have been me. I could have been a mother.* She took a long swig and set the bottle down hard, causing the beer to foam over the top. *I've wasted my life.*

"Wasted," she mumbled.

"What?" asked Ceren, sopping up the beer with her napkin.

"Huh?" Judith looked up, unaware she had been thinking aloud. Then she saw the erupting foam still flowing down the sides of the bottle, like life ebbing away. "I said, what a waste . . . of beer."

Feathered Serpents

"The world will never starve for want of wonders, but for want of wonder."

~ G.K. Chesterton

The next morning, they met their driver in the hotel lobby. As he removed his sunglasses, Judith did a double-take. "He looks like a short, Latino version of Al Pacino," she muttered.

"Good morning, ladies," he said. "My name's Juan. The university sent me to be your tour guide and driver to Puebla." Reaching for Judith's trunk, he added, "Let me help you with that."

"I got it." She shot him her dour, school-marm expression.

He turned to Ceren. "Miss, can I help you with yours?"

"Definitely," she said with a big smile. "This is Judith, and I'm Ceren."

"Judith and Karen?" he asked.

"SAIR'n," she said, pronouncing phonetically, "as in serendipity. Ceren's Turkish for young gazelle or fawn."

"Might as well be Bambi," muttered Judith, fixing her with a disapproving stare. *She's so much like I was forty years ago . . . ambitious but . . .* "She's so damned naïve."

"It's close to Spanish," said Juan. "*Cervato* is fawn."

He opened the car's back door for them and lifted the baggage into the trunk. As he drove through Mexico City's traffic, he began a stream of conversation about the sites they passed.

"This is the *Plaza de la Constitución*," he said, pointing to the *Zocalo*. "Across the plaza is the National Palace, and on the north side is the Metropolitan Cathedral."

"Will we pass Mt. Tepeyac on the way?" asked Judith.

"Ah, the site of Our Lady of Guadalupe's Basilica," said Juan. "Not on today's route, but it's scheduled for later this week. What interests you about Mt. Tepeyac?"

"We're pooling our resources and coauthoring a book," said Ceren. "Judith's a professor of Anthropology, and my area's Art History."

"Team work," said Juan, nodding as he kept his eyes on the traffic.

"Grant collaboration," Judith corrected, her tone curt.

Ceren jumped in. "I'll spend most of my time at the shrine's Art Museum, studying and writing about the paintings, particularly the oils of the sixteenth and seventeenth centuries."

Juan nodded. "What about you, Judith? What calls you to the basilica?"

"Call is the right word," Judith said, marginally warming to her subject. "I'm compelled to study the relationship between Our Lady of Guadalupe and *Tonantzin*."

"So you know about the Aztec goddess, *Tonantzin*." Juan smiled at her through the rear-view mirror. "Not many *gringos* know about *Tonantzin*."

"I don't," said Ceren. "Who's Toe-Nancy?"

"Toe-NAN-zeen," he said phonetically. "Mt. Tepeyac was *Tonantzin's* sacred hill for centuries. Then, after Juan Diego met Our Lady of Guadalupe on its slopes, it became sacred to Our Lady."

"What became of *Tonantzin*?" asked Ceren.

"That's exactly what I'm documenting," said Judith. "Some legends say *Tonantzin* and Our Lady of Guadalupe are one and the same. I'd like to get to the bottom of this myth . . . see if there's any truth to it."

"Who hasn't heard the rumors that local gods were sometimes the basis for saints?" Ceren asked. "As the saying goes, where there's smoke . . . ." Her smile and shrug finished her sentence. "Was she a fertility goddess?"

"In Aztec mythology, *Tonantzin* was the earth mother or mother goddess since she gave birth to a Mesoamerican god."

"Just as Our Lady of Guadalupe is the mother of Christ," added Juan.

Through the reflection of the rear-view mirror, Judith watched his eyes glance at Our Lady's image attached to the dashboard.

"She was also the patroness of birth and of women who died while giving birth," said Judith, "very similar to Our Lady of Guadalupe, who's the Patroness of the Unborn. Those are only a few of the similarities."

"Does anyone worship *Tonantzin*, anymore?" asked Ceren.

"I've read that some do, but that's exactly what I want to explore." Leaning forward, Judith asked, "Juan, do you know of anyone who worships *Tonantzin*?"

"Not personally," he shrugged, "but I know some *curanderos* call on her help when performing spiritual healings."

"What are *curanderos*?" asked Ceren.

"Folk doctors," said Juan.

"They're shamans that use ancient practices from the Aztecs, or even Toltecs, to heal people," added Judith. "It's really amazing how spiritual ideas fuse. If it's true that *Tonantzin* survives as Our Lady of Guadalupe, it's an example of how each generation of the faithful breathes new life into ancient beliefs."

Ceren's eyes narrowed. "How do you figure that?"

"The Aztecs incorporated Toltec gods into their religion," said Judith. "That's a proven fact. Now, if saints are recreations of Aztec, or any other indigenous gods, today's worshippers may be keeping alive traditions and customs that could stretch back to the beginning of time."

"Did you know that *Tonantzin* is sometimes associated with *Iztaccíhuatl* or White Woman Mountain?" asked Juan.

"No, I was unaware of that." She quickly searched through her purse for a pen and scrap of paper to make a note.

"Some think *Iztaccíhuatl* is another form of *Tonantzin.*"

"Really," said Judith, scribbling.

"But you've heard of the folklore of *Iztaccíhuatl* and *Popocatépetl*, haven't you?

"Yes," said Judith, "that I have heard. Supposedly, *Iztaccíhuatl* was a princess, and *Popocatépetl* was a warrior."

"That's one of the myths," said Juan, "but, no matter which version, in the end, both *Iztaccíhuatl* and *Popocatépetl* are turned into mountains by the gods, and *Popocatépetl* becomes *Iztaccíhuatl's* consort." He took his eyes off the road momentarily and turned toward them. "Look to your right after we turn this corner. If there isn't too much haze, you'll see *Popocatépetl* in the distance."

"Popo-what?" asked Ceren.

"Po-po-ca-TEP-et-l," Juan said phonetically. "It's an active volcano, the second highest peak in Mexico. The name in Aztec *Nahuatl* means Smoking Mountain."

"That must be what I saw from the plane yesterday. Where?"

He peered through the passenger's window until it came into view and then pointed it out. "You should be able to see it . . . now. Look to your right."

"I just see haze and clouds," said Judith, pinching her lips together in frustration.

"Parts of those clouds are volcanic gases." Again his finger pointed toward the smoking peak. "Look right through . . . there."

"I see a spire of smoke," said Ceren, her large, brown eyes widening.

"That's the gas escaping. Look underneath that."

"Oh, yes, I can just make out the volcano's peak!"

"All I see are smog and clouds." Running her fingers through her hair, Judith scratched her head impatiently.

"Don't worry, you'll get better views from Puebla and Cholula," he said. "We'll stop at the pyramid in Cholula this morning and be in Puebla for lunch."

ॐ

"That's the San Gabriel monastery," said Juan. "We're entering the San Andrés part of Cholula. The Toltecs conquered this city from the Olmecs in the thirteenth century," he said, pointing. "There, where you now see the monastery, they built a temple to *Quetzalcóatl*, the feathered serpent."

Above the monastery, Judith watched a backlit contrail climb upward and then undulate in the wind. "It doesn't take much imagination to see a feathered serpent slithering through the sky."

Juan smiled. "For two thousand years, this pyramid has been a religious focus."

Even in the distance, she could see the grass-covered, pyramid-shaped hill.

"Now, the *Nuestra Señora de los Remedios* Sanctuary tops it, but the pre-Spanish pyramid was sacred to *Chiconahuiquiahuita*."

"That's a mouthful," said Ceren. "Chico . . . what?"

"*Chiconahuiquiahuita*, it means Nine Rains. When sixteenth-century Franciscans discovered pagan idols here . . . on what they thought was a hill . . . they dedicated it to the Virgin and built a church. Our Lady of the Remedies is now the patroness of Cholula, so, you see, the pyramid continues to be a place of pilgrimage."

"Not unlike Mt. Tepeyac," said Judith, nodding at the parallels.

"How could the Franciscans confuse a pyramid with a hill?" asked Ceren.

"For centuries, even before the Spaniards arrived, it was overgrown with weeds. Locals called it *Tlachiaualtepetl*, or man-made hill. It was so wild, it was hard to recognize as a pyramid. Still, its base is the largest in the world."

"I've read that. The Guinness Book of Records says it's the largest pyramid, as well as the largest monument ever constructed anywhere in the world," said Judith. "Its total volume is larger than the Great Pyramids of Giza."

Viewing its perimeter, Ceren shook her head. "Its base doesn't look as large as pictures of Egyptian pyramids."

"That's because so much of its base is buried," said Juan. "What you see is maybe half the pyramid's actual height. Some say a serpent lives beneath it."

"A serpent," repeated Judith, "*Tonantzin*? In her *Coatlicue* aspect, she was sometimes portrayed with a head and garment of writhing snakes."

"That could also be her *Chicomecoatl* aspect," he said, "where she was known as the Seven Serpents."

"Or it could be *Tonantzin* in her *Cihuacoatl* aspect, as the wife of the serpent," said Judith.

He shrugged and said, "Maybe it's *Quetzalcóatl*, the feathered serpent. Maybe it's the biblical snake, the devil of the Garden of Eden."

"What about Our Lady of Guadalupe's snake?" asked Ceren. "In paintings, she's sometimes depicted as standing on a serpent. Why is that, anyway?"

"Good question," he said. "Her name in *Nahuatl* is *Coatlaxopeuh*, which sounds very close to the Spanish word Guadalupe. *Coa* means snake. *Tla* means the, and *xopeuh* means to crush or tread on. So in *Nahuatl*, Our Lady called herself the one who crushes the serpent."

"Maybe it represents her crushing the serpent religions," said Ceren.

"Maybe." He hunched his shoulders.

Then recalling her dream, she added, "Perhaps a phallic symbol referring to her pregnancy?"

Raising her eyebrows, Judith nodded as she continued scribbling. "I had no idea serpents played such an important role in this area."

"Who knows which legendary snake lives beneath it, but one thing's certain," said Juan. "The pyramid offers excellent views. From Our Lady of the Remedies Church at the pyramid's top, you can see the peaks of the *Popocatépetl* and *Iztaccíhuatl* volcanoes."

"Does the church have any talavera tile in it?" asked Ceren.

"You like talavera?" he asked.

"Yes, it's so ornate, so baroque."

"The dome of the cupola at Our Lady of the Remedies Church is covered with it," he said. "But if you like talavera tile, you'll love the *Santa María Tonanzintla* Church. Inside, it's decorated with gold and bright yellow, red, white, and blue-colored tiles. It's trimmed with stucco shaped like maize, snakes, angels, Francis of Assisi, Christ, *Quetzalcóatl*, and the Virgin Mary."

"Snakes and *Quetzalcóatl* adorning a church," repeated Ceren, tilting her head to the side. "Amazing."

"Why's it called *Santa María Tonanzintla*?" asked Judith, ears perking. "Does this church have anything to do with *Tonantzin*?"

"Before the Spanish arrived, this area was sacred to her," he said. "The people linked *Tonantzin* with their source of life . . . maize. Then the monks replaced their mother goddess with the Virgin Mary and built a church over her shrine."

"Interesting . . . ."

"More interesting, the residents won't let the Catholic diocese or the state of Puebla have any authority over their church. When they want Mass said, they hire a priest."

Molé Poblano

"Hearing nuns' confessions is like being stoned to death with popcorn."
~ Bishop Fulton Sheen

When they arrived at Puebla in time for lunch, Juan suggested a restaurant half a block from the university.

"It used to be a noble family's home," he said. Double-parked on the busy street, he pointed. "It's just through that door."

"What about our baggage?" asked Judith as they hopped out onto the bustling sidewalk.

"No worries," he said with a quick smile. "I'll deliver it to your rooms."

Judith closed the door and thumped it twice. "Thanks."

As he pulled away, Ceren returned his wave. "Thanks, Juan."

"Might as well get this over," said Judith, her lips tight, as she dialed her cell phone.

"Get what over?"

"Calling my sister, *the Sister*."

"Where does she live?" asked Ceren.

"Here." Judith inhaled deeply through her nostrils.

"Here? In Puebla?!"

"Yup." Then speaking into the phone, she said, "This is Judith."

Ceren delicately stepped away out of earshot, pretending to admire a nearby storefront's candy displays.

"Ready?" asked Judith a moment later.

"That was fast," said Ceren. "Wasn't your sister home?"

"Yeah, she's joining us for lunch," Judith said over her shoulder, as she strode toward the restaurant.

Hurrying after her, Ceren raised her eyebrows but kept her thoughts to herself. *Is this how Judith treats her sister? How am I ever going to get along with that woman?*

A cadre of waiters, all wearing dark, if not shiny, well-worn suits, greeted them at the door. As the maitre d' led them to their table, they walked through the refurbished, colonial courtyard into the surrounding restaurant that was a converted hacienda, complete with balconies and antique paintings.

Ceren lingered, admiring the time-darkened paintings that lined the walls. A vine-covered trellis created a dropped ceiling for the covered courtyard. She stared up into the trellis's dappled light and sighed, breathing in the atmosphere. Linen and small vases of fresh flowers graced each table.

After they were seated, Ceren lifted the tiny vase. She inhaled the flowers' fragrance, and tried to identify them while Judith began wiping the silverware clean with her napkin.

"Can I get you something to drink?" asked another of the waiters.

"*Cerveza, por favor,*" said Judith, rearranging the utensils.

"Bottled water, please," said Ceren, omitting her usual smile in the solemn waiter's presence. As her eyes tracked the room's artwork, she spotted a nun wearing a habit.

She smiled politely, and the woman smiled back, almost as if recognizing her. The woman spoke to the maitre d' and crossed to their table.

"Faith?" she asked, addressing Judith. She leaned over, as if to hug her, but, with a well-timed shrug, Judith avoided contact.

"How long has it been?" the nun asked, straightening up.

"Not long en . . . ." Judith muttered, rolling her eyes, pursing her lips into a grimace. "Awhile."

"What brings you to Mexico?" she asked, as if oblivious of Judith's rebuff.

"My health," said Judith, holding up her bottle mockingly. "*Salud.*"

"All right," said the nun, drawing in her breath. "How is your health? You're looking well."

"You, too," Judith said sarcastically, her quizzical, gray-green eyes running up and down her sister's clerical clothing. Again she held up her bottle in a mock toast. "Here's lookin' at you, kid." She took a swig. Then, using her bottle as a pointer, she gestured toward the newcomer. "Ceren, meet my sister, *the Sister.*"

"Please, call me Pastora," she said, turning to Ceren, beaming. "I feel I know you already."

"You do? Why?"

"You're the spitting image of Faith forty years ago." Then giving Judith a sly look, she added, "It has been a while. Could this be your daughter?"

Judith started to speak but began choking. The waiter, hovering nearby, quickly poured her beer, and she took a long draft before answering.

"You know I never had children."

"A lot can change in forty years," Pastora said. "The family hasn't heard from you in thirty, thirty-five years. Who beside God knows what you've been doing?"

"I don't need a lecture on family relations," said Judith, her face flushing. "Besides, I keep in touch with Aunt Tillie. Who do you think gave me your phone number?" Her cold stare was confrontational.

"Won't you sit down?" interjected Ceren, sensing the rift. She pulled out a chair for Pastora.

"Thank you, dear," she said with a warm smile, appraising her. "You're the Faith that I recall."

Ceren gave her shoulder a friendly hug as she pushed in her chair.

"Can I get you something to drink, Sister?" asked the waiter, setting another plate.

"Water, please." Pastora turned to Ceren. "Have you ever tried *Molé Poblano?*"

"I've never heard of it." Ceren shook her head.

"It's a specialty of Puebla, a dish that some say a nun created for a bishop. It's made with turkey, roasted chilies, almonds, peanuts, sesame seeds, and chocolate."

"Chocolate, I like it already," said Ceren with a grin.

"Another, *Señor*," said Judith, draining her glass and motioning to the waiter.

He nodded and asked, "Are you ready to order?"

Pastora asked, "Faith, will you try the *Molé Poblano?*"

She shrugged.

"Three orders of *Molé Poblano*," Pastora said, "with extra *molé* on the side, please." Turning to Judith, she said, "After all this time, I was stunned to hear from you. Seriously, what brings you to Puebla of all places?"

She took a deep breath. "I'm doing research on a book about *Tonantzin* and Our Lady of Guadalupe."

"Perhaps I can help you with the background of Our Lady, but I'm not familiar with Tonan . . . ."

"*Tonantzin*," Judith said loudly, almost belligerently, "the Aztec goddess, who's the basis for Guadalupe." Her eyes challenged Pastora's.

"Interesting," said Pastora evenly. Then she turned her attention to Ceren. "And what brings you to Puebla?"

"I'll be researching the art history aspect of Our Lady of Guadalupe."

"Really? Art history's my passion. We'll have to visit the basilica's art museum together."

"I'd like that," said Ceren, warming to Pastora.

Judith rolled her eyes. "What have you been doing?"

"As you know, I became a religious after Father passed away. I was assigned to Mexico City, not far from the basilica, until seven years ago, when I was transferred to Puebla."

"Was assigned, was transferred," mimicked Judith. "Haven't you done anything on your own in the past forty years?"

"I do what God directs me to do."

"But who gives the commands? Bishops, priests?"

"The religious superiors are servants of God, as am I. We're all His instruments if we let Him speak through us."

"But where are your choices?"

"God gives us the choice every day of walking with Him or of trying to walk life's path on our own."

"It's so passive," said Judith, rolling her eyes.

"It's a choice between actively believing in Him and passively accepting a default life where we follow the herd."

"And you believe these priests have the God-given right to order you about your life?"

"I believe the assignments are the will of God. All things work according to God's plan."

"Yes, I also believe everything happens for a reason, that all things work out for the best," said Ceren. Leaning toward Pastora, she smiled.

"Cock-eyed optimists," Judith muttered, scowling.

Ceren could not hear the rest of the words, but she could see her struggling to control her tongue. Then the waiter poured Judith's beer, and she lifted her glass in salute.

"I'll drink to that," Judith said.

"You seem fond of beer," said Pastora. "I don't recall your drinking. When did you start?"

"You should remember." Judith stared at Pastora, her flinty eyes piercing her. "Almost forty years ago, just after I had the abortion."

Pastora flinched, and Judith shrugged. Biting her lip, Ceren looked on as Pastora silently watched with wounded eyes.

"Forty years is a long time to hold on to hard feelings," Pastora said slowly. "To paraphrase your earlier question, haven't you moved on, moved forward in the past forty years, or have you simply moved away?"

Judith scoffed.

"Let's put the past to rest," said Pastora. "I'd really like to start over, get to know you." She held out her hand. "If not sisters, can't we be friends?"

Judith tentatively reached out her hand but, at the last moment, changed direction and picked up her glass. Looking straight ahead, past her sister, she took a long draft of beer. A silent moment passed. Pastora worked her jaw, took a deep breath, and turned her attention toward Ceren.

"Although I'd hoped you were Faith's daughter, apparently you're not related. Do you have any children of your own?"

"No . . . ." Scrunching her nose, Ceren smiled impishly. "Well, sort of."

"What she's trying to say is that she's knocked up," said Judith, sneering, her body turned at an oblique angle to her sister.

"You're with child, how delightful!" said Pastora, squeezing Ceren's hand. Her face lit up in a little-girl grin. "Congratulations!"

With a gleeful smile, Ceren hunched up her shoulders. "Yes, I'm so excited." Putting her hand over her heart, she said, "I just found out last week."

"Last week! And you took this assignment? How does your husband feel about your being in Mexico?"

"He, well, that is . . . ."

"She's not married, so don't hound her," said Judith, scowling, eyes narrow and dark gray. "She's a big girl . . . free to make her own choices!"

"I'm simply asking." Pastora's eyes were wide and guileless.

"Yeah, right," said Judith, pursing her mouth. She took a deep breath and then took another draft of beer. "Don't let her harass you," Judith said, turning toward Ceren. "I've been this route before."

"That's all right," said Ceren quietly, her hands brushing imaginary crumbs from her lap. Addressing Pastora, she said, "We're married. We've just kept it quiet."

"What?!" Judith's open stare mirrored her doubt.

"A Justice of the Peace married us," Ceren said, feeling the heat rush into her cheeks. Then turning toward Pastora, she added, "But we plan to be married in church in November."

"Anyone I know?" asked Judith, her eyes narrowing.

Ceren swallowed. "Actually, yes . . . Dr. Witunski." In the ensuing pause, she could almost hear the wheels turning in Judith's mind.

"Yeah, right," said Judith at last, finishing her drink, "when pigs fly. He's already married, chippie, and he'll never leave his rich-wife meal ticket, not for you, not for anyone."

"You're mistaken," said Ceren, forcing herself to stay calm. "We were married five weeks ago."

"Five weeks ago?" Judith's mirthless laugh sounded like a cackle. "Five weeks ago, his drunk of a wife was drying out on her annual trek to the rehab center . . . oh, excuse me, what the jerk euphemistically refers to as her 'weight-loss clinic.'"

Ceren felt the blood drain from her face. "Jarek's divorce isn't common knowledge."

Sneering, Judith leaned toward Ceren until her face was inches away. "Five weeks, you say . . . he must have married you the moment his wife left town. How long was your engagement? An hour?"

Double that, two hours. Ceren groaned inwardly. *Can there be any truth to this? Why would she lie to me?* She stared hard at Judith, trying to understand the basis for her words. *Am I the world's biggest idiot, or has she had too much to drink?*

"It was a whirlwind courtship," Ceren said finally, pressing her lips together, her chest heaving.

Judith stared back, as if appraising her, then took another long draft of beer, draining the bottle. "If he married you, as you say, that makes the jerk a bigamist." She gestured toward her with the empty bottle. "Accept it, and the sooner, the better."

Both Pastora and Ceren paused awkwardly as the waiter brought out their order.

"Oh, good, here's our *Molé Poblano*," said Judith, smirking, appearing to enjoy the strained silence. "I'm starving. Let's eat." Then turning to the waiter, she held up her bottle, adding, "Another one, *por favor*."

ॐ

After lunch, Pastora asked, "Would you like to try Puebla's famous sweet-potato candy?"

"Thanks, I'll pass," said Judith, her signature grimace masquerading as a smile. With a dismissive wave, she walked off, preferring her own thoughts to company.

So Jerk's the father. She snorted. *That explains his eleventh-hour substitution of Ceren for Roger Lauber.* Shaking her head, she snorted again. *Times change, but circumstances sure don't. Why else would Jerk have replaced a premier anthropologist with this glorified grad assistant if he weren't trying to keep her out of sight.*

Her chest heaving, Judith recognized the parallels with her own pregnancy so long ago. She thought of her advisor and felt sick to her stomach. She recalled her early days of pregnancy so vividly that waves of nausea washed over her. Beads of sweat broke out on her upper lip. Feeling shaky, she leaned against a cool, brick storefront for support. *It's like morning sickness all over again. What is this? A physical response to my past, my memories?*

Every time she thought of her pregnancy, another round of nausea overtook her. Breathing slowly, deeply, she waited for the cramping and nausea to pass. Suddenly the image of her old advisor popped into her mind, and she saw the connection. History was repeating itself. Jerk was the embodiment of her old advisor, another academic predator, preying on students' naïveté and trust. *I see it clearly now.* Gagging, she pressed her trembling hand against her mouth to keep from vomiting.

ॐ

"Ceren, how about you? Would you like to try Puebla's sweet-potato candy? It's delicious," said Pastora, turning toward her. "We make it at the convent."

"I really should register and unpack," said Ceren, fingering her cell phone. Distracted, she watched Judith turn down an alley, out of sight. *I've got to talk to Jarek and straighten this out.*

"Don't feel you have to leave, too," said Pastora. "As long as you have your apartment's address, I can walk you home."

"Thanks. I am a little turned around." Ceren looked up one street and down another. Then her eyes met Pastora's, and something in the woman's crinkled, smiling eyes convinced her to stay. "Why do you call her Faith?"

"Faith's her given name. Judith is the name she chose at Confirmation."

As they turned onto the side street, Ceren asked, "How long has it been since you saw her?"

"Too long," Pastora's words were a sigh. "Other than at Father's funeral, it's been nearly forty years."

"Yet you're both in Puebla now," said Ceren, shaking her head. "God's weird."

Simultaneously, Pastora said, "God works in mysterious ways."

Ceren chuckled, recognizing a kindred spirit, and gave Pastora a friendly hug.

As they passed shop after shop that displayed candy arrangements, Pastora asked, "Can you guess the name of this street?"

"Candy Street?" said Ceren, eyeing the many sizes, shapes, and colors of candy.

"Exactly, *Calle de los Dulce*," said Pastora, "Street of the Sweets." She held open the door of one of the shops and waved Ceren in. "This one carries the candy our convent makes."

Giving them small samples, the shopkeeper said, "This is *pina*-flavored candy made from yams. This one's *limon*, and this one's *fresa*."

"Delicious, I can almost taste the yams," said Ceren, enjoying the gooey concoction. "What are these called?

"*Camotes*. They're a traditional Puebla candy," said Pastora.

"I'll buy a box for Jarek."

"Is Jarek your . . . ."

"Husband," said Ceren, finding it difficult to wrap her lips around the word. "It all seems so new, so novel." Ceren lowered her voice to confidential tones. "We've kept it a secret."

Pastora cocked her head sideways. "Why's that?"

"Until his annulment's final, he doesn't want to announce it." Her cheeks burning, she felt the need to explain. "He only recently divorced, and, as a university dean, he's concerned the department faculty won't accept me." She took a deep breath, feeling a great weight had been lifted from her shoulders.

"As a new bride, that must be difficult for you to keep secret," said Pastora.

"I was just thinking how good it feels to share that information. You and Judith are the first to know." She laughed, relief flooding away the strain. "It's so unreal. In some ways, I hardly feel we're married at all." She looked at her left hand. "I don't even have a wedding ring." She shrugged. "Not a real one, anyway," she added, with a self-deprecatory laugh.

"I can see where a civil wedding may not seem . . . genuine." Pastora spoke slowly, as if choosing her words carefully. "But you said you're planning to marry in the Church soon?"

"Yes," said Ceren, taking a long, cleansing breath, "next month, just as soon as Jarek gets his annulment."

"Is he excited at the prospect?"

"I don't know." Ceren paused, thinking. "He hasn't really discussed his feelings about it."

"He's married to you," said Pastora, a crease forming between her eyes, "but he hasn't discussed his feelings with you?"

Hearing her words repeated made Ceren grimace. She shrugged, trying to make light of it. "He did say he's looking forward to a fresh start."

"Are you getting married in Puebla?" Pastora's eyes went from troubled to twinkling. "I know a lovely chapel."

"I . . . I'm not sure." Biting her lip, Ceren hesitated. "Everything's happened so fast, especially with this research trip, that we really haven't had time to discuss our wedding plans."

"Are you sure Jarek's serious about this commitment?" Pastora's laugh lines deepened. "Judith's words were thought-provoking, even if she said them after several beers . . . ."

Ceren took a deep breath. *I can't let her words bother me. Judith obviously doesn't know, and Jarek wasn't kidding about the faculty not understanding.* Then rubbing her forehead, she composed herself.

"Jarek's only recently divorced. We haven't had time to settle into any routine yet."

"Marriage is a vocation, and not everyone's called."

"I'm sure I'm called to this vocation!" It bothered Ceren that she had to force her enthusiasm. Needing reconfirmation, she took out her phone and checked the time. "In fact, he'll be calling me in fifteen minutes." She turned toward Pastora. "We made a pact. Every day, wherever we are, we'll drop whatever we're doing and call each other at three o'clock on the dot."

Fifteen minutes later, Ceren was in her cramped, efficiency apartment, sitting on the edge of her single bed, phone in hand. As the minutes ticked by, she glanced at the dorm-sized room, looking but not seeing, instead, mentally listing the topics she wanted to discuss with Jarek.

She absentmindedly reached for the earrings dangling from her ears. Fondling the intricately inlaid lapis lazuli and opal, she recalled how Jarek had surprised her with them on their wedding day. Their smooth, cool touch brought a smile to her lips as she mentally replayed their first weeks together.

They had met at the new-faculty orientation meeting. Ceren could not take her eyes off him as he gave the welcoming speech. After the meeting, over coffee and cookies, Jarek approached her.

"I don't think we've been introduced." Wearing a boyish grin, he held out his hand. "I'm Jarek Witunski, the Dean of the Humanities Department."

Ceren took his hand and felt an instant tingling. A shiver traveled up her arm and down her spine, leaving her awed, speechless.

His cerulean blue eyes fixed on hers as he continued the one-sided conversation. "You're the new lecturer hired through the grant, aren't you?"

She nodded and, finding her tongue, said, "Yes, in the Art History Department."

"I'm sure you'll make an excellent addition to our faculty."

Squirming beneath his inflexible gaze, she mumbled, "Thanks."

"Are you new to Austin?"

She wished his eye contact weren't so intimidating, yet, flattered by his attention, she shyly shook her head. "I grew up in Austin but attended Rutgers."

"So this is a home-coming."

Even his questions sound like statements. Impressed by his self-assurance, she felt small, vulnerable . . . yet somehow protected under his wing. She nodded as she took in his appearance. The wide, silver streak in his shock of light-brown, wavy hair lent him an air of distinction that Ceren found captivating. Her eyes traveled down to his left hand. No ring. She looked up into his compelling eyes and fell under his spell.

"The meeting ran late." Checking his watch, he said, "It's nearly one. Have you had lunch?"

Breathless, too swept away to speak, she shook her head.

"Then let me properly welcome you back to Austin and to our department. Do you like Tex-Mex?"

They found a *taqueria* on Congress Avenue.

"This is my favorite restaurant," he said, opening the heavy, wooden door for her.

With a cry of surprise, she said, "Although it's been years, I remember this place." Nodding, she took in the antique, Mexican artwork and photographs hanging on the painted brick walls. "My father used to take me here as a child." She smiled at the memory. "He said it had the only authentic Mexican food in Austin."

"Your father and I share that opinion." His disarming smile caught her attention. It was then she noticed the resemblance, and she found herself staring. "What?" he asked, eyes twinkling.

"I knew you reminded me of someone." She chuckled self-consciously. "You have more in common with my father than this *taqueria*. You have his blue eyes." Responding to his raised eyebrows, she grinned. "Yes, my Latino father had blue eyes."

"That's right, your last name is Hernandez. So you're of Hispanic descent?"

"Half," she said. "My mother was Turkish."

"I may have his blue eyes," he said with a slow grin, fixing his glacial gaze on her. "But I can assure you, I feel no paternal compulsion toward you."

Despite the hot August day, his icy blue eyes sent pleasant shivers down her spine. Intrigued, Ceren wanted to learn more about him. "What's your heritage?"

"With a name like Jarek Witunski?" He chuckled. "Half Czech and half Polish."

"Can I take your order?" asked the waiter, pencil in hand.

Jarek turned toward her. "Would you like to begin with iced tea, salsa, pico de gallo, guacamole, and taco chips?"

Giving a laugh of disbelief, Ceren rested her head on her hand and stared at him. "How on earth did you know?"

"Know what?"

"This is what my father and I used to do . . . come here on Saturday mornings, munch on finger foods, and just catch up. We talked about everything."

Immediately feeling connected, Ceren found herself opening up to Jarek. Chin still in hand, she gazed at him.

He was so unlike the boys she met at school . . . mature, worldly, and so very attractive. Again she felt a pleasant quaking sensation in the pit of her stomach.

Still talking three hours later, instead of lunch, they ordered dinner and margaritas.

"So you lived in Manhattan? Did you ever visit the Manhattan Metropolitan Museum of Art?"

"Nearly every week," he said. "My wife and I lived in a brownstone two blocks away."

Wife? She stiffened. "I didn't realize you were married, Dr. Witunski." Inwardly, she cringed as she watched his response.

"'Were married' is a good choice of words." He snickered. "Past tense, I was married." He held up his bare left hand.

Not realizing she had been holding her breath, Ceren took a deep breath and then sighed. "So . . . you're divorced?" The tone came out brighter than intended.

He nodded.

"It must have been a difficult decision."

Grimacing, he shrugged. As if deep in thought, his normally clear eyes clouded over. "It's really not something I care to discuss yet." He paused. "It's recent and still raw."

"Of course." Ceren sat back in her chair suddenly feeling awkward. She picked at her burrito as she tried to think of something to say.

"Excuse me a minute? I have to make a call."

"Sure." Through thin lips, she gave a polite, tight smile.

His wooden chair protested as he rose, scraping across the tiled floor.

Watching his back as he walked toward the men's room, she rolled her eyes. She certainly handled that gracefully. Noting his empty plate, she sighed and made an attempt to finish her burrito before he suggested they leave.

Five minutes later, Jarek returned, noticeably more relaxed, wearing an engaging smile. "You know, it's nearly dusk. Have you ever seen the bats emerge from under the Congress Avenue Bridge?"

Did she misread him? She scoured his face for clues. "No . . . well, actually yes, but not in many years, not since my—."

"Let me guess. Not since your father took you, am I right?"

She chuckled as she nodded. "That's true."

"How would you like to see them fly out tonight?"

She touched her napkin to her lips. "I'm afraid I've taken enough of your time, Dr. Witunski. I wouldn't want to impose on your hospitality." She complimented herself for her professional tone, but looked up at him expectantly, hoping he'd object.

"Nonsense, this is the most fun I've had since . . . since my divorce." His blue eyes twinkling, he flashed his disarming smile again.

His smile contagious, she found herself smiling back.

She felt so relieved . . . . No. Reprieved.

ح

They met the next afternoon to tour San Antonio's art galleries and ended up having dinner together in Kyle. The following day, they went kayaking on Town Lake and sampled tandoori chicken from one of Austin's gourmet food trailers. On Sunday, they met for brunch at an open-pit barbeque in the Hill Country and then toured the winery. Under an ancient, live oak, Jarek swept her into his arms and slowly kissed her.

It was like nothing Ceren had ever experienced. She felt lightheaded, giddy. After they pulled apart, her head tilted back as if too weak to hold itself up, it occurred to her.

She was in love.

Two weeks after they met, Jarek took her to a romantic, Italian ristorante in a converted limestone train depot built in the 1870s. "To celebrate our second anniversary," he said, toasting with Asti Spumante. On a candle-lit table, graced with bone china and a linen tablecloth, they dined on grilled Gulf-Coast shrimp and Texas T-bone.

"More wine?"

"Oh, I think I've had enough," She covered her glass with her hand.

"One last toast?" He cocked his head to the side, questioning, inviting.

She rolled her eyes, caving, knowing he'd won. "Well," she moved her hand aside, "maybe just a sip, enough for one final toast on this fabulous evening." Open, relaxed, she smiled at him, completely trusting, smitten.

"This may sound a tad forward," he started, watching her, "but I have to speak at a Southwest Art seminar at Sul Ross University in Alpine this Thursday. All faculty members are invited." His eyes blazed momentarily as he fixed them on her. "Would you be interested in attending?"

She hesitated, unsure what he was really asking.

"It's a six-hour drive, but we can make it there and back in a day," he added quickly, giving her a reassuring smile.

"Oh," she laughed nervously, "so we wouldn't be spending the night?"

"Absolutely not." Taking her hand in his, he tilted his head back and peered at her. "What did you think I was asking you?"

She chuckled self-consciously as she glanced away, unable to meet his piercing blue eyes. "I don't know."

Tightening his grip on her hand, he gently tugged, until she faced him. "Ceren, in case you haven't noticed, during these past weeks, you've become the most important person in my life. Do you think I'd do anything to jeopardize our relationship?"

She raised her eyebrows. *Relationship?* She took a deep breath.

"Well, do you?"

She managed a cockeyed grin.

"Well?"

"I don't know what to think. You're moving so fast, my mind's reeling." She groaned. "I'm not used to this kind of attention. You're talking to someone who's never . . . ." She paused, screwing up her courage. "Someone who's rarely dated and, even then, never seriously." She looked up at him through her long lashes. "Maybe you've been through this before, but this is all new to me."

ح

Jarek picked her up the next morning at five. They talked non-stop across Interstate ten, passing through the Hill Country, barely noticing as the foothills gave way to the peaks and plateaus. Pausing only at Fort Stockton for gas and coffee, they were in Alpine by eleven, in the heart of the Big Bend Region's high desert.

Ceren sat in the auditorium that afternoon, proudly watching Jarek give his talk and enthusiastically leading the sparse applause when he finished. Following the discussions, they toured the artwork display, side by side, chatting like colleagues, shoulders barely touching.

When Ceren reached for his hand, Jarek sidestepped and subtly shook his head.

"What's wrong?"

"Let's step out a moment," he said over his shoulder, leading her to an exit. Outside in the desert heat, he checked that they were alone before turning to her.

Ceren did a double-take, barely recognizing him. All hard hollows and shadows in the harsh light, his face was a stern mask. As if reprimanding a child, he looked and acted like a different person. Who was this?

"So many people know me in university circles," he said. "It's better if we keep a low profile in public." He lifted his mouth in a half-grin, a sparkle momentarily glimmering in his cold eyes. "At least, for a while."

Stiffening, she stood to her full height. "Are you telling me you're embarrassed to be seen with me?"

He scowled and shook his head. "No, nothing like that." Quickly glancing sided to side, as if checking whether they were being watched, he took her hand in his. "It's just so soon after my divorce, I don't want to raise any eyebrows in these stuffy, academic circles."

Working her jaw, her chest heaving, she looked off into space, counting to ten.

He tugged at her hand. "Does that make sense?"

"No." Squinting in the glare of the bright, desert sunlight, she turned toward him and stared, seeing him in a new light. "You'd said I'm important to you, that we have a relationship. I believed we had a future . . . but now you want to keep 'a low profile.' What? I'm not good enough for your academic cronies, is that it?" Glancing at the door, she added, "What is it you want me to do, sneak around? Hide, like we're doing now?"

"No, with you I can be myself, but here," he paused, gesturing to the campus, "here, I'm the Dean of the Humanities Department representing our university. I have to observe certain protocols. You can understand that. All I'm asking is your patience during this transition, just that we act professionally in public, and even then just for a month or so until my divorce is yesterday's news."

She tried to read his face. His glaring expression had relaxed into a wounded facade. Though his expression seemed convincing, she peered into his eyes, looking for deeper truths. Only a frosty, arctic blue barrier stared back, no answers, no insights. She blinked at the inconsistency, the contradiction.

"I'm not sure what to think."

Suddenly she felt trapped, vulnerable, totally reliant on his good graces, even to drive her back home. Pulling her hand from his, she clenched her jaw.

"It was a mistake coming here with you. I see that now." She took a deep breath. "If I recall, Amtrak runs between Alpine and Austin?"

"Ceren, what are you thinking?" He pressed his fingers between his eyes as if gathering his thoughts. "Please don't do something reckless. You're the best thing that's happened to me, and I don't want to lose you."

"You have an odd way of showing that."

"Look, I . . . ."

He paused while a group strolled past, waiting until they were out of earshot.

Groaning in disgust, rolling her eyes, Ceren turned her back on him and stomped off.

"Ceren . . . *Ceren!*" When she picked up her pace, he ran after her. "Ceren, where are you going?" He caught her arm, turning her toward him in an about face.

She wrenched away. "How dare you grab me?"

"Ceren, what can I do?" Reaching into his pocket, he pulled out his car keys. "If you're set on returning to Austin, I'll drive you back. We can leave now, just please listen . . . ."

She turned on her heel and began walking.

"Where are you going?"

Over her shoulder, she called, "None of your business."

"Ceren, please, wait up, I'll drive you . . . just wait a minute 'til I get the car."

She strode through the massive parking lot toward town.

Watching her progress, he ran to his car. Within five minutes, he rolled alongside her, matching her pace. "Ceren, this is ridiculous. It's got to be over one hundred degrees. Get in."

She ignored him.

"Ceren, it could be miles to the train station. I don't know where it is, but I don't recall passing any tracks on the way. It could be miles from here."

Lips pressed together, she kept her eyes focused ahead of her.

"Ceren, whatever I said, I didn't mean to upset you. I'm sorry."

Still keeping up her pace, she turned to look at him.

"Please get into the car. I'll drive you back to Austin."

Chewing her lip, she slowed her stride.

"We can leave right now if you like."

Chest heaving, she stopped.

"This isn't some ploy?"

Shaking his head, he grimaced. "No ploy, just disaster recovery." He leaned over and pushed open the passenger door. "Please get in."

Still debating, she hunched her shoulders. "It's difficult to trust you now." She motioned toward the university buildings. "What you showed me back there scared me. It made me realize I don't know you . . . at all. These past two weeks have been wonderful, *had* been." She grimaced. "Now that's changed."

"Ceren, this is all my fault. What can I say? What can I do to make it up to you?"

Shaking her head, she got in. "Just drive."

At the intersection, he asked, "Do you want to take Highway 118 or US 67?"

Turning her profile to him as she looked out the side window, she shrugged.

Thirty silent miles later, he said, "Except for coffee, we haven't eaten today. Do you want to stop for lunch?"

"I want to go home."

"We're on our way back." He stifled a sigh as he pulled into a parking lot. "I just wondered if you'd like to stop for a bite."

She stared hard at him. "I want to go home!"

"All right, stay in the car." He turned off the engine and opened the door. "It's your choice whether or not you care to join me, but I can't drive all the way to Austin on an empty stomach."

She looked at the steakhouse's rustic-chic exterior. The smoky scent of a mesquite-wood grill wafted in from the driver's side, and her stomach growled.

She couldn't make it to Austin without eating, either. Her spirit was willing, but her flesh was hungry.

She sneered as she pushed open her door, annoyed at being sabotaged by her own body. She walked past Jarek without making eye contact and led the way in.

Inside, Ceren's eyes were drawn upward to the vaulted ceilings and rough-hewn beams. An open-pit grill was visible off the main dining area. Chandeliers crafted from wagon wheels radiated overlapping circles of light, casting a warm, soft glow over the round tables and semicircular booths.

"Two?" asked the waitress, leading them to a corner booth. Jarek pulled the table out for Ceren.

"Thanks," she said with a perfunctory smile as she picked up the menu. Refusing to make eye contact with him, she sat at the very edge of the crescent booth, not sliding over, forcing him to walk around the table to the other side.

Taking his cue, Jarek sat at the opposite edge of the curved booth. Although seated as far apart as possible, when Ceren looked up from her menu, she found herself face-to-face with him across the table. Rather than make eye contact, she focused on the tiny vase of wildflowers between them.

Steel guitar music played lightly in the background. Ceren heard the muted patois from the other tables, but, lips firmly pressed together, she refused to make polite conversation.

"Anything to drink?" asked the waitress.

"Water, please," said Ceren.

"I'll have water and," he pointed to an item on the menu, "the half-bottle of Merlot."

"Back in a minute to take your order."

Narrowing her eyes, Ceren scowled at him and then averted her eyes, opting to people-watch instead. At the nearest table, a young couple chatted animatedly, heads close together, their eyes glittering. Ceren looked away, embarrassed, her nostrils flaring.

She felt like a voyeur, peering through their pheromone fog. She couldn't watch them, not then, not while she and Jarek were . . . what?

48

She stole a glance at him. She couldn't even call it breaking up, not when they'd dated for only two weeks.

Mentally groaning, she looked in the other direction, glimpsing an older couple at the next table. Apparently at ease with their lull in conversation, their eyes met and crinkled at the edges. She saw their entwined hands under the table and looked away. She was surrounded by young lovers and happily married couples. It hadn't been her day. Ceren's chest heaved in a barely audible sigh.

"What?"

Startled by his voice, she glanced at Jarek. "Nothing." She looked away and saw the waitress approaching with the wine and two glasses.

The woman placed a glass in front of Jarek and poured a sample for his approval. When he nodded, she placed a glass in front of Ceren and began pouring. "None for me," she said, holding up her hand, but it was too late.

"No harm done," Jarek said, smiling at the waitress. "We'll just pour our own, thanks." He turned toward Ceren. "Don't worry. If you don't want it, I'll drink it." His warm, easy smile gave no indication of any earlier disagreement.

What was she feeling so uncomfortable about? Was she over-reacting?

"What would you like?" The waitress stood, pencil in hand, looking at Ceren.

"Oh." Caught daydreaming, Ceren started to pick up the menu, but then recalled her selection. "I'd like the petit fillet, please."

"And for you, sir?"

"I'll have the filet mignon."

Her pencil paused mid-order, the waitress hesitated. "Might I make a suggestion?"

"Sure," said Jarek, listening attentively.

"Since you're both ordering tenderloin, why not get chateaubriand for two?" She winked. "It's a whole lot more romance for less money."

"That's a great idea. What do you say?" he asked.

Surprised by the enthusiasm in his voice, Ceren turned toward him, wanting to see his expression, read his meaning. He focused his blue eyes on her. She noticed the frosty eyes crinkling at the edges, warming into a smile.

She started to protest but couldn't think of any logical objection, not with his eyes piercing hers. Instead, she managed a shrug. "It's a steak, however you cut it."

Congratulating herself on her show of indifference, she turned away from him, staring at the grill's dancing flames across the room, ignoring the eyes she felt drilling into her. She heard wine being poured but refused to look.

"Ceren."

The voice sounded nearer, and she peeked. He had moved closer, close enough to touch glasses.

"How about a toast to better days?" He held up his wineglass.

Crossing her arms, she rolled her eyes. Her chest moving in a silent sigh, she turned her back to him, pretending to watch the grill's flames.

"Ceren, I can't change how you feel, and I won't try . . . promise . . . ." His tone persuaded her to look. When their eyes met, his lips parted in an intimate, exclusive smile.

Just for her. Suddenly she felt singled out, special . . . and something else. When he looked at her like that, she felt secure, safe. How could that be?

"Just through lunch, can we be friends again?" He raised his eyebrows questioningly, his blue eyes peering so hard, they seemed to see into her soul.

The gesture was endearing . . . and vaguely familiar. *Why?*

She stared, suddenly recognizing it. Swept with nostalgia, she was a nine-year-old girl again, looking into her father's eyes, anxious to please, all too ready to conform. She instinctively trusted that he had her best interests at heart, that any suspicions were unfounded.

"Can we be friends?"

Finding it difficult to say no, she opened her mouth to answer. Then she remembered Jarek's earlier behavior. Pursing her lips together, she turned away.

"Ceren . . . ."

His voice sounded closer, and she turned. He had crossed the distance and was sitting beside her.

"Through lunch only, how about a truce?" He held out her wineglass.

She grimaced, deliberating.

"Consider it a peace offering." He raised his eyebrows along with the wineglass.

She squirmed in her seat, feeling the tug of wills, but when she looked into his blue eyes, she realized the take-over had begun. Accepting her glass from him, she clinked it to his.

"Truce."

The chateaubriand was their conversation starter. Both giving and taking, they fell into the role of two friends enjoying lunch and a lively conversation over a glass of wine.

Ceren looked at him in the chandeliers' soft glow. Though she had not forgotten the seminar's episode, she tried to view it from Jarek's perspective.

As a university dean, of course he had certain appearances to maintain. That was understandable. All he asked for was her patience, and even then just for a month. She took a deep breath. She could do that for him, couldn't she?

She squinted. Or was he ashamed of her, ashamed to be seen with her? It was as if he was hiding her, or hiding when he was with her.

Crossing her arms, she grunted as another thought entered her mind. As her dean, she'd be reporting to him when the semester started. Furrowing her forehead, she scrutinized him, wondering how that would impact their relationship.

"What are you thinking?"

She watched his eyes. "It just occurred to me that I'll report to you when classes start. Basically, you'll be my boss."

He nodded slowly. "That's true, and not to bring up a sore subject, but that's exactly what crossed my mind this afternoon . . . you, your reputation in the academic community." Ducking his head to peer directly into her eyes, he smiled. "I'm a known quantity at the university, but you, more to the point, the faculty's perception of you, is what I'm concerned about." Leaning into her, bracing his hand on the table, he positioned himself so their faces were inches apart. "I'm only thinking of your standing at the university."

"How so?"

"You've worked hard to get where you are. For someone your age, you're way ahead of the curve. A university lecturer on the brink of defending your doctorate, you're only months from reaching your goal." He leaned in. "You're on track to becoming a tenured professor. I don't want anything or anyone to interfere with your career, especially me."

She puckered her eyebrows. "I'm not following."

He sighed, hesitating, as if choosing his words. "As well as you've done for yourself, you're in a vulnerable position. Face it. You have a semester-to-semester contract in a grant-funded position. These positions can continue for years, or they can vanish if funding disappears . . . or if your peers report any unprofessional behavior. You may not realize it, but you're high-profile. The university's a fishbowl. Though you may not recognize their faces yet, the academic community will be watching you, what you do, where . . . and with whom . . . ."

Taking in his words, she inhaled, arching her neck.

"Ceren, I only have your best interests in mind." He leaned closer into her space. "I care for you . . . deeply. I don't want to see you hurt." He pressed closer, his presence overwhelming.

"Really?" Rather than pursued, she suddenly felt cornered, pushed too far. Her gut instinct said, push back. She narrowed her eyes, fixing them on him, moving into his space, forcing him to back off.

As if responding to her body language, he leaned away.

"I'm hearing a lot of words, but what I witnessed earlier didn't impress me." She sat up straight. Throwing her head back, she challenged him. "What's the old adage? Actions speak louder than words."

"What," he swallowed and started again. "What do you want me to do?"

"For one thing, don't foist your own insecurities onto me. If you feel you're high profile, living in a fishbowl, admit it." She inhaled sharply. "Don't project it on me."

Shaking his head, he dismissed her suggestion with a groan of disbelief.

She crossed her arms and looked him squarely in the eyes. "For another, if you're so concerned about my reputation, don't ask me to sneak around. Show me you're proud to be seen with me. Prove it."

"And how do you propose I do that?" His eyes widened. "Propose?"

Tight-lipped, she stared him down. "If you're going to play word games, forget it." She stood up. "I've wasted enough time here. Let's get going."

He pushed back the table, left a tip, and stood up. "Ceren . . . ."

Turning her back on him, she hurried toward the exit. They returned to the car in silence, but, as he opened the door for her, Jarek leaned over and whispered, "Marry me."

"What?" She blinked in the sunlight. *I couldn't be hearing him right.* She looked at him closely, lip reading.

"Ceren, I'm serious. Marry me."

Peering at the blue eyes that could have been her father's, gazing at her future boss, the dean, Ceren stared mutely at the man before her. She gasped as it occurred to her: father figure and authority figure rolled into one. She felt lightheaded.

"I have to sit down." She swung into the bucket seat, suddenly drained.

Jarek shut her door and slid into the driver's seat.

Not turning her head, she mumbled. "This is so surreal."

"Ceren . . . ." He reached for her hand. "Ceren, look at me."

As she turned toward him, she stared. No longer icy, his blue eyes were warm, liquid as they gazed at her.

"You were right. Words are cheap. I want to prove how important you are to me." He kissed her fingertips. "Be my wife."

She squeezed his hand. "Jarek, yes!" Leaning over the console, she threw her arms around him and kissed him.

Moments later, she broke away, catching her breath. "When?" she gasped. "When do you want to set the date?"

He glanced at his watch, then grinning, said, "In about two hours."

"What?"

"New Mexico's two hours away. If we hurry, we'll be married before the courthouse closes."

Her jaw slack, she stared at him. "What's the rush?"

Grinning, he shrugged. "What's wrong with spontaneity?"

She paused, mentally listing the reasons. Then she looked at Jarek's boyish expression and opted to mention only the most essential. "Well, for one thing, isn't there a waiting period?"

His grin widening, he shook his head. "Not in New Mexico."

"This is all happening so fast." She chewed her lip. "I'd feel better if we had some family or friends . . . ."

His raised eyebrows stopped her mid-thought. "Ceren, if it's a big wedding you want, we'll have one. We can renew our vows in church later, but let our elopement be an adventure, something we can tell our grandchildren."

She brightened at the thought. "When do you want to get married in church?"

Chuckling, he playfully held up his hands, as if fending her off. "One wedding at a time, please."

శ

At 3:35, her cell phone rang. So tense, she nearly dropped it, taking it from its case.

"Hello," she said breathlessly, relief conquering annoyance.

"Hi, how's my baby?"

"He's doing . . . ." She stopped mid-sentence, realizing Jarek was asking about her, not their child. "I'm fine, missing you."

"Yeah, me, too," he said. "Look, gotta' make this quick. A department meeting just came up."

"Oh, I met a nun today, who—"

"Have them wait five minutes, Peg," he called to his assistant, his voice muffled. "You met a nun, you said?"

"Yes, Judith's sister, and they got me thinking about our wedding —"

"I'll be finished with this call in a minute," he said, his hand partially covering the receiver. "Please close the door on your way out." Speaking into the phone, he said, "You were saying . . . ."

She sighed, rolling her eyes. *Skip the introduction. I'd better get straight to the point.*

"Where are we holding our Church wedding, Mexico or Texas?"

The silent pause was nerve-wracking. Ceren heard his office phone ring in the background.

"This afternoon is a madhouse," he said finally, drawing in his breath and releasing it. "I'll . . . I'll have to call you tomorrow."

Tomorrow . . . is he being evasive? No, he's just frustrated with his hectic schedule.

"You poor darling, you're overworked. I can hear it in your voice. When are you coming to Mexico?"

"Uhm . . . ." He coughed, paused with his hand over the phone, and then cleared his voice. "Sorry, what was that you were saying?"

"I said, when are you coming to Mexico?"

"Uh . . . December, I believe . . . ."

She heard something in the background. *Voices?*

In a strangled voice, Ceren said, "December? I thought we'd have our church wedding in November."

"Did I say December?" He clicked his teeth and then sighed. "I'm trying to do three things at once, preparing for this meeting. You know I meant November."

Not really. She paused, breathing deeply, regaining her balance. "Okay, so then we're getting remarried here in Mexico next month, is that what you're saying?"

Again she heard silence and then a muffled voice in the background.

"Gotta' go," he whispered into the phone.

The line went dead. Feeling adrift, she held onto the cell like a lifeline.

Like Winning the Lottery

"Angels can fly because they take themselves lightly."

~ G.K. Chesterton

"Good morning," Judith said, addressing the assembly of graduate students. She glanced around the classroom, noting the bank of windows on the back wall and the intent faces staring at her from behind the marred, blonde-oak desks.

Picking up a piece of chalk, she wrote 'Culture of Death' on the worn blackboard, and then turned toward her class.

"Welcome to today's lecture about culture, specifically the culture of death. It's my privilege to be here with you in the land of the Aztecs, only seventy-five miles from *Tenochtitlan*, the ancient center of the Aztec culture. Consider the word culture. It comes from the Latin word *colo*, which means to cultivate. It's also the root of agriculture and cult. The farmers' cult was agriculture. They cultivated their produce, and their produce fed them. Their culture kept them alive. What would be another way of saying that?"

Several students raised their hands.

"You," she said, pointing to a student in the back.

"Without the protection of their culture, they would have died."

"Yes, life and death, culture is a paradox. It can either nurture or ruin us. For instance, medicine, pharmaceuticals, drugs, can heal us . . . or they can destroy us. Just being alive, ever being born is like winning the lottery. Over ninety percent of all people ever born are dead. Roughly sixty percent of them died before reaching the age of five. This doesn't take into consideration natural disasters, like tsunamis, earthquakes, or volcanic eruptions. Nor does it take into account birth defects or plagues. Do you feel lucky to be alive?"

When no one answered, she repeated loudly, "Do you feel lucky?"

"Yes," the students said in unison.

"Speaking of lucky, during intercourse, each ejaculation contains fifty- to two-hundred-million sperm, yet a womb contains only one ovum. You are the result of the fastest sperm."

She waited for the giggling to subside and then continued, knowing she had the class's attention.

"Think of the odds of you being born. Life is vulnerable. The culture of life is fragile. Now think of the culture of death: genetic or gender domination, wars, jihads, and ethnic cleansings. Consider droughts, floods, bombs, and traffic accidents. Is it easier to be born or stay alive?"

Half the students said, "Being born," while the other half said, "Staying alive." A student in the back began singing the lyrics, "Stayin' alive, stayin' alive," and the assembly broke into laughter.

Judith grinned, knowing when to go with the flow. "Life is like the old Bee Gees song, *Stayin' Alive*. It's nearly as mathematically challenging as being born. Culture can save lives or end lives. What about capital punishment? Claiming an eye for an eye, courts can sentence a murderer to the electric chair. What about disease? If a patient with an incurable disease arranges an assisted suicide, is that euthanasia? What about abortion?"

The room went silent. Judith surveyed the group, pausing momentarily at some of the faces, wondering. *How many of these students have been touched by abortion? I was only a year or two older when I had mine.*

"When death solves a problem, the culture becomes one of death. Now, turn back time. Instead of our present culture of death, think of the Aztecs' culture of death. Why did they practice human sacrifice?"

Several students raised their hands.

"You," she said, pointing.

"It was an offering to their gods."

"Can you tell me more?"

He shook his head.

"How about you?" she said, calling on another.

"They offered animals, flowers, and even pottery that they smashed, so it would not be reused. Anything could be used as an offering, but blood was the most valuable."

"Good," said Judith. "A creation myth tells of *Quetzalcóatl* offering blood from a wound in his penis to give people life. Some Aztecs sacrificed their own blood by using cactus thorns or slivers of obsidian to cut their tongues, ears, and genitals. It was an act of atonement for their sins. Heart extraction was the highest form of sacrifice. Why was that?"

"They believed a person's heart was his center of being."

"Yes, but why? What else?" Judith asked, pointing to another.

"Aztecs believed each person's heart was a small piece of the sun . . . ."

"And," Judith prompted when the student hesitated.

"And that the sun needed human blood to rise each day."

"What ended the Aztec culture of death?" Several students raised their hands. "You," she said.

"The Spanish conquistadors."

She pointed to another.

"The Catholic Church."

Judith called on a girl in the front.

"Our Lady of Guadalupe," she mumbled.

"Our Lady of Guadalupe," Judith repeated loudly enough for all to hear, "and that is our next topic of discussion . . . ."

෭

The following morning, Juan picked them up at their apartments. As Ceren climbed into the back seat, Pastora showed up.

"I'll get in the front," said Judith, pursing her lips in her school-marm imitation, "so you two can talk."

"Oh, no, sit with your sister," Ceren said, swinging her legs and getting out. "You haven't seen each other in so long, it'll be good for you to catch up."

"Nope," said Judith, getting into the passenger seat. "I'll discuss *Tonantzin* with Juan. You two chit-chat."

With a brusque wave, she shut the door, ending the conversation before Ceren could argue.

"I'm glad we'll get a chance to know each other better," said Pastora as Ceren sat next to her. "I feel I already know you. You really do resemble Faith when she was your age." Raising her voice, she leaned forward. "Faith, don't you think Ceren looks like you did forty years ago?"

Judith spun around to look at Ceren. Looking at her, as if seeing her for the first time, she opened her eyes wide in recognition and then narrowed them. "Not in the least. Why would you say that?"

"Look at her eyes and the way her pulled-back hair highlights her cheek bones. She's the spitting image of you . . . the way I remember you," Pastora said. "Don't you see the resemblance?"

"No, not at all," said Judith, curling her lips into her habitual grimace. She turned her back to them.

"I think the resemblance is uncanny," said Pastora, shrugging off Judith's dismissal.

"Maybe you're trying too hard to find the sister you knew," said Judith, her back still toward them.

"Maybe you're right." Pastora sighed. Turning to Ceren, she added, "I do feel I've missed so much of Faith's life. When I look at you, so eager and fresh, I see Faith just starting out in life." She sighed again. "Hard to believe it's been forty years."

"Faith was her given name, but Judith is her confirmation name, right?" Ceren asked.

"In honor of Saint Jude," said Pastora.

"Patron saint of lost causes," Judith chimed in from the front seat without turning to face them.

"I see." Ceren's eyebrows lifted. Then she turned toward Pastora. "What was your name before you became a religious?"

"Amaryllis, or Maryl for short."

"What a beautiful name. Other than the flower, does Amaryllis have any meaning?"

"It means shepherdess in Greek."

"As Pastora means shepherdess in Spanish," said Ceren. "At least you were able to keep your name."

"Yes, I'm pleased it worked out that way." She shrugged. "Maybe it was divine intervention."

"Maybe it was dumb luck," said Judith from the front.

Ceren lowered her voice as she turned to Pastora. "What was Judith like forty years ago?"

"Faith was open, trusting," said Pastora, her eyes lighting up at the memory. Then her eyelids drooped as she sighed. "Unfortunately, Faith wasn't able to keep her name, at least, not its essence. Somewhere along the way, she lost her faith, and, with it, her identity."

"What do you mean, she lost her faith?"

"She lost her faith in mankind. She used to trust people. At one time, Faith believed in God, but . . . something changed. Now she teaches about gods and goddesses."

"Do I hear my name being used in vain?" Judith asked sharply. She turned to face the back seat. "Here we go again with the 'religious studies versus theology' argument."

"I've never heard the two compared before," said Ceren, "religious philosophy versus theology."

"Yes, a great many people fail to distinguish between the two," said Pastora, speaking louder. "They major in religious studies without a firm understanding of their religion, and they can get off track."

"Off track of what?" asked Judith. "A well-worn path that's been so heavily traveled, it's a rut, not a route?"

"Is that what you call religion: a rut?" asked Pastora. "As I said the day you arrived, God gives us the choice of walking with Him or walking life's path alone."

"An unexamined life isn't worth living," said Judith.

"Examination is good for the soul," said Pastora, "but faith uses both logic and scripture. I like Anselm of Canterbury's definition of theology: *Credo ut intelligam*, faith seeks understanding."

"You're the believer, and I'm the scholar," said Judith. "You passively accept what you're taught in Sunday school, while I continue to search for the truth."

"You call it religious studies when you look for links between an Aztec goddess and Our Lady of Guadalupe?"

"Absolutely." Narrowing her eyes to slits, Judith stared her down.

"Some would call it heresy."

"Others would call it research."

"Faith, how could we have been raised in the same house?" Spreading her hands, she motioned to her habit. "How could the same upbringing make you a heretical professor and make me a nun?"

"Two sides of a coin, I guess," said Judith with a shrug.

"You teach about gods, not God."

"That's not true. I cover the Old and New Testaments in the spring syllabus," said Judith.

"When you finally do refer to the God of the Old Testament, your discussion isn't scripture-based, faith-based, it's face-based. You take any religion at face value and turn the sacred into the secular, if not into the profane."

Judith's neck became taut, the cords stiff and pronounced.

"You take divinity and turn it into propaganda," said Judith, the blood draining from her lips.

"You lecture about a generic god/force/higher consciousness/universal energy that's so new-age ecumenical, it barely distinguishes Pepsi from holy water," Pastora said.

Shaking her head, Judith gave a barely audible groan.

Responding, Pastora said, "I sat in on your lecture yesterday."

"Good, maybe you learned something."

"Yes," she nodded, "I learned the sister I recall has struggled along life's path. You've chosen to go it alone."

"Damned straight!" said Judith. "That's the first thing you've said that makes any sense."

"I'm not talking about men or family," she said. "You've struggled because you've chosen to walk life's path without God."

"And you," Judith sputtered, her face flushing red, "you . . . you . . . ." Jabbing her fingers into her forehead, she shut her eyes and sucked in her breath through clenched teeth. A moment later, she started again. "You wonder why we don't get together more often."

She abruptly turned her back on the women and started a conversation with Juan.

ॐ

Miles before they approached the entrance, they saw parades of people walking toward the basilica. Many carried floral arrangements.

"Why is that group carrying a banner?" asked Ceren.

"That's the Garcia family," said Pastora. "See their name on it?"

"It's definitely the extended family," Ceren said, looking at the long column of people.

"This sidewalk down the center of *de Guadalupe* was planned for such processions," said Pastora. She pointed at the wide walkway that ran the length of the tree-lined boulevard.

"Look," Ceren said, "there's a man walking on his knees. How far are we from the basilica?"

"Half a mile," said Juan.

"He's going to walk there on his knees?"

"Such is the faith of the devout," said Pastora.

Judith smirked but kept silent.

"I'll let you off as close as I can to the entrance," said Juan, "but I can see the barricades ahead. Just call my cell when you're finished, and I'll pick you up at the same place I let you off."

"Okay," turning toward the back seat, Judith said, "since you're both going to the art museum, and I'm starting at the new basilica, let's meet at four o'clock. Is there a central location?"

"Yes," said Pastora, "let's meet by the Bell Tower in the Atrium of the Americas. It's in the middle of the large, open plaza. You can't miss it. It looks like a pre-Columbian god, but it's really just a collection of clocks." She counted off on her fingers. "It has a circular carillon, sun dial, Aztec calendar, and astronomical clock showing all the constellations of the Zodiac."

"All right, already," Judith said, frustrated, splaying her fingers stiffly. "It's a clock. I get it. We'll meet by the clock and decide what we want to do then." Sighing, she turned toward Juan. "Just drop me off here."

ᛣ

Judith jumped out as the car came to a rolling stop. With a brusque wave, she strode toward the basilica. She inhaled deeply, glad she could finally breathe. Confined in the car with her sister and the others had been stifling.

After nearly forty years, seeing Maryl again is . . . she rolled her eyes . . . *purgatory and hell rolled into one.* She took a deep, cleansing breath, and then snorted. *Pastora—I'll never get used to calling her that. Her name may have changed, but she hasn't. Still the disapproving, goody-good girl.* Sneering, she gave an indignant snort. Then the memories came unbidden, one after the other, starting like rain drops, then turning into a downpour. *Nothing would please her. Nothing. Never could please her, no way, no how, no matter what I did. Never. Seemed I could never measure up—never can—never* . . . .

In the swarming basilica, she walked down the main aisle toward the revered tilma, but crowds of people kept her from getting closer to the painting. Again, she felt short of breath, even claustrophobic in the teeming masses. She noticed a back exit and slowly squeezed her way through the throngs toward it.

Once outside, there was air, light, and Tepeyac, the hill sacred to both

Tonantzin and Our Lady of Guadalupe. She stared at the moss-covered rocks, comparing the character of the craggy hill's natural beauty to the cement-covered plaza.

This, I can relate to. She could almost see how the place had looked five hundred years prior. Water seeped and flowed from the sides of the hill. Lush ferns, yuccas, and gigantic poinsettias seemed to grow in stone. On closer inspection, she saw they cropped up through tiny crevices.

Finding a path, she followed it up the hill. Immediately, the scenery began to change. The path widened into a cement sidewalk and swelled with people. Immaculately manicured, grass-carpeted areas were roped off to the public. Instead of a mountain, it now looked like a vertical, inaccessible park.

She watched parents lift little girls onto chipped, wooden horses while photographers snapped their pictures against images of Our Lady. She saw lovers stealing kisses and young marrieds holding hands, the very pregnant wives looking like children themselves. Everywhere Judith looked, she saw pregnant women or grandmothers, proudly holding new-born babies.

I can't get away from it. She began feeling that familiar pang of loss. She felt jealous of the expectant women and young mothers. With an exasperated sigh, she even felt jealous of the grandmothers. *Damn, they're probably younger than I am.*

She climbed to the top of the hill and stopped at the Saint Michael chapel. In front of the edifice, two winged angel statues stood guard. Judith felt drawn to their massive figures.

From their vantage position, the statues overlooked the entire basilica complex and plaza. She held the banister tightly and, keeping her weight on her heels, stretched forward, peeking over the edge, not trusting the stone balustrade, feeling unsteady. *Am I getting vertigo?*

From behind, she heard someone giggling. Now what? Hoping to catch the culprit in the act, she turned quickly and saw the hem of a dress just as the girl ducked behind the statue of Michael.

Deciding it best to disregard it, Judith returned to gazing down on the gardens and buildings of the Villa.

Again she heard giggling, but she ignored it. Instead, she rested her arms on the banister and tried to imagine what the hill had looked like five hundred or a thousand years before. The giggling persisted, gradually getting louder until it was impossible to ignore. Although it sounded like a little girl having fun, Judith did not particularly relish being the subject of the girl's mirth.

Without turning her head, she could see a figure in her peripheral vision. Then it became a kind of game. If Judith turned her face ever so slightly, the girl dove behind St. Michael's statue. Yet Judith sensed more than saw her creep out again the moment she turned her gaze forward. After five minutes of the giggling give-and-take, Judith pivoted quickly and caught a glimpse of the child.

The dark-haired girl was wearing an ankle-length, dazzling white, Mexican wedding dress. *Maybe it's a costume?* She vaguely wondered why the girl would be wearing such a vintage, crocheted dress.

Judith looked at her watch. Nearly three o'clock, and she still hadn't seen the tilma. She left her perch and walked back to the basilica. Although it was just as crowded as it had been, she joined the long line of pilgrims snaking toward the viewing area. At least it was moving quickly despite its swollen size.

Wisdom to Know the Difference

"Change is inevitable. Progress is optional."

~ Tony Robbins

At 2:55, Ceren looked at her watch and gasped. Her hand flew to her mouth.

"Ohmigosh," she mumbled through her fingers, "I didn't realize the time. I've got to get outside, so my cell can get better reception. Jarek'll be calling at three."

"All right," said Pastora, rushing to keep up with Ceren's stride. "It's too beautiful a day to stay indoors, anyway."

They hurried down the marble grand staircase of the art museum and out the front door into the atrium. Checking the signal, Ceren immediately turned up the volume of the cell.

"I don't want to miss his call," she said with an apologetic smile, glancing sideways at Pastora.

"I can see that." After they mulled around several minutes, waiting for the call, Pastora said, "Let's walk while we wait."

They began climbing the path through the Tepeyac Garden. Ceren held her phone in her hand, checking for signal strength. As the minutes ticked by, her attempt at conversation gradually gave way to pursed lips and grinding teeth.

What is this with him? This is the second time in as many days Jarek's missed our call. Out of sight, out of mind? Could he be losing interest? She drew in her breath as another thought crossed her mind. *What if something's happened to him?*

Not until they passed a diminutive replica of Tepeyac Hill, complete with miniature cacti and multi-colored stones, did Ceren stop.

"It looks like a Bonsai mountain," she said with a forced laugh.

"I'm surprised you noticed," said Pastora.

"What do you mean?"

"You've barely taken your eyes off your phone."

Ceren gave a resigned sigh. "You're right." She checked the time: 3:21.

"He isn't going to call, is he?" asked Pastora, her mouth twisted in a sympathetic half-smile.

"You're probably right again," she said, putting her phone away.

They resumed their walk uphill on the switch-back path. Water cascaded from the mouths of a dozen gargoyles in the retaining wall.

"There's a freshwater spring in the mountain," Pastora said. "Supposedly, that's the source of this water."

Distracted, Ceren grunted politely.

"How did you meet him?" Pastora asked.

"Jarek?" Ceren asked, enjoying the sound of his name, the choice of topics engaging her in the conversation. "We met at a new-faculty orientation meeting." She smiled. "It was love at first sight."

"I don't have a lot of experience in that area." Pastora gave a self-deprecating laugh. "How did you know it was love at first sight? Had it happened to you before?"

"Oh, no," said Ceren, shaking her head. "I never really had a serious boyfriend before Jarek, never had time."

"But you're so young. Certainly you must have dated in school."

"Not really, I was always too busy studying for scholarships or working part-time jobs. I never had time."

"Weren't your parents able to help with your tuition?"

"No," she shook her head. "My mother died while I was in high school. I made her a promise to finish my education."

"You've done more than that. You have a master's degree, I believe?"

"Yes, I'm actually ABD, just need to defend my dissertation, and I'll have my doctorate."

"Your mother may not have helped with tuition, but you could say that she was an inspiration."

"Yes," said Ceren, brightening, "you could definitely say that."

"What about your father?"

"He passed away my freshman year at college."

"So you're an orphan," said Pastora, clicking her teeth "just like Faith. Do you have any siblings?"

"I was an only child." Ceren shrugged. As they passed a group of life-sized statues, she asked, "What's this?"

"It's the *La Ofrenda* monument," said Pastora, "showing the Virgin of Guadalupe receiving gifts from the native people."

"They're so lifelike." She looked at the surroundings. "And the waterfall creates a beautiful backdrop."

They politely waited while a mother snapped a picture of her family in front of the monument. Then they stepped around several visitors, who were kneeling in worship.

"I need to sit down," Pastora said with a sigh, pointing to an empty bench.

A man selling home-made popsicles from a push-cart asked, *"¿Quieres comprar una paleta?"*

"Sí, dos, por favor," said Ceren.

While they ate the sticky popsicles, Pastora said, "You so remind me of Faith, uh, Judith. She wasn't always the bitter woman she is today. Like you, she was young when our mother died."

"Yes, but she had you."

68

"That's true. I became her surrogate mother. Also like you, Faith pushed herself to succeed in school. She was always an over-achiever, simply driven."

Grunting, Ceren nodded her head in agreement. "I can relate."

"She, too, was twenty-six when she defended her dissertation. Maybe that's why you remind me so much of Faith before . . . ." Pastora's voice faded off as her eyes focused on the statue of Our Lady. Lost in thought, she lost track of the conversation.

"Before the abortion?" Ceren finally asked.

"That's right. She mentioned it, didn't she?" Pastora turned to look at her. Ceren nodded. "Then I wouldn't be telling any family secrets behind her back if I tell you about it." Again she gazed at the statue of Mary. "You know, Our Lady of Guadalupe is the Patroness of the Unborn?"

"Mmm-hmm."

"Then I have a confession to make." She leaned closer, lowering her voice. "I've always felt at least partially responsible for Faith's change."

"Why?"

"Faith came home for Christmas vacation after her final semester of post-graduate classes. She planned to work on her dissertational defense over the break, so she could start teaching at the university in the spring semester."

"That's pushing it," said Ceren, grunting, shaking her head in empathy.

"It's what you're doing."

"That's true," Ceren said with a shrug. Grimacing, she saw the parallel.

"She just wasn't herself. She seemed preoccupied, barely noticing Father or me that Christmas. Instead of her usual self, she was withdrawn, moody. She'd lock herself in her room for hours. Father and I thought she was preparing for her defense. If she weren't in her room, she was on the phone, speaking with her advisor. It was the only thing she'd talk about."

"What, the defense?"

"That and her advisor," said Pastora. "Finally, on New Year's Eve, it became obvious that something else was bothering her. Although she didn't say anything was wrong, her eyes were red and swollen from crying.

Father asked if something were wrong with her dissertation. She burst into tears, ran to her room, and slammed the door . . . ."

"What was wrong?"

Pastora leaned back against the bench, her expression suddenly drawn, wilted. The corners of Pastora's eyes sagged, her smile drooped in a parody of a tragedy mask as she recounted the event.

ह

"Father asked me to check on you," said Maryl, speaking through the door.

"Go away," Faith shouted.

"Father's health really can't take this drama. You know he needs his rest."

Maryl heard the lock click. She opened the door, but, without an invitation, stood waiting in the doorway.

"What's wrong?"

"You might as well know . . . I'm pregnant."

"Pregnant?" Maryl quickly stepped inside and shut the door. "By your advisor?"

Faith hesitated, then sniffing, wiping her eyes with a Kleenex, nodded.

"Oh, Faith," Maryl put her arms around her, "does he know?"

"Not yet." She wiped her nose. "He promised to come home with me, meet you and Father."

"Why the delay?"

Closing her eyes to gather her thoughts, Faith shook her head. "Every day there's another reason." Opening her eyes, she fixed them on Maryl. "Then this morning, I found out I'm pregnant."

"You have to call him, tell him."

"I have been calling him, but I haven't been able to reach him." Faith's fear showed in her tear-stained face.

Maryl gently let her go, picked up the phone, and handed it to her. "Try again. He has to take responsibility."

Faith nodded, took a deep breath, and began to dial.

"Do you want me to leave?" asked Maryl, stepping toward the door.

"No." Faith managed a faint smile that broadened when a male voice answered the phone. "May I speak to Tim?"

The voice droned at the other end of the line.

"Oh." Her voice dropped an octave, like a deflated bagpipe. "Do you . . . could you take a message?"

Again, the voice droned through the phone.

"Well, when do you expect him back?"

Maryl could hear a voice, but no words.

"What!" The color drained from Faith's face as her eyes leapt wildly.

Alarmed, Maryl grabbed her sister's hand. "What's the matter?"

Faith motioned her to be quiet while she listened. Tears gathered in the corners of her eyes and then started trickling down her cheeks.

"Yes, that . . . that is a surprise . . . . Me? I, uhm, I'm a friend," Faith said slowly, "a good friend, Faith, Faith Truman." Her mouth trembling, she added, "Tim must have mentioned me, Faith Truman." She swallowed.

Maryl watched her, trying to make out the other side of the conversation, but all she could hear was the whine of a voice through the line.

"Yes," Faith said, wiping away the tears, "tell him . . . tell him the mother of his child . . . ."

"His child?!" Maryl winced as she heard the voice shouting through the phone. "Is this some kind of sick joke?"

"The mother of his child is going to abort his baby, your grandchild," she continued, her voice rising. "Thanks for raising a real son-of-a-bitch!"

Trembling, Faith slammed down the receiver. Maryl blinked and drew back her head as if she had been slapped.

"You don't mean that, do you?" she asked.

Reaching for Maryl, Faith broke into tears. "Yes," she said between sobs, "I do mean it."

Maryl held her against her chest, hugging her. "What just happened on the phone?"

Faith could only sob.

"Who were you talking to? What could they have said to make you think such a thing?"

When the tears finally subsided, Faith looked into her eyes. "It was Tim's father. He said he can't get a message to him because Tim eloped."

Maryl tried to speak, but no words escaped.

"I'd rip this thing out of me right now if I could."

"You don't mean that."

"Oh, yes, I do! I'm getting an abortion. I don't want anything to remind me of him. He's done enough damage," Faith said, her wet eyes glaring. "I especially don't want his baby around to ruin the rest of my life!"

ॐ

"Wow." Ceren sucked in her breath as she absorbed the knowledge. "I can see why Judith is so bitter."

"All through New Year's Eve and New Year's Day, I pleaded with her, trying to reason with her," Pastora said. "I even offered to raise the baby for her, but she was obstinate." She turned to Ceren with a wry smile. "That part hasn't changed about Faith, although everything else has."

"But I don't see how you could possibly blame yourself for the abortion," said Ceren. "It sounds like you did everything in your power to prevent it."

"There's more," said Pastora, pursing her lips as her expression hardened. "Finally, on January second, our Father's birthday, I offered to drive her into Manhattan to the abortion clinic."

Ceren abruptly leaned forward. "Were abortions legal back then?"

"They were in Manhattan," said Pastora, meeting her eyes.

"So you drove her to the clinic, and that's why you feel guilty?"

"No, I offered to drive, but Faith saw right through me. She said, 'You'll just try to talk me out of it and end up driving me somewhere else.' Instead, that morning, she took the bus to New York City alone, got the abortion, and came back in time for Father's birthday dinner."

"Did your father ever know about it?"

"No, both Faith and I put on cheerful masks, although, as I recall, she looked so pale. Father never knew, thank God. Two months later, he passed away in his sleep. His funeral was the last time I'd seen Faith until this past week."

Pastora's chin quivered. She swallowed and looked down at her hands, blinking.

Ceren lightly touched her shoulder. "Hearing from her, seeing her again after all this time, must have been quite a shock for you."

Eyes still cast down, Pastora nodded.

"She must have changed over these forty years."

"On, no," Pastora looked up, eyes red. "She changed overnight. When she left to take the university position, she began using her confirmation name, Judith . . . ."

Arching her neck, Ceren grunted. *Poor kid, and she was my age.* As on the flight to Mexico, Ceren saw the parallels between Judith and her. The ambition, the competitive spirit, the pride, even the academic, father-figure choice of men . . . . She stopped.

Why would a thought like that enter my head? Jarek's nothing like Judith's advisor. Jarek loves me, married me . . . still . . . . The idea gnawed at her until Pastora's woebegone expression woke her from her reverie, and her thoughts returned to Judith. For the first time, Ceren viewed her in a more charitable light, saw her as a vulnerable colleague, a sister in the sorority of womanhood.

"How incredibly sad that a person of her gifts considered herself a lost cause."

"Exactly. From that time on, she's been this driven, cynical woman that you see today. She insulated herself, shutting out everyone, including God. She trusts no one and apparently believes in nothing. Her independence is her armor."

Forty Flashbacks and a Break

"Sometimes the best way to figure out who you are is to get to that place where you don't have to be anything else."

~ Anonymous

Behind the basilica's altar, Judith edged her way forward slowly as the walkway funneled the jostling crowd into one narrow lane. Ahead, she could see that, after the people squeezed through the bottleneck, they could choose from four moving sidewalks. These passed directly beneath the tilma, encased high above the walkways and altar.

Judith chose the lane closest to the tilma. Her eyes drawn upward by the vertical, gold-tone blocks, she craned her neck, mouth gaping, as she slowly passed beneath the image of Our Lady of Guadalupe. Encased behind thick glass and mounted within several gilded frames, the nearly five-hundred-year-old, cactus-fiber cloak looked vibrant. Where had she seen these colors before? The tilma's colors reflected the luminous hues of Painted Buntings' feathers and Blue-Swallowtail butterflies' wings.

The Virgin's blue mantel attracting her attention, she lifted her eyes. Barely making out the star motif, Judith recalled the tradition that the stars represented the constellations as seen from Tepeyac on the night of December 12, 1531.

Then the golden rays surrounding the Virgin caught her eye. Not a nimbus or large halo, the rays clothed the image with the sun, like the Woman of the Apocalypse. Squinting to see better, she saw the tassels of the sash, the cummerbund worn high. She drew in her breath. That had been a sign to the Aztecs that the Virgin was pregnant.

But it was the dusky, Mona-Lisa face that captured Judith, her tender expression: eternal, solemn, serene, yet youthful. The Virgin's face held her attention, silently speaking to her. Without warning, her chest ached. Buried memories and hidden indiscretions flooded her, rushed from her like a bleeding wound.

Suddenly, she recalled the title of Our Lady of Guadalupe: Patroness of the Unborn. She inhaled sharply.

Hairs rose on the back of her neck, and she felt chilled.

She recalled her aborted baby with a deep, mourning grief, not simply a sense of loss. No longer scar tissue, muscle memory dulled by time and denial, it was a fresh gash, its nerve-endings raw and hemorrhaging. Although the walkway's ride beneath the tilma lasted moments, it felt like hours, days. Judith was outside time.

The years fell away like unstrung pearls from a broken necklace. A yoke she had worn, burdening her for forty years, was now broken. Without its numbing weight, she was free, free to feel the pain.

As if a surgeon's knife plunged into her, trimming away the emotional plaque and cholesterol that had squeezed shut her heart, she grieved for her baby. No more denial. No more rationales. No more justification. Shoulders drawn up, elbows tucked into her sides, she hung her head, cringing from the guilt. Making a fist with her left hand, she gripped her bag tightly. And no more blaming everyone but herself.

How could I have overlooked my own role in the abortion? It's time to take responsibility.

She stepped off the moving walkway in a trance. As if she were having a mini stroke, Judith saw bursts of flashing lights. Like a strobe effect, a series of flashbacks to the abortion bombarded her.

In her mind's eye, she saw herself walking into the abortion clinic. The waiting room was filled with people—boyfriends, mothers, sisters, friends, husbands—all waiting for the babies' deliveries to death. She surveyed the pairs of sad eyes that looked up at her, knowing her reason, the only reason, for being there.

Alone, petrified at what lay ahead, intimidated by their expressions, their censure, their pity, she stood tall, raised her chin, strode to the registration desk, and announced in a strong, clear voice that she had an appointment. She wasn't going to show fear. She wasn't going to accept their judgment, their condemnation, their pity. She was tough. She could and would do whatever it took.

Next she saw herself in the clinic's anteroom along with seven other young women wearing nothing but hospital gowns and paper slippers. As they waited for their names to be called, each told her story of how she came to be there. They would never see each other again. Why not be honest? The stories were different yet the same: gullibility, love gone wrong, selfish abuse, one-sided love.

She snorted, mirthlessly laughing at herself. Passion without purpose had led us to this place. The stories helped pass the interminable minutes, helped keep her mind off what lay ahead.

An attendant handed each a summary of abortion statistics. One fact captured her imagination. One girl was not pregnant but insisted on having the procedure performed, anyway. *What was she thinking? What am I thinking? What am I doing?* Beginning to hyperventilate, she exerted all the self-control she could muster just to slow her breathing, slow her pulse.

When the attendant called her name, Faith, she wondered where her faith was. She blindly, numbly followed the attendant into the examination room.

Within minutes, several men entered the room. One began to roughly explore her uterus with his ungloved hand. His hand still inside her, he proclaimed she was four months' pregnant, too far along to perform the abortion. She struggled to sit up.

"That's not true." His hand still inside her, he forcibly pushed her back onto the examination table from the inside of her pregnant belly. She struggled against the pressure and mounting pain. "I can't be three months' pregnant, if even that," she argued, gritting her teeth against the pain.

Insult had been added to injury. She glared at him. She didn't want to be here in the first place. Now, this incompetent abortionist was man-handling her and threatening to withhold the abortion she needed. Much as she wanted to get off that table and stomp out of the room, she needed his help.

Finally, he removed his hand from inside her. After a short consultation with the other men, he conceded she was within the time frame to perform the abortion, and a young assistant led her into the operating room.

Faith was both relieved and terrified. She had just fought to go through with the abortion, but all she wanted to do was flee. She had won the skirmish, but now she was going to lose the baby.

"Are you sure you want to go through with this?" The assistant's eyes drilled into hers, and Faith wondered if something in her expression or body language had tipped her off.

"I wish I didn't have to, but I have no choice."

"If you're unsure, I can stop it."

Faith hesitated, recalling Maryl's offer to raise the baby.

Before Faith could respond, the attendant opened another door, leading to the doctors' scrub room.

"She isn't sure," said the girl. "Don't do it. Don't do this abortion!"

Faith saw the doctors poised over the sinks, hands and arms lathered to their elbows, looking up at her and the attendant.

"No," she said too loudly, panicking, horrified at the thought of having come this far only to be denied now. "They have to. There's no other way. I don't have any other choice. Not really . . . ."

Again she had fought to have the abortion despite her fear, despite her ambivalence. Twice obstacles had intervened, but now there were no more opportunities to change her mind, no more options. In moments, she would abort her baby. She felt like an animal caught in a trap, willing to do anything to escape, even gnaw off its own leg.

The next thing she recalled was holding the attendant's hand as they put her feet in the cold stirrups, and they began administering the anesthetic. This was it, the moment.

What if I don't wake up from this? What if God punishes me for killing my baby by letting me die on this table?

She looked at the doctors hovering over her, shadowy figures against the glare of the operating lights. *I don't trust them. What if they botch this abortion? What if this leaves me sterile or worse? What if I pay for their mistakes—and mine—with my life?* She breathed deeply. *Maybe it would be just punishment for destroying this baby. Oh, God, I'm so sorry . . . . If I should die before I wake, I pray . . . .* "Hold hard," the attendant said, tugging at her hand, reminding her to focus on her hand.

Faith looked at her, the only person in the room she trusted. Terrified, she felt tears run down the corners of her eyes. A sob escaped as she gratefully squeezed the girl's hand, hanging on for dear life . . . and death.

The next flashback found her waking up from the anesthesia on a hospital bed.

Eyes still closed, she heard a voice ask, "Why is that girl crying?"

Faith peeked through half-open eyes and recognized one of the girls from the waiting room.

"Some of them do that," said an attendant, shrugging. "Cry."

"Is she all right?"

"She'll be fine."

Faith lay there, hurting inside and inside. Both her womb and soul ached.

Too weak to sit up, she lay on her hospital gurney, looking at the other recovering women. Two rows of gurneys lined the walls. The long, rectangular recovery room simulated a hospital ward, except for its fast pace.

As each post-abortion patient recovered, her gurney was wheeled away, and another took its place, methodically, like clockwork. Watching the cycle of death as her anesthetic wore off, Faith almost felt detached—until the pain began.

The cramps were stronger than during her heaviest period. Originating in her abdomen as a feeling of pressure, as the anesthetic faded, the cramps became a steady ache that developed into increasingly painful spasms and uterine contractions . The pain became severe, radiating to her pelvic region, sacroiliac, and lower back. She bit her lip to keep from groaning.

Pulling up her legs to relieve the pressure put her into a fetal position. As she gently rocked herself to relieve the pain, she squeezed back the tears stinging her eyes. *My baby should be in a fetal position, not me.*

She felt the blood flowing between her legs and, with a sinking heart, knew it wasn't menstrual blood. It was her baby's. Becoming nauseous at the thought, Faith gagged. *I killed my baby. That little person will never grow up, never smile, never laugh, and all because of me.* She started shaking and couldn't stop.

ॐ

Numbly swept along by the crowds, Judith gradually became aware of her surroundings. Her hands were shaking, and she needed air. The lump in her throat choked her. The weight in her chest pressed on her lungs, squeezing out the oxygen. She had to get away from the crushing stream of pilgrims. She found an exit, but her trembling hands had trouble opening the heavy door. Finally, she escaped into the bright sunlight.

Occasional nightmares had had this effect on her over the years, but never had she had a series of waking flashbacks to the abortion. Gasping for air, waiting for the shaking to subside, she leaned against a wall, collecting her thoughts.

What just happened? Am I losing my mind?

Again she heard giggling. She looked around but saw no children nearby. Then, she remembered the time and checked her watch. It was nearly four o'clock. Still gulping air, she began walking toward the Bell Tower at the atrium's center.

Pastora and Ceren were waiting for her.

"Are you all right?" Pastora asked, noticing Judith's gasps for air.

"I'm fine, just hungry," Judith said, breathing deeply, trying not to hyperventilate.

"There's a food court by the market place," said Pastora, pointing to a multi-colored conglomeration of tents just off the plaza.

They found a *taqueria* with picnic tables in front, where they could sit while enjoying their open-faced *tortillas*.

"Did you see the image of Our Lady on the tilma?" asked Ceren.

"Yes," Judith mumbled between bites, keeping her eyes down, concentrating on her *tostada*.

Her aloof behavior ended any polite chit-chat, as intended, and Ceren and Pastora resumed their conversation. Along with the *tostada*, Judith digested her experiences with the flashback vignettes and the giggling girl.

"What?"

"Are you finished?" Pastora repeated.

Judith looked blankly from her empty plate to her sister. "Yeah."

"You seem distracted," said Pastora, a concerned furrow growing between her eyes. "Are you all right?"

"I'm fine." Judith stood up brusquely. "Do you want to tackle the older basilica?"

"Maybe we should call it a day," Pastora said, the concerned furrow between her eyes a contrast to her smile lines.

"Is there time to find a tee shirt before we leave?" asked Ceren. "I promised Jarek I'd find him one at the basilica."

"Sure," Judith said instead of her customary response, 'Jerk.'

Ceren and Pastora exchanged looks.

"Or, if you're not feeling well, we can leave now," said Ceren.

"I'm fine."

The food court and souvenir shops were connected. Tent after tent offered tee shirts for sale, along with rows upon rows of rosary beads, plaster images of the Virgin, and other pious trinkets.

Suddenly, Judith heard the giggling girl. She tried to ignore it. When the giggles became too loud to disregard, she peered around but saw nothing.

"Did you hear anything?" she asked.

"Like what?"

"Laughter, giggling," she said, still searching.

Again Ceren and Pastora exchanged glances.

"Maybe we should call it a day," said Ceren. "I can find a tee shirt another time."

The giggling sounded closer. Judith turned and caught sight of the girl's scalloped, crocheted hem just around the corner.

She bolted after her, turned the corner blindly, and tripped over a tent stake. When she hit the ground, pain flooded through her right hand like a flash of light.

Ceren and Pastora rushed to help her up.

"Are you all right?" asked Pastora, the crease between her eyes deepening.

"I'm fine," Judith lied, standing up, refusing their help.

When she tried to brush herself off, she screamed in pain. Her right hand hung limply and had already begun to swell.

"That's it," said Pastora, taking charge. "We're taking you to a hospital."

"I'm fine. It's just sprained," she said, watching the purple color in her hand deepen and spread.

"Yeah, sure. You're going to the hospital."

ॐ

It was midnight before they arrived home. Using one hand, Judith shuffled through her purse, trying to find her keys. The purse strap slipped from her shoulder, and the purse tumbled to the floor, strewing its contents everywhere.

"Damn it!"

She awkwardly wielded her right arm in the cast and sling as she sank to her knees and gathered the coins, comb, keys, and hospital paperwork that were strewn across the hallway.

"Do you need any help?" Pastora asked.

"I got it," snapped Judith, her lips white and pinched.

Pastora watched as Judith gathered the items and threw them into her purse. Mumbling under her breath, Judith struggled to her feet. Pastora held out her hand, but Judith shook her head.

"I'm all right." Judith glared at her sister.

Wearing a weary smile, Pastora shrugged. Judith tried to fit the key into the lock and open the door. Try as she might, she couldn't push in, as she turned the key, and twist the door handle simultaneously with one hand.

After the third attempt, she said, "Well, are you just going to stand there, gawking?!"

With a crooked smile, Pastora silently took the keys, unlocked the door, and held it open.

"I can't believe I broke my finger," said Judith. "I've never broken a bone before. I've always taken such good care of myself." She eyed the cast. "So much plaster for just a finger. And of all times . . . ."

"It could have been worse," said Pastora.

"Yeah, right."

"It's only a finger that's broken," said Pastora, "not your wrist or arm. You only have to wear that cast for a month."

"A month?! It's an eternity. I couldn't even open the door." Pointing with her good hand, Judith sat down on the bed with a sigh. "How am I going to do research, let alone dress myself, eat?"

"I can help you," said Pastora quietly.

"You've got your own work to do," said Judith.

"This is more important."

"No, thanks. I'll be fine." Shoulders heaving, she took a deep breath."I can take care of myself."

"Mmm-hmm, show me. If you can undress and shower by yourself, I'll leave you to your own devices, but, if you can't do these simple things . . . what choice do you have except for me to help you?"

Choice. Her ears perked at the word. Memories flooded her before she realized her sister wanted an answer. "Fair enough," said Judith slowly.

She began to remove her cardigan sweater that had been pushed up to her elbow. It would not fit over the cast. She tugged and pulled, but, try as she might, she could not budge the sweater.

Pastora calmly watched her sister's actions without saying a word.

Judith shot her a mutinous look and groaned with frustration. Then she rummaged through her desk drawers, rifling their contents, slamming them shut until she found a pair of scissors.

"Are you serious?" asked Pastora. "Do you plan on cutting up all your clothes?"

She walked to Judith, took the scissors from her hand, and then gradually stretched and pulled the sweater over the cast.

"Faith, let me help you."

"I don't need . . . ."

"That's just it. You do need help, and I'm freely offering it. Quit being so obstinate. Besides, you really don't have a choice."

"I don't have a choice," she repeated softly, remembering her words from the flashbacks. Her shoulders slumping, she sighed.

"That's better," said Pastora.

"I feel defeated, helpless."

"You helpless?!" Shaking her head, Pastora chuckled but then, seeing Judith's stooped posture, became serious. "Everyone needs a helping hand now and then, even you. This is simply your turn."

Judith looked at her sister, actually seeing her, not grimacing at fabricated shadows of her, not resenting trumped-up ghosts, not avoiding eye contact. Just seeing her for what she was, a good person. *She's not the ogre of my childhood, the ramrodding disciplinarian I recalled, the person I always blamed . . . .* She snorted.

"You're being awfully generous," said Judith, "after . . . after the way I treated you all those years . . . and these past days."

"That isn't important now. With your arm in a cast, let me be your helping hand. I want to do this." Pastora paused. "Judith, do you have any plans for lunch tomorrow?"

"No, why?"

"There's someone I'd like you to meet."

౽

83

"This is Father O'Riley," said Pastora.

Turning toward her sister so he could not see her, Judith narrowed her eyes in a disapproving scowl, irritated that Pastora had coerced her into meeting with a priest. Apparently unaware, Pastora held out her chair for her, giving Judith no choice but to graciously join him for lunch.

"Pastor emeritus," he said, raising an eyebrow. "I'm retired, you know, put out to pasture."

"Father, I'd like you to meet my sister, Faith."

"Judith," she snapped, more loudly than intended. Exhaling, she pursed her lips, feeling the muscles contract in her face.

After watching her reaction, he turned toward Pastora. "Have you lost your 'faith'?" Then pointblank he asked Judith, "Or have you?"

Pastora ducked her head, hiding a chuckle. "I see you two have a lot to talk about." Turning to Judith, she added, "Call me when you're finished with lunch. I can help . . . ."

"Nonsense," he said with a dismissive wave, "do you think I'm so feeble I can't escort your sister home?"

"I was just about to say something similar myself," said Judith.

She studied Pastora, developing a burgeoning respect for her shrewd insight. Initially annoyed at the set-up, Judith smiled begrudgingly, warming both to her sister and the irascible gentleman.

"Call me if you need me," said Pastora, her eyes twinkling.

Judith waved her off and studied her lunch partner's face, lined with decades of concern. She judged him to be in his eighties. As she began reevaluating him, she recognized a kindred spirit behind his clerical clothing.

"Pastor emeritus," she said, "yet you still wear a white collar. Are you only semi-retired?"

"That's a polite way to put it." He snorted contemptuously. "Still in my prime, and they forced me to retire, but I still say seven o'clock Mass every morning."

"Once a priest, always a priest," said Judith, their eyes meeting in understanding. "So much of our identity is tied to our vocation."

"Yes, my vocation has been my life."

"Can I get you something to drink?" asked the waiter.

"Yes, *cerveza*, please," Judith said automatically.

"Beer?!" Father O'Riley looked at her sternly. "If you're going to drink, do it right."

Turning to the waiter, he ordered two shots of tequila.

"And bottled water, *por favor*," Judith quickly added.

"The best tequila is made from one-hundred percent agave, not the run-of-the-mill vodka that's only flavored with tequila," he said.

The tequila came in two pony-sized shot glasses. Judith lifted hers and then hesitated.

"What's the matter?"

"Where's the lime and salt?"

"That's for *gringos* who don't know any better," he said. "Tequila's made for sipping and savoring."

"I thought it was only used in margaritas."

"Heathen."

They both chuckled and toasted with their glasses.

"*Salud*, to your good health," he said, looking at her cast.

"I'll drink to that." Judith rolled the tequila around her mouth, as if tasting fine wine.

"It has a mellow, distinct flavor, hasn't it?" asked Father O'Riley.

Nodding, she savored the clear liquor, identifying the flavors. "Have you always been a priest in Puebla?"

He took another sip before answering. "No, I attended seminary in the States." His eyes clouded over.

"What happened?"

"Politics and too many years."

"Can you be a little more specific?"

"Vatican II," he said cynically.

"I don't understand."

"A reversal of policy changed everything." He sighed. "I'm sorry. I'm just bitter, despite forty years."

"Forty years," she repeated softly, "you, Moses, and I've had to deal with forty years of wandering."

"What's that?"

"Nothing," said Judith. "What was it about Vatican II that kept you from your goals?"

"The seventies were turbulent times," he said, "for society and the Church." He looked at her. "Maybe you're too young to remember."

"Oh, I remember only too clearly," she said dryly. "So how did that affect you?"

"I was groomed in the old ways, and then passed over by those who embraced the new. My views were not simpatico with my bishop's."

Judith nodded and sipped the tequila.

"I was labeled 'traditional' and 'conservative,'" he said. "Once you're labeled, you're marginalized, and when you're marginalized, you're left sitting on the sidelines."

"So what happened?"

"Time and again, I was passed over for promotion by younger men with ideas more in keeping with the times." He looked at her. "If I say so myself, less qualified men rose with the Church's hierarchy."

"You were a wallflower at a dance," she said, lifting the corner of her mouth wryly.

He chuckled at the analogy. "A closer parallel might be that I was the last one picked for the team."

"So you're bitter because you've been a priest and not a bishop?"

"Not exactly. I loved," his cataract-dimmed eyes focused on hers, "I *love* being a priest, a pastor of a flock, but I feel . . . ."

"Unfulfilled?" she asked.

"Exactly, I was groomed to be more, and now I feel I've failed God's plan for me."

"Ouch." She sucked in her breath and downed her tequila with a flick of her wrist. "Another?"

At his nod, she held up two fingers and caught the waiter's eye.

"*Dos mas?*"

"*Si.*" Returning her attention to Father O'Riley, she said, "I can relate."

"You can?" His tired eyes smiled. "How?"

"First, I need another tequila," she said as the waiter set down the drinks. "*Salud.*"

"*Salud.*" Father O'Riley sipped and repeated his question.

"Forty years ago, I had an abortion," she said, half expecting to shock him.

He nodded slowly. "Go on."

"I truly believed, or, at least, I convinced myself that I had no alternative. That if I had the baby, my future would have ended before it began." She took a deep breath.

"You weren't alone." His eyes pulled down as he focused on her. "Millions of women felt that way, continue to feel that way."

"To be honest, it didn't bother me for decades."

"How do you feel about it now?"

"It's odd. Yesterday, while I viewed the tilma of Our Lady of Guadalupe, I had a series of flashbacks so real, so tangible, I could feel the ache after the abortion."

"This isn't uncommon," he said. "Post-abortion trauma is well documented. It can be suppressed or delayed for years." He shook his knobby finger. "But something always triggers it, as happened to you yesterday. For God, there's no sense of time. He's eternal. What happened in the past, and what will happen in the future, seems to God as if it's happening in the moment."

Judith nodded and told him of the giggling girl.

"That is odd." His eyes lit up as he leaned into her. "Yesterday was the first time you've been aware of this?"

"Yes. I first heard her by one of the angel statues in front of the St. Michael chapel."

"Angels are messengers of God." His fingers played at his chin. Then, with a shrug, he raised his palm, questioning. "Maybe God's giving you a message."

"Some message." Judith snorted. "It was when I tried to catch this giggling wonder that I tripped and broke my finger."

He smiled wryly. "God works in mysterious ways."

"That's what my sister tells me."

"Sometimes, we're meant to live life's mysteries without ever knowing the reason."

She held up her sling. "But this is a punishment."

"It is?" He studied her. "For what?"

"I don't know, maybe delayed retribution for killing my baby."

"Maybe," he said, tilting his head to the side. "How does this broken finger affect you?"

"I can't bathe, dress myself . . . ." She counted off a litany of woes.

"Seems to me, you're being tested," he said, sipping his tequila.

"Tested?"

"Yes, this hardship on you could be characterized as punitive, but, from what you're telling me, I believe God's testing you."

"Testing me for what?"

"That's something only God knows."

"I think God's punishing me."

"What about Job?" He sipped his tequila. "Do you think he was punished or tested?"

She snorted. "Punished, definitely!" Itemizing on her fingers, she said, "He lost his children, servants, livestock . . . . He lost everything, even his position in the community."

"He lost his wealth, but he didn't lose his health or his wife."

"Now that's debatable," she said hotly. "If I remember correctly, Job was covered nose-to-toes in maggot-infested boils that stank so badly, even his wife couldn't stand him."

"But she did stay with him, and, ultimately, Job passed God's test. If memory serves me, he recovered to grow wealthier than ever and sire another ten children with her."

"And his suffering was all for what?" She scoffed. "A wager."

"It was a test. Job passed it and was rewarded. He became a wiser, more prosperous person because he persevered, matured, and remained faithful."

"Job's problems all started because of a bet between God and the devil." Her eyes challenged his. "Where's the virtue in that?" When he didn't answer, she added, "It doesn't make sense."

"Whatever God allows doesn't have to make sense to us." Father O'Riley's cataracted eyes twinkled. "God has a problem. He thinks He's God."

She chuckled wryly and then gestured with her casted arm. "Call it what you will, but I think God's chastising me."

"You could approach this as a penance, as a means to atone for past sins." He raised his eyebrows. "Who can say but God, but I believe this is a test, and you have a lesson to learn from it."

"Really?"

"Really." His wizened face stared into hers. "You say your abortion was forty years ago. Moses and the Israelites wandered forty years before they found the Promised Land."

"Forty years," she repeated softly, "with two steps forward, one step back."

"We wax; we wane. We evolve; we devolve." He nodded.

They sipped their tequila in thoughtful silence.

"Judith, have you been to confession since the abortion?"

She snorted then lifted her eyes to him. "Several times over the years, but I've never felt forgiven."

"That's not uncommon. It sounds to me that you haven't forgiven yourself."

"That's probably true, but, after so many years of not being forgiven—"

"Of not feeling forgiven," he interrupted. "There's a difference."

"What's the difference?"

"Everything can be absolved except despair. That's the one sin that's unforgiveable."

"I'm not following." Squinting, she shook her head.

"If you've been forgiven, which you have, and you still don't believe God's forgiven you," he looked at her sternly, "that's a sin against the Holy Spirit. That's despair."

"Great, add on another sin." She threw up her hands in resignation.

"Have you ever joined a post-abortion retreat?"

"No." She reached for the tequila.

"Join one. It'd do you a world of good." His cataracted eyes peered into hers. "You've been forgiven, Judith, but you're not yet healed."

She shrugged as she sipped the tequila. *Someday, I'll join a retreat. Maybe, but now isn't the time.* Recalling the posters and signposts in front of churches about post-abortion reconciliation, she also recalled purposely looking the other way.

He watched her. "Have you ever heard of PASS?"

"Pass?"She raised her eyebrow questioningly.

"Post Abortion Stress Syndrome. It isn't a mainstream topic. Few admit it even exists, but there's mounting evidence that many women experience psychological distress following an abortion. Often, it doesn't surface for years."

Judith grimaced uncomfortably.

"When men return from war with PTSD—"

"With what?" She squinted, unfamiliar with the term.

"Post Traumatic Stress Disorder, society doesn't blame the man and defend the war. No, it realizes the war triggered the man's stress, but society seems less supportive of post-abortion stress. It blames the woman and defends abortion. It either holds the woman responsible for any trauma, since it was her choice to have the abortion, or it dismisses the concept of PASS as an anti-choice myth, labeling the woman either whore or anti-feminist."

"Interesting that you've chosen an analogy of war and abortion," she said, brightening, seizing an opportunity to change the topic. The conversation was becoming too emotionally involving. Judith preferred her comfort zone: academic distance. "In her *Cihuacoatl* aspect, *Tonantzin* was the goddess of battles and birth. She was the patron of warriors and women."

He shook his head. "You're missing my point."

"I was simply linking our conversation to my work." She shrugged and, with a practiced flick of the wrist, downed her tequila.

He fixed his rheumy eyes on hers. "Judith, do you realize you're displaying two common symptoms of blocked grief: alcoholism and workaholism?"

"What—?" She opened her mouth to speak, but indignation made her speechless. *Who the hell died and made you Pope?*

"Forgive me, Judith. I don't mean to be critical, but you may not be aware of your denial. I simply want to bring these classic indicators to your attention. Many women, perhaps millions, feel as you do, unforgiven, that you're being punished. You're not alone. This is a syndrome." He held out a shaking, arthritic hand. "Forgive an old man for being tactless?"

Jaw working, she hesitated. His words still stung like venom, but his trembling hand remained suspended, waiting. She drew in her breath, recognizing yet resenting the truth. Despite her wounded pride, she felt a budding respect for him. *He doesn't pussyfoot around.* With a wry chuckle, she reluctantly extended her hand and shook his.

"A post-abortion retreat might help you resolve old issues."

She nodded solemnly in agreement. *Maybe it would at that. Just not now.* Then she smiled and picked up her menu.

"Didn't we come here for lunch?"

ॐ

Later that afternoon, Pastora asked, "How was lunch with Father O'Riley?"

"He's very insightful," said Judith, her nod a tacit affirmation of the man.

"Good, I'm glad you hit it off. He's been lonely and needs a friend."

Judith looked at her sister in surprise. "I thought you wanted him to keep me company."

Like Living on Top of a Volcano

"Unless there is a Good Friday in your life, there can be no Easter Sunday."

~ Bishop Fulton Sheen

When Jarek missed their three o'clock call again, Ceren's unproven concerns began to solidify into real fear. She called his cell at three-fifteen and left a message. When he had not returned her call by four o'clock, she began dialing every fifteen minutes.

As the quarter hours ticked by, she felt less and less sure of Jarek's commitment to her. At five o'clock, he answered.

"Jarek, I—"

"Oh, it's you," he said, lowering his voice. "Look, I have to keep this line open."

"But you haven't called all week."

"This is important."

"And I'm not?" When he didn't answer, she asked slowly, "Is that what you're telling me?"

His voice chilly, he said, "I'm expecting a call."

"I'm expecting, too . . . your baby. I'm expecting your call. I'm expecting you to . . . . Hello?"

Ceren heard muffled voices, as if he were covering the mouthpiece while speaking to someone. Then it sounded as if the phone were being passed.

"Who is this?" demanded a woman's voice.

"Who's this?" Ceren sputtered.

"This is Mrs. Witunski, Dean Witunski's wife. I've heard all about you and your vicious lies."

"I don't know what he's told you, but—"

"Listen, you little whore, never call my husband again, or I'll have you dismissed, and you'll never work again, here or in any university. If you know what's good for you, you'll quit spreading rumors and keep your mouth shut."

The phone went dead in Ceren's hand.

Ceren angrily redialed his number. No answer. She called his office line, and the assistant answered.

"Dean Witunski," she said as casually as she could muster. Still, her breathing was jagged.

"Who may I say is calling?"

She felt like saying 'Mrs. Witunski, Dean Witunski's wife,' but instead she said, "This is Professor Rodriguez."

The assistant's tone was icy. "Dean Witunski is not in."

Again the line went dead.

Her breathing labored, Ceren began dialing his cell number but stopped midway, imagining what had occurred. Judith was right. He is a jerk. She ran different scenarios through her mind, how he had gotten back with his wife . . . or, as Judith had said, had never left her.

"What an idiot I am, what an imbecile! How could I have ever believed him, believed in him?" Unaware she was thinking out loud, she shouted, "How could I have defended the jerk, the bigamist?!"

She threw herself on the bed, sobbing. *What am I going to do? After this semester, I can't imagine the university renewing the contract . . . not if Jerk had married me while still wed to his first wife.*

What if our marriage isn't legal? What if he has no intention of being a husband to me, a father to our child? How will I earn a living while I'm pregnant . . . or even after I have the baby?

Her sobs gave way to tears. *My plans, my dreams of raising a family with Jarek were nothing but fantasies built on lies. Now what? My career, my reputation are ruined. What will I do?*

"What'll I do?!" she shrieked at the top of her lungs.

At a loss, she picked up the nearest book, "Raising Baby with Smiles," glanced at its title, and, enraged, threw it at the dresser, shattering the mirror.

"I hate you! I hate you!" she screamed, oblivious to the insistent knocking at her door.

"Ceren, are you all right?" Judith's voice came through the door.

Ceren buried her head in the pillow, stifling her sobs, and pretended not to be home.

The knocking persisted.

"Ceren, I know you're in there. Are you all right?"

When she failed to answer, the knocking became louder.

"Go away," Ceren finally called.

"Are you all right?"

"I'm fine. Please go away."

"You're not fine," called Judith. "Either you open this door, or I'm getting the janitor to open it for me."

Pinching the bridge of her nose and tightly squeezing her eyes, Ceren gathered her faculties before unlatching the door.

"You're far from fine. That's obvious." Judith looked at her tear-stained face. "What happened?" Holding her arm gingerly, Judith invited herself in and sat down.

"Nothing happened." Ceren brushed away the tears. "I stubbed my toe."

"Right." Holding up her arm in the cast, she said, "And I'm wearing a diamond bracelet."

When Ceren did not speak or sit, Judith said, "It's Jerk, isn't it?"

"Yes," Ceren involuntarily sobbed. "You were right."

"I've got a pretty good idea of what happened," said Judith, "but tell me, anyway."

"He is a jerk."

"So it's over, I presume?"

"Oh, big time!" She angrily wiped her eyes with her hand. "He'd promised to call every day. The first day I didn't hear from him, I worried but thought something important had come up."

"Go on."

"When he hadn't called for several days," said Ceren, "I began calling him."

"Did he return the calls?"

"What do you think?" Their eyes met in understanding.

"And just now," Judith gestured to the shattered glass littering the room. "What did Jerk say to bring on all this?"

"It was nothing he said." Her eyes wet with tears, Ceren added, "It was what his . . . his wife said . . . she . . . ." Nearly choking, Ceren swallowed her anger and hurt. "She called me a whore, said never to call her husband again, and told me to keep my mouth shut if I knew what was good for me."

"The coward," said Judith, snorting, shaking her head.

"She didn't sound like a coward to me," said Ceren.

"I meant Jerk, what a cowardly little man."

Blinking, Ceren thought it through. "You're right. He just tried to lie his way out of it . . . again . . . and then let her fight his battle for him." Realization beginning to set in, Ceren said, "Let her have him. He isn't worth it."

"She either doesn't know the whole story, or she's bluffing, trying to scare you off," said Judith. "Sue him for bigamy. Start a paternity suit, naming him as the correspondent. A blood test will quickly prove Jerk's the father."

"But making it public would ruin my professional reputation as well as his," said Ceren.

"Call his bluff." Judith sneered. "Jerk stands to lose a whole lot more than you if this becomes public. Since you're a member of his department, he's technically your supervisor. The law's clear about sexual harassment . . . and bigamy."

"I can't believe how naïve I was," she said, her chin dropping to her chest.

"It doesn't matter," said Judith. "He lied to you, took advantage of your inno . . . took advantage of you. They know and I know, if this were brought before the board of regents, he'd be suspended."

"Doesn't he have tenure?"

Judith shook her head. "I told you he got the dean's position by default . . . and with his wife's money. It's temporary and meaningless, but he used that position to take advantage of you."

"I don't know," said Ceren, taking a deep breath.

"Trust me. My last husband was an attorney. We're still on speaking terms. I'll call Sam tonight, and he'll take care of things."

Ceren gave a half-smile. "But I'm pregnant. Can Sam take care of that, too?"

"We didn't see eye-to-eye on everything," said Judith, "but he's the best there is in the business." Pausing a moment, she added, "I bet he could even find you adoptive parents for your baby, if you like."

"With such an uncertain future, maybe I should get an abortion and be done with it," she said, thinking out loud. "The more I think about it, you were right the first time we talked . . . right about Jerk and right about getting an abortion."

Judith became silent, listening to her own words repeated.

"I don't want any part of him. I especially don't want his child growing in me. It's not too late. I'm only eight weeks pregnant."

"Ceren, maybe you ought to consider adoption."

"You're the one who was so adamant about my getting an abortion. What did you call it, a missed period, a worm, a clump of cells?"

Judith flinched. "Yes, I said that. I believed that. Only . . . ."

"Only what?"

"I've believed this for forty years," said Judith, speaking slowly. "Only now I'm beginning to wonder if that's true, if that clump of cells isn't actually a baby, an immature baby . . . ."

"And I've always been against abortion . . . until now," said Ceren. "Part of me wants to get rid of it, be done with it, and be done with the Jerk."

Seeing how distraught Ceren was, Judith said, "It's been a rough day.

Let's get something to eat, and you'll feel better."

"Food isn't going to make me feel better," said Ceren. "The only thing that will is getting rid of reminders of the Jerk."

"Look, to have a paternity case, you need a baby," Judith said sternly. "Don't do anything rash until I speak to my ex-husband and we get his advice, okay?"

Ceren shrugged.

"C'mon, let me buy your dinner."

"Thanks, but I'm really not hungry." She looked at the mirrored confetti strewn across the room. "Besides, I have a little cleaning up to do."

Ceren let Judith out and began sweeping up the mess. How could she have been so stupid?

Her cell phone rang. Despite her anger, her hurt, her hopes rose.

"Hello," she said tentatively, wishing caller ID worked in Mexico.

"Ceren, my darling," said Jarek.

"Of all the men in the world, why did I have to pick you to get me pregnant?!"

"I don't blame you for feeling that way," said Jarek slowly, as if testing the waters. "After what you've experienced, you have every right to feel that way."

Rage rose in her throat like acid reflux. "You bastard! So you're back with your first wife, or had you ever left her?"

"Ceren, you have it all wrong. I lost my cell phone and only found it today. My w . . . my ex-wife happened to be in my office, signing the final paperwork, when you called."

As he spoke, she clutched her chest, wondering. *How can two parts of my body, my heart and mind, work so disjointedly. I despise him yet still love him. Love's not something I can switch off as easily as my phone.* She sighed. *I'm not dumb enough to believe him, yet maybe this time he'll redeem himself. After all, he is my husband, for better, for worse. I've got to give him the chance . . . .*

"Are you telling me the truth?"

"Of course, I am."

"Paperwork, then you're saying the annulment's final?"

"You took the words right out of my mouth."

"It is?" Tears welled up. "You're separated?"

"We've been emotionally separated for months."

Something didn't sound right. She paused. Whether from naïveté or the inability to confront him, she felt embarrassed to ask, but was compelled.

"So . . . so we can be married in church now?"

"Why else would I be calling?"

"You're not answering me." Catching onto his game, she took a deep breath, trying to keep her rising anger in check. "Since you're being so evasive, let me rephrase that. *When* are we getting married in church?"

"We still have to file the paperwork," he said, "and then get the judge's blessing."

"What kind of sick game are you playing? Since last summer, you've been telling me you are divorced, that you're just waiting for the annulment. Lately, you've added 'except for' lawyers, paperwork, filing, or judges."

"You're twisting my words . . . ."

"This waiting game of yours is like living on top of *Popocatépetl*."

"Popo . . . on what?" His irritation came through his tone.

"A volcano," she said, ready to explode herself. "Have you ever told me the truth?"

"If you're going to be unreasonable, I'll just hang up . . . ."

His words hung in the air like the smoke over *Popocatépetl*, quietly threatening.

Ceren paused, debating, her desire to believe him overwhelming her better judgment. *Despite everything that's happened, I still want to be with him.* She groaned. *But it's so hard to stand up to him. Why?* Rolling her eyes, she sighed. *Why, other than the fact he's a father figure, authority figure, and my boss rolled into one? I realized this the day he proposed, but I didn't think it would be this hard to stand up for myself.* She scratched her head.

Once again, the phone line was the horse hair holding the sword of Damocles over her head.

"I'm listening," she said finally.

"Good, that's showing maturity."

She bit back a snide remark, instead saying, "I'm listening, but only if you have something worth hearing."

"What do you want to hear? That we'll be married in church?" he asked impatiently.

"That's what you've been telling me for months. What I want to hear is when."

"I wish I could tell you."

"When we met, you said you were divorced, just waiting for the annulment to finalize. When the Justice of the Peace married us in August, you told me we'd be married in the Church by October, which is nearly over, I might add." Suddenly brightening, she had an idea. "Come to Mexico. Aren't they supposed to have fast-track divorces here?"

"So?"

"So maybe annulments are faster here, as well?"

"You obviously don't understand the complexities of this," he said, ending with a derisive sigh.

"What's so complicated about it?" she asked sarcastically. "And don't patronize me!"

"If you're going to be childish about this, there's no sense in continuing this conversation."

"Strange you mention child. Have you once asked about the baby? About me? Do you recall that I'm pregnant with your child?

"How could I forget?" he asked drily.

"This conversation is going in circles. Are you marrying me or not?"

"Yes."

"When, next month?"

"How would you like a Christmas wedding?"

"Are you setting the date?" she asked, stifling a deeply-felt sigh.

"Possibly . . . ."

"You're so irritating," she said. "Yes, no, December?"

"What are you babbling about?"

"Marriage, I'm making this simple for you. Yes, no: are you marrying me in the Church in December?"

"If the filing . . . ."

"This is a simple yes-no question. What's your answer?"

"Yes."

"December what, the first?" she asked.

"Now what?"

"What date? Set a date in December."

"Oh, the twenty-third . . . tentatively . . . ."

"Are you capable of making a decision?" she asked.

"Ceren, this position as dean is far more demanding than I'd anticipated."

"So?" she hissed.

"So, until we're actually married in the Church, have you considered . . . not having this baby?"

"Not having . . . ." She struggled to contain her anger, not wanting to jump to any conclusions. *I'll give him the benefit of the doubt.* She breathed deeply, slowly, counting to ten. "What are you suggesting?"

"Once we're married, we'll have a dozen children. In the interim, this would buy us time."

"What would buy us time?" Her voice rose. "Are you suggesting I get an—"

"Hear me out." The tone of his voice changed. "Your reputation wouldn't be compromised just because the courts move so slowly."

"So you're concerned about my reputation," she said sarcastically.

"Exactly. You know how much you mean to me. I wouldn't want to see your character harmed in any way."

"Mm-hmm, didn't the woman who claimed to be your wife call me a whore and say I'd never work again in a university? Didn't she threaten to, what was it, 'have me dismissed?'"

"She has a volatile temper when she's been drinking. Don't listen to anything she says."

"You didn't defend me then. Why should I believe you're concerned with my reputation now?"

"I can't reason with her when she's been drinking. She's not even coherent. Why do you think I divorced her? She doesn't understand me. Ceren, I can talk to you, something I've never been able to do with her."

"Talk to me?" she repeated, scoffing. "You're unbelievable. You talk at me. You only lie to me. Now you want me to have an abortion, just so 'my reputation,' as you put it, isn't compromised."

"That's right. My only concern is you. I wouldn't want to see you harmed in any way."

She groaned in frustration. "But it's okay to abort the baby?"

"We'll have others. Don't be selfish, Ceren. Think of what I'm giving up for you."

"You're not giving up anything. You've had your cake and you've eaten it, too. From the start, you told me you were divorced, yet here we are, discussing your wife. You're the most self-centered person I know. Don't you dare call me selfish!"

"What about my position as dean?" he asked, changing his approach. "Don't you care if I have a job to support us?"

"What are you getting at?" she asked.

"I'd lose this position if anyone suspected—"

"If anyone suspected you of what, sexual harassment, bigamy? I see. Your only concern is about you, your reputation, and your job. All's well while I'm out of sight." Then recalling Judith's words, she added, "But you'd be in hot water if I sue for bigamy or bring a paternity suit against you, wouldn't you?"

"Ceren, that line of talk is pure nonsense. We're two consenting adults, who love each—"

"Love?" She laughed scornfully. "This is the first time that word's entered our conversation."

"You know I love you. How can you think otherwise?"

"Very easily." She snickered. "Tell me, have you ever intended to announce our wedding, or do you want us to keep our marriage a sordid secret forever?"

"Why do you insist on doubting me?"

She groaned. "That reminds me, how did you manage to live with me as man and wife while you're still married to her?"

"I've told you." His impatience came through his tone. "I'm divorced."

"Where was she during that time?"

"If you must know, she didn't take our divorce very well. She went on one of her binges and then checked herself into a rehab clinic."

"Presumably to dry out." Nodding, she mumbled, "That agrees with Judith's version."

"What?"

"I said," Ceren sneered, "weren't you afraid she'd call at an 'inopportune' time?"

He took a deep breath and blew it out through his nostrils. "It was a lock-down program."

"Which means . . . ."

"She could accept calls, but she couldn't call out."

"How convenient for you. Incidentally, where did you find your phone?"

"My phone?" Sounding perplexed, he paused. "Oh, you mean my cell phone. Oh, uh, it was, uh, in the, uh, in the car, under the seat."

"Mmm-hmm . . . very convincing." Rolling her eyes, she shook her head slowly. *This guy is unbelievable.* "And, since you love me so much, as you've recently stated, why did you let your . . . that woman insult me like that?"

"I told you," he said, raising his voice. "She has anger issues, especially when she's been drinking." He took a deep breath. "Look," he started again in a silken, persuasive voice. "I'm getting the annulment as soon as I can."

How does he do that? He changes personas faster than a chameleon changes color.

"We're so close now. Can't you be patient just a little while longer?"

"What's patience got to do with anything? What about our baby? A few minutes ago, you wanted me to get an abortion."

"It's not an abortion. It's just a D&C, a simple office procedure, and it's over. My w . . . ex-wife's even had it done." His tone became honeyed. "After we're married in church, we'll have a houseful of children."

"A D&C," she repeated, mocking him, ignoring the carrot he dangled in front of her.

"Yes, dilation and curettage," he said, sounding clinical and detached. "It's an outpatient procedure."

"It's a euphemism for abortion." She sniffed. "If you really want to have children, as you say, why kill this one?"

"It's complicated." He sighed. "I'm just so miserable without you, I . . . I have an idea!" Suddenly, his voice became animated. "Come back for the weekend. We can spend it together, and I know a doctor who'll squeeze you in."

"Squeeze me in?"

"That's right."

"For a D&C?"

"Exactly," he said.

"But you want kids?" She rolled her eyes.

"A houseful!"

"Just not this particular one," she said, trying to keep the sarcasm out of her voice.

"Come back this weekend, and we can make it a romantic retreat, a honeymoon."

"What about a romantic getaway, but, instead of getting an abortion, we get married in the Church?"

"Ceren, you know that isn't possible, at least, not just yet. Have the D&C, and we'll be properly married after Christmas."

"I thought you said by Christmas? And before that, November, and before that—"

"Don't be unreasonable. Look at everything I'm giving up for you . . . a house, a home—"

"So now you're trying to make me feel guilty?" She forced a laugh. "You think everything is you, you, you. You don't do anything that isn't in your own best interest." She snickered again. "Listen, you're the one who told me you were divorced, not the other way around, so, if anyone should feel guilty, it's you. Finally, I get it. Judith was right."

"Judith?" His fear came through the phone. "You haven't told Dr. Truman you're pregnant, have you?"

"Not only that I'm pregnant," she said, her self-satisfaction coming through her voice, "but that you're the father, and that you married me before finalizing—"

"How could you talk about our private lives?" he asked, his breathing becoming labored. "This is our personal affair."

"Affair, that's a perfect choice of words." Glancing at the broken-mirror splinters still scattered across the floor, she grunted. *Looks like shards of broken dreams.* Sighing, she rubbed her forehead. "I've also told her about your broken promises to me."

"What . . . ." His tone started as a reprimand but ended as a question. "What did she say?"

"That I should sue you for bigamy and start a paternity suit against you . . . ." She let the words hang in the air. "Have a nice day."

She disconnected and turned off her cell. Looking at herself in the broken mirror, she shook her head. *The bastard. How could I have believed him? What was wrong with me? His lies are so transparent.*

Pursing her lips, she took a deep breath. *It's time I admit it: our 'marriage' has been a sham from the very start. I knew it. I knew it! I should never have listened to him.* She sighed. *I should have followed my instincts.*

Why couldn't I see that before I got pregnant? She thumped her forehead and groaned. *If it weren't for this baby, I wouldn't want anything to do with the jerk. and I certainly wouldn't want a church wedding. Just get a quiet annulment to get on with my life.*

She clutched her stomach. *But, whether it's convenient or not, I have this baby to consider. He or she needs a father, or at least needs a legal name.*

Then she remembered Judith's words from that first night in the café. "Lose it. Get rid of it . . . . Don't ruin your career, your life, because of some stupid mistake. Take care of it!" She narrowed her eyes, analyzing the idea, weighing its possibilities.

Without a baby, there'd be nothing holding me back from dissolving this . . . this . . . I don't even have a word for our relationship. I can't even call it a common-law marriage. It's . . . it's . . . it isn't anything. Frustrated that she had no word for their marriage, tears welled up. She dropped her forehead into her hands and recalled the day Jarek had proposed, their wedding day, the first time she had brought up having a church wedding.

ૐ

Chuckling, he playfully held up his hands, as if fending her off. "One wedding at a time, please." With a kiss to seal the proposal, Jarek raced toward Pecos, Texas, and then on to Carlsbad, New Mexico. Even with a frantic, last-minute search for the county clerk's office, they had their marriage license in hand, had said, "I do" in front of the county judge, and were out the door before the courthouse closed at five.

Standing beneath an ancient live oak on the courthouse grounds that hot August afternoon, they planned their next step.

"Where would you like to spend our first night together, Mrs. Witunski?"

Mrs. Witunski. The words sounded musical, magical. She couldn't believe she was a bride, a married woman. Taking a deep breath, she studied the attractive man beside her, finding it difficult to think of him as her husband.

"Well?"

"Sorry, I'm still reeling from all that's happened today. My mind's playing catch up. Then glancing at the street sign, she said, "Carlsbad Caverns is only twenty-seven miles away." She smiled shyly, feeling bashful. "Maybe we could stay near there and visit the Caverns before we head back to Austin?"

"You mean, if we find time this weekend." He looked at her pointedly, and she felt the heat rise in her cheeks. She took a deep breath, realizing more was ahead.

Too self-conscious to meet his eyes, she stared instead at the wedding license still clasped in her hands. She still couldn't believe they were married. Maybe if she reread the certificate, reality would sink in. Snickering at herself, she scanned its contents. Suddenly she gasped.

"What?"

"Jarek, did you fill out this field wrong?"

"Which one?" He looked at the certificate she held out.

"For Marital Status, you put 'Single.' Shouldn't you have put 'Divorced'?"

"Oh, that." He waved off the idea. "Rather than bring it up, I just didn't mention the previous marriage."

She drew her eyebrows together, a furrow forming between her eyes. "This couldn't somehow affect the legality of our marriage, could it?"

"Of course not." He dismissed it with a shrug. "They don't care about the details, just that I'm free to marry you."

"I don't know . . . ." Rubbing her eyebrow, she debated whether they should correct the paperwork. "Maybe we should go back—"

"The courthouse is closed for the weekend."

She winced. "I'm just uneasy about this. I wonder . . . ."

She looked at the certificate, fingering it. She'd better ask if it was valid, just to be safe. Caught in a moral dilemma, she looked back at the office building. Maybe it was still open? Fingers nervously playing at her lips, she watched as the guard locked the door behind him. There was her answer.

Forehead creasing, she peered up at Jarek. "Maybe we should wait until Monday morning, just spend the weekend here . . . as friends . . . and then straighten this out—"

"What a worry wart I've married." His lips curling into a smile, he took her hand is his, gently drawing her to him. "This is definitely a case where less is more. The less said, the less red tape, and the more time we'll have together this weekend as legally wed man and wife." He pulled her to him in a tender kiss.

Sensing the strength of his body pressed against hers, she felt her tension, all her worry drain away. The elopement, their whirlwind wedding suddenly took shape. She could finally put her mind around it.

Then mid-kiss, she started chuckling.

Stiffening, Jarek tilted his head back to look at her. "Is it something I did?"

It took her a moment to recover from a case of the giggles. "I'm . . ." she caught her breath. "I'm sorry. I just thought of something that struck me funny."

"Yes . . . " He eyed her dubiously.

"Judging from your expression, you might as well be asking if I've lost my mind." She sighed. "I know it sounds silly, but, when you kissed me, an image popped into my head of Snow White when the Prince woke her."

His left eyebrow cocked, he looked at her skeptically.

"Your proposal, our marriage has happened so fast, none of it seemed real, not until you kissed me just now and brought it all to life." She took a deep breath, collecting her thoughts. "It's as if your kiss grounded me, made this whole idea take root, have any substance." She pressed against him, hugging him, digging her fingers into his back. "You're the only thing tangible in this . . . fairytale. I keep thinking I'll wake up to find it's all been a dream."

ॐ

"Judith, what a surprise," said Sam, the warmth coming through his voice. "It's great to hear from you."

"It's good to hear your voice, as well," she said, genuinely surprised to mean it.

"How're things going? Are you still at the university?"

"Actually, I'm doing research in Mexico. Grant money," she added.

"Glad you're pursuing your goals," he said. "I know how important that is to you."

Judith heard the sincerity in his voice. Instead of getting to her point, she had the sudden urge to know more about him.

"And you, what are you up to?"

"The usual, divorce cases, paternity suits . . . ."

She paused. Although it had been two years since their no-fault divorce became final, Judith felt uncomfortable. What had seemed like a good idea minutes ago now placed her in an awkward position.

"Actually, that's what I'm calling about."

"Our divorce?"

"No," she cleared her voice, "a colleague needs advice regarding a paternity suit."

"Shoot."

After explaining the situation, Judith asked, "So does she have a case?"

"For openers, they'd need a DNA sample, either from an amniocentesis or CVS."

"What's CVS?"

"Chorionic villus sampling, a procedure where a needle extracts genetic information from the uterine wall."

"That doesn't sound pleasant," said Judith, wincing.

"Incidentally, neither test is performed past the twenty-fourth week. How far along is she?"

"She isn't showing yet. I believe she's nearly two months' pregnant."

"I take it your colleague doesn't anticipate the father admitting to his paternity?"

"It seems unlikely," she said.

"In that case, they'd have to sample the alleged father's DNA and compare."

"Thank you, Sam," she said. "I appreciate the information." Again she paused. "Well, I just called . . . ."

"Does she have an attorney," he asked quickly.

"No," she said, glad to prolong the conversation. "Can you recommend one?"

"What about me?"

"You?!" Caught off-guard, she said, "That's a generous offer, but don't you have a full docket?"

"I'll clear it."

"Just like that?" she asked, unconvinced.

"Just like that." After a self-deprecatory chuckle, he added, "Of course, I'd have to meet my client."

"Of course," she said, tongue-in-cheek, matching his tone.

"Where in Mexico are you?"

"Outside of Mexico City in Puebla." She warmed to the idea of seeing him again, but recalled his hectic schedule only too well. "Seriously, Sam, your calendar must be full."

"So what if it is? Judith, I'd . . . ." He paused, catching his breath. "What would you say to showing me around Puebla next weekend?" When she hesitated, he added, "For old time's sake."

She heard the smile come through his voice.

"I suppose you should meet with your client," she said, struggling not to chuckle.

ح

Ceren dumped the last dustpan of glass splinters into the trash as she heard a knock. Brushing off her hands, she opened the door.

"Sr. Pastora, come in." Following her stare at the broken mirror, Ceren added, "I had a little accident."

"Are you all right?" Pastora asked.

"Anyone else would have said, 'Seven years bad luck.'" She snickered.

"Did you hurt yourself? You look flushed."

"The broken glass didn't hurt me," Ceren said.

"Then what did?"

Ceren relayed the story.

"So this Jarek is married to two women. Now what?"

"He wants me to get an abortion."

"What do you want to do?"

Ceren found it difficult to meet Pastora's eyes. She stared down at her hands.

"I'd wanted this baby more than anything."

"Past tense," said Pastora, "wanted."

"If Jarek and I could be married in church, I'd still want it, but . . . ."

"It," repeated Pastora. "What about now that his annulment appears . . . unlikely? What about the baby?"

"I," Ceren looked up to read Pastora's eyes, "I want it, the baby, the marriage in church, but I don't see how I can have one without the other."

Ceren gave a sigh of relief that she had voiced her thoughts, yet her chest ached, realizing where that line of thought could lead.

"You know, you have options," said Pastora. "Even if you decide not to raise the baby, there are so many infertile couples who'd love to adopt him or her. Think of the gift you'd be giving them, literally, the gift of life."

"I have to be realistic." Ceren rubbed her temples. "It's still seven more months that I'd have to support myself." Rolling her eyes, she added, "That is, if I still have a job next semester."

"There are crisis pregnancy centers where unwed mothers can stay."

Ceren shook her head. "I'm sorry, Pastora, but I don't want to live in a dormitory."

"Sometimes, infertile couples supplement the mother's income during the second and third trimesters."

"I know you're trying to help, but . . . ."

"This isn't the time," Pastora said, looking around the small room, "or place." Then her eyes lit up. "You need to be uplifted. Ceren, have you seen the Chapel of the *Rosario*?"

She shook her head.

"It's breathtaking. Vaulted, gilded, New Spain Baroque, it's a work of art. I often go there to feast my eyes, while I meditate on the tangible faith of the artisans who created its beauty for the greater glory of God."

"Well . . . ."

"The Church of *Santo Domingo* has one of the most elaborately decorated chapels in Mexico. It's a ten-minute walk," said Sr. Pastora, "seven, if we hurry." She smiled that hopeful, little-girl grin, and Ceren chuckled despite herself.

"Okay, you convinced me."

Ceren automatically picked up her cell phone with her keys.

"Do you need that?" Pastora asked, looking at the phone.

"Nope," she said, slowly replacing it on her dresser. "I don't need to keep that line open any longer."

As they started toward the door, Judith knocked.

"Good timing, would you like to join us?" asked Pastora.

"Where are you going?"

"To the Chapel of the *Rosario*," said Pastora. Her eyes twinkling mischievously, she added, "It's such an important part of the area's religious anthropology, that is, from an academic view. Why don't you join us?"

"All right," said Judith, holding a pair of blue topaz earrings in her hand. "But only if you'll put these on for me."

"They're lovely." Taking them from her hand, Pastora studied them in the light. "Are those stars I see in them?"

"Yes, that's the Lone Star Cut. Blue topaz is the state gem of Texas," said Judith.

Pastora placed them in Judith's ears. "I've never seen you wear them."

"They're from Sam," Judith said, the corners of her mouth tilting up in a shy grin.

Ceren and Pastora exchanged glances.

"Who's Sam?" asked Pastora.

"You never met my ex-husband?"

"I thought his name was Ed."

"He was my first husband. Sam was my second."

"Faith, I never met either of your husbands. In fact, I didn't know you'd been married a second time."

The two sisters' eyes met.

"I forgot how long it's been since we lost touch, how little we've shared of each other's life," said Judith.

"So you've been married and divorced twice?" asked Pastora, her usual smile morphing into a subtle scowl.

"Annulled the first time, and divorced the second . . . . Why?" she asked sharply.

"So where's this chapel?" asked Ceren, sensing the tension. "Did you say it's close by?"

Dancing Angels and Onyx

"The Rosary is the best therapy for these distraught, unhappy, fearful, and frustrated souls, precisely because it involves the simultaneous use of three powers: the physical, the vocal, and the spiritual, and in that order."

~ Bishop Fulton Sheen

Ten minutes later, they entered the chapel.

"You said it was a work of art," said Ceren, staring at the gilded ceiling and onyx stonework, "but I wasn't prepared for this masterpiece."

"This chapel is where I come to meditate," said Pastora, whispering. "The artistry is a small reflection, a shadow, of the magnificence of God's creation." She pointed to the architecture. "The dome is coated with ornate sculptures in gold-leaf-covered plaster. On the walls, golden vines frame six paintings, depicting the mysteries of the rosary."

Ceren and Judith stared, wide-eyed, speechless.

"In its day," continued Pastora, "this chapel was considered the eighth wonder of the world. See the statue of the Virgin of the Rosary? It's surrounded by saints, serpents, dancing angels, martyrs, and a heavenly orchestra of cherubim. Its style is *Churrigueresque,* Spanish Baroque."

"It's beautiful," said Ceren in a hushed voice, moving toward the altar.

She sat in the front pew, attracted to the craftsmanship of the gilded altar, onyx pillars, paintings, and Talavera tile. She read and re-read the words inscribed, "*Palabra de Dios,* Word of God."

"The Dominican order began building the Church of *Santo Domingo* in 1532," said Pastora. Knowing that history appealed to Judith, she stressed the intellectual over the spiritual. "That was only a year after work began at Our Lady of Guadalupe's basilica."

Nodding, Judith sat in a pew near the exit.

"Sit closer to the altar," Pastora urged in a whisper. "You'll be able to see the details better."

Judith shook her head. "I like to sit where I can make a hasty retreat."

"Why?"

"It's been years, decades, since I sat in a chapel," said Judith. "I don't want to feel trapped."

"There's so much of you I don't understand," said Pastora, shaking her head.

"There's so much of me I don't understand," said Judith, sitting back in her seat.

Sr. Pastora nodded. "Like I said, this is my favorite place to meditate." She gently touched Judith's shoulder. "I'll be back."

A moment later, Judith saw a shadow cross over her. She turned, expecting to see her sister. No one was there. She looked from side to side. No one was near.

Ceren was still seated in the front staring at the artistry of the chapel. Across the pew from her was a very pregnant Mexican woman fervently praying the rosary. Shrugging off the shadow as her imagination, Judith wondered what was going through the pregnant women's minds.

She recalled the regret she had felt at the basilica, wishing she could undo what she had done forty years before.

Again, shadows swept and swirled in front of her, so close that she ducked, thinking someone had come up behind her. She turned again quickly, but no one was there.

She remembered the goose bumps she had felt in the presence of the tilma, recalling that Our Lady of Guadalupe is the Patroness of the Unborn.

Suddenly, she felt a presence, as if someone had sat down beside her.

"Could it be?" she whispered to herself, wondering if she were hallucinating or simply experiencing an overactive imagination.

Again she ducked, seeing, feeling the shadows that played in front of her eyes. Certain that someone was behind her, she turned abruptly. No one was there, but the feeling that someone was seated beside her seemed stronger.

Judith tried to do something she had not done in years: pray. She prayed for her baby, for her lost innocence, for her ex-husbands, for her sister, for Ceren and her baby.

Again she saw a shadow, but she did not turn until it touched her shoulder.

"Faith," said Pastora, "unless you want to stay for Mass, we should leave."

"We just got here," said Judith, stretching, as if waking up.

"That was over an hour ago," said Pastora softly. "Would you like to stay longer?"

"No, that's okay." Then Judith reached for her sister's arm. "I had the strangest sensation."

"What?"

"Shadows," Judith sighed, "I don't know how to describe it, but it seemed shadows kept crossing in front of me and behind me."

Sr. Pastora smiled. "I told you this chapel was a shadow of the magnificence of God's creation."

"But I mean actual shadows, so close, they felt as if they were above my head. I mean, I actually ducked, they seemed so close."

Sr. Pastora nodded.

"You've felt this?"

"Not as you describe it, but this is God's house, after all," said Pastora. "Why couldn't there be shadows of souls here? God works in mysterious ways."

"I even felt . . . ." Judith stopped just short of describing the sensation that her baby, her forty-year-old baby, had sat beside her in the pew.

"Felt what?"

"Oh, nothing important," said Judith, embarrassed by such an irrational thought. "Here comes Ceren," she said, glad for the interruption.

"What a peaceful, beautiful chapel," said Ceren. "It's easy to see why this is your favorite place."

"Here's a little something to remember the chapel by," said Pastora. She held up two rosaries, giving one to each woman.

"Onyx?" asked Ceren.

"Yes, it's the local stone here."

"It looks more like moonstone, it's so translucent," Ceren said. "How appropriate, a rosary from the *Rosario* Chapel. Thank you." She kissed Pastora's cheek.

"I don't recall the last time I held a rosary," said Judith. She reached for it with her good hand and suspended it from her hand in the cast. It rotated, letting the light reflect through it. Then, holding her cast out of the way, she hugged her sister.

"Thank you."

Pastora started to speak, then cleared her voice and tried again.

"Just a remembrance," she said. "We'd better leave before Mass starts." Turning aside quickly, she brushed a tear away.

ॸ

That evening, after Judith's shower, Pastora helped her remove the waterproof sleeve from her cast.

"You never knew that Sam and I had married?" asked Judith.

"Or that you'd divorced," said Pastora, "until you mentioned it recently."

"But you knew I'd married my first husband?"

Pastora nodded while she helped Judith slip into a nightgown.

"Did I write you about the annulment?"

"Aunt Tillie mentioned you'd separated."

Judith shook her head, vividly recalling that January day forty years before when she returned from the abortion. The look on Maryl's face had spoken volumes. She didn't have to voice her condemnation.

Her expression said how much I'd let her down. What a failure I was, how I hadn't lived up to her expectations—never would—never could. That feeling of failure has stayed with me my whole life, no matter what I've accomplished, no matter what awards I've earned.

Jaw working, wanting to open the lines of communication, but not knowing where to begin, Judith regarded her sister.

"How can you be so kind to me after all those years I ignored you?"

"It's simple," said Pastora. "You need my help now, and I'm glad to give it."

"You don't . . . resent me?"

"I can't say I'm not saddened by all the years we wasted, but resent you?" She shook her head, adding, "Of course not."

Pastora hung up the towels and tidied the sink.

"For someone who's always had to be so damned independent, I feel very vulnerable now," Judith said, raising her casted hand. "I can't even shower or dress myself. This is all very . . . humbling."

"It's all right, Faith. I'm glad to help."

Judith looked at her sister. "Why do you still call me Faith? Nobody else does."

"It's the way I remember you," said Pastora, her eyes focusing on past memories. "You were such a trusting little girl. When you were born, I told Mother that you were my baby."

"Really?"

"Nine years' difference is a lot to a child."

Judith nodded.

"Did you know it was my idea to name you Faith?"

"No, I'd never heard that. Why did you choose that name?"

"Even as a newborn, you couldn't take your eyes off me. You used to follow me with those big eyes. You'd cry if anyone else picked you up." She chuckled at the memory. "Father said you only had faith in me, so it seemed logical to call you Faith."

Judith smiled, trying to remember her childhood.

"Why did you change it to Judith?"

"I never changed it legally, but I hated the name Faith growing up."

"Why?"

"Faith Truman . . . do you have any idea what fun the kids had with that name . . . at my expense?"

"No, I guess I was too preoccupied with Mother to realize that," said Pastora.

"That's right. You were basically Mother's nursemaid while she was ill." Judith touched her forehead as a thought occurred. "You were barely more than a child yourself when Mother died."

"Almost fifteen."

"You seemed so grown-up to a six-year-old. I'd forgotten how young you were to take on the role of mother." Judith looked at her sister, reappraising her. "You were very strong."

"You didn't think so at the time." Pastora chuckled ruefully. "What was that you used to call me?"

"Little Miss Mother." Judith giggled. "I thought you were insufferable, forcing me to eat my vegetables and brush my teeth. Oh, and what was it that I'd always say when you told me to do something?"

"Who died and made you Pope?"

"That's it!"

They chuckled, remembering the taunt.

"I hardly remember our mother," said Judith. "Looking back, you were the closest thing I had to a mother."

"You were gypped," said Pastora. "In many ways, you were an orphan."

"Why do you say that?"

"Mother died when you were six, and Father never really recovered.

You never met him, at least, not the man I recall before Mother took ill." She looked hard at Judith. "I can see why you became so independent."

"I had you," said Judith.

"Yes, but . . . ."

"I resented you telling me what to do."

"Like when I tried to talk you out of taking St. Jude as your patron saint."

"That was how I saw myself," said Judith, "a lost cause."

"Or the time you . . . ." Pastora stopped.

"The time I what? Got the abortion?"

Judith's features hardened. Her eyes took on the look of flint.

"Maybe it's time we got this out in the open. Yes," said Pastora, "you've seemed to resent me since that New Year's. Why?"

"Oh, I don't know." Judith sighed, recalling past hurts and recent revelations. "You always acted like such a know-it-all. You had all the answers, but I felt you didn't, couldn't comprehend what I was going through."

Pastora began picking up and putting away articles of clothing.

"Sit down!" said Judith with an exasperated sigh. "Please. You're doing exactly what you used to do, create busy work."

"Idle hands . . . ."

"Are the devil's playground," finished Judith. "You've always said that. Please sit down and listen. We've started this. Let's finish."

Judith struggled to suppress her annoyance as Pastora finished arranging the earrings and rosary beads on the dresser and finally sat on the bed.

"You were saying . . . ."

"You were quick with the answers," said Judith, "but you never . . . you never experienced life outside of Father's house or the convent. How could I take your advice when you didn't know what you were talking about?"

"As you say, I haven't had your . . . worldly experience," Pastora said slowly, as if picking her words, "but the advice I gave you was sound: two wrongs don't make a right; forgive; choose life." Her eyes pleaded with Judith. "All I ever wanted was to help you in the best way I knew."

Judith mentally repeated the adages, and then snorted. "Your advice doesn't sound nearly as glib now as it had then."

"Truth is truth. It's we who change," said Pastora.

"It's we who change," Judith repeated slowly, softly, listening to it with her inner ear. "Yes, if we're lucky, God does help us change."

"You mean, if we're blessed," said Pastora. "That's His grace at work in us."

Judith turned toward her sister. "Can I share something with you?"

"Of course." Alarmed by Judith's intensity, Pastora's smile faded.

"Didn't you wonder how I had your phone number? How my research 'just happened' to bring me to Puebla?"

"It was quite a coincidence." Pastora met Judith's eyes.

"More than a fluke," said Judith. "I asked Aunt Tillie for your address and phone number. I could have stayed anywhere near Mexico City, but I chose Puebla."

"So maybe you weren't as reluctant to see me as you let on," said Pastora, raising her eyebrows.

Judith sniffed. "Maybe deep down, I wanted to see you. After all these years, I just didn't know where to begin."

"You don't have to see the whole staircase to take the first step," said Pastora. "Just have faith."

Judith smiled wryly, hesitating. "I'd meant to contact you after the first marriage," she said in a strangled voice, finishing her thought silently. *But, when it ended in annulment, how could I admit another failure?* She started again.

"I'd meant to contact you after I married Sam, but . . . ." Judith rubbed her forehead, summoning the courage to speak her thoughts. "When that marriage ended in divorce, I was too embarrassed to admit yet another failure." She took a deep breath, centering herself. "The look on your face that day I returned after the abortion," she swallowed, "I couldn't bear to see that expression in your eyes again, hear the disappointment in your voice."

"Faith, if I'd only known—"

Judith held up her good hand, interrupting. "I'm on a roll. Please, let me finish." Judith focused on her sister's face. "I've resented you for forty years . . . but maybe it's time to release those feelings, let go the antagonism that's kept us apart. After all, it was only an expression, a look in your eyes, that, truth be known, in my mental condition that day, I could have misinterpreted." She took a deep breath. "I have to face it. I'm the one to blame, the one who's kept us apart." She snorted. "Just me, myself, and I."

Pastora paused, her expression hidden as she focused on her hands, kneading them, massaging them.

Impatient to hear her response, Judith chafed as the pause stretched into what seemed minutes.

When Pastora finally looked up, her expression was refreshed, as if she'd just returned from a relaxing vacation. She smiled gently, and Judith stifled a sigh of relief.

"Faith, I've never taken a psychology class in my life, but it sounds to me as if you're coming to terms with your guilt for your abortion."

Lips and eyelids pressed tightly together, Judith nodded.

"But could it be that you still feel . . . shame? They're not the same thing, you know."

Judith blinked, letting that sink in.

"From what I'm hearing, somehow, over the years, you seem to have associated me with your sense of shame. By avoiding me, you've avoided confronting it, but that didn't deal with its root cause, the feeling that you had let me down."

"It's more than plausible. It's possible." Judith took a deep breath. "No matter my successes, I've always felt inadequate." Groaning, she shook her head. "It's been so frustrating."

Pastora nodded. "Shame's often a cover-up for feelings of vulner-ability . . . and judgment."

Judith shot her a wounded look of betrayal.

"*Self*-judgment," Pastora quickly added. "I've read that at the center of shame is some deep-seated belief that you're not worthy of being loved . . . which is simply not the case." Pastora smiled warmly. "Faith, guilt is rooted in our actions, but shame's rooted in our internal story, our beliefs about ourselves."

Judith digested that. "I have a confession to make."

"Father O'Riley can. . . ."

"No," Judith laughed, "not that kind of confession." Then she became serious. "Something happened to me that day we visited the Basilica of Our Lady of Guadalupe."

"You mean meeting the giggling girl," said Pastora.

"She certainly played a role," said Judith, recalling it all too vividly, "but there was something else."

"What?"

"I visited the tilma."

Pastora inhaled deeply, nodding, as if knowing what she was about to hear.

"As I passed beneath it, looking up," Judith shivered. She gave a self-effacing chuckle. "I still get chills, even at the memory."

"Go on," murmured Pastora.

"I was bombarded with many layers of recollections, emotions. It was like living two lives simultaneously, then and now."

"Then?" asked Pastora.

"When I had the abortion," said Judith. "In a flash, I relived that entire month and the years that followed." Her eyes drilled into Pastora's. "I had buried those memories of you, the baby, the abortion, under forty years of denial."

Biting her lip, Pastora nodded.

"Looking up at the tilma, I remembered the title, Our Lady of Guadalupe: Patroness of the Unborn. Suddenly, I felt a gangrenous wound had opened. I won't say I felt cured, but . . . ."

"You felt healing had begun?"

"Yes," hissed Judith in a sigh. "I felt the poison, the pus, that putrid hatred begin to drain away." Turning toward her sister, she reached for her arm. "I felt so incredibly sorry and so very accountable."

"Faith," said Pastora, covering Judith's hand with her own, "I do believe you've experienced a conversion of the heart."

The Hollow Men

"Art, like morality, consists of drawing the line somewhere."

~ G.K. Chesterton

"Good morning," Judith said, addressing the grad students. "Welcome to today's lecture about the culture of death, the second in a series. It's my privilege to be here with you in the land of the Aztecs and Spanish missionaries. Tell me about the Aztecs' culture of death."

Several students raised their hands.

"You," she said, pointing to a student in the back.

"The Aztecs believed in maintaining a cosmic balance between life and death."

"Can you tell me more?" she asked, pointing to another student.

"They believed human hearts and blood nourished the gods," said a girl in front.

"Yes, the Aztecs believed human lives needed to be sacrificed for life to continue," said Judith. "They recognized an interdependence of life and death."

She drew the path of the sun on the board.

"In Aztec mythology, gods sacrificed themselves daily in order for the sun to rise. Human blood offerings gave the gods strength. The Aztecs sacrificed children to the rain gods to repay them for abundant harvests. In their world view, death produced life. What about today's culture of death?"

Several students raised their hands. Shielding her eyes from the sun pouring into the room, she pointed to a student near the windows.

"You must be enlightened," she said with a smile. "What can you tell us about today's culture of death?"

"It's like T.S. Eliot's poem, *The Hollow Men*."

"How so?"

"We're the hollow men," said the student, paraphrasing. "We're the stuffed men . . . . Paralyzed force, gesture without motion."

"Okay," said Judith, "so how does that reflect today's culture of death?"

"We don't live life fully," said the girl. "We only go through the motions. At least, the Aztec culture of death was part of its religion. Today's culture of death is secular."

Someone's cell phone rang, and the class chuckled.

Trying to restore order, Judith asked, "And why do you say today's culture of death is secular?"

"For one thing, there's a breakdown in manners and common courtesy."

"We can attest to that," said Judith, eyeing the errant student with the phone. "Which reminds me, People, please turn off all cell phones prior to class. What else?"

Several hands went up. As Judith pointed at each, they called out their answers.

"Breakdown in relationships."

"Uninhibited lifestyles."

"Uninhibited sex," someone called from the back, amidst giggles.

"Eating disorders."

"Drug and alcohol abuse."

"Pornography."

"Okay," Judith said, returning to the poetic student, "you're saying that modern society is filled with hollow people, trying to escape their emptiness." She drew stick figures on the board. "How does that make us a culture of death?"

"In trying to fill our meaningless lives," said the girl, "we pursue only pleasure, so anything that's not pleasurable is an inconvenience or, at worst, a burden. Unwanted pregnancies, physically . . . or mentally . . . deficient embryos, female embryos, sick, wounded, or handicapped people, and the elderly are viewed as nuisances to be aborted or euthanized."

Judith inhaled as she arched back her neck, internalizing the girl's line of reasoning. *Amazing how much we learn from our students.*

"Point well made," said Judith, nodding. "If the destination's self-seeking pleasure, we hollow people are on a death march."

After class, Judith walked to Father O'Riley's favorite restaurant, musing about her graduate class. Despite the decades she had spent studying the Aztecs and their culture of death, T.S. Eliot's poem, *The Hollow Men,* had never entered her mind in connection.

Her lip lifting in a half smile, she shook her head and chuckled. *What a fresh perspective the poem gave!*

Teaching is a two-way street. I'll leverage these students' stories, ideas, and questions, and their enthusiasm will spark the next book or next year's syllabus. That's their gift to me.

She breathed deeply. *I only hope my students take what I give them, draw from it, build on it, and that it prompts them along their paths.*

ॐ

Judith waved Father O'Riley over to the table.

"The tequila's on its way," she said.

He chuckled as he sat down.

"I heard your lecture today."

"What did you think of it?"

Before he could answer, the waiter set down the tequila and a second lunch menu.

"What's the special today?" Father O'Riley asked. Before the waiter could answer, he said, "I'll have that, whatever it is." His stern face relaxed into a smile. "Is it any good?"

Chuckling, the waiter said, "It's an excellent choice, *Señor*."

"What is it?" asked Judith.

"*Chiles en nogada*," said the waiter, "my personal favorite."

"Chilies and walnuts?" she asked.

"You're translating directly," said Father O'Riley. "It's a poblano chili filled with picadilla, topped with walnut-cream sauce, and sprinkled with pomegranate seeds. It's not only a traditional Puebla dish, it's very patriotic."

"Patriotic?" she asked. "Why's that?"

"You'll see."

"Make it two," she told the waiter. Then raising her glass, she turned back to Father O'Riley. "I've taken the liberty of ordering our tequila today."

"So I see."

"It's a triple-distilled silver."

"Ah, you're showing off your newly learned expertise, Judith." They both chuckled. "A few more tequila tastings, and you'll be a connoisseur." Picking up the snifter by its base, he tilted it to one side. "Why am I doing this?" he asked, his raised eyebrow questioning her.

"You're checking for beads."

"You're a quick student." He sipped it slowly. "Roll it around your tongue. Let your taste buds analyze it."

"Do you like it?" she asked.

"It's smooth, with a long finish . . . a good choice."

She lifted her glass. "*Salud!*"

"*Salud!*"

As the waiter set the *chiles en nogada* in front of them, Judith's eyes lit up.

"I see why it's patriotic," she said, looking at the colorful entrée. "The green cilantro, white sauce, and red pomegranate seeds have the colors of the Mexican flag."

After savoring the entrée, Father O'Riley raised his eyes. "Now to answer your question about the lecture, I like the way you contrasted the Aztecs' human sacrifices with our present culture's human sacrifices. The former appeased their gods, while the latter displeases God."

Her mouth full, she nodded.

"You also mentioned a paradox between the cultures of life and death."

"Yes, of all the people who've ever lived, ninety-four percent of them are dead," she said, swallowing. "Life's a game of chance."

"Life's a gift to be cherished," he said. "Perhaps the older we get, the more we appreciate it."

"Maybe," she said, recalling the past. "There's a certain logic in the culture of death."

"Yes, the logic is to eliminate the problem by killing it, whether by capital punishment, euthanasia, or abortion. Has the person committed a crime? Kill him. Is the person old or incapacitated? Kill her. Is the baby unwanted?"

"Kill it," she said, sighing. "How I bought into that culture. How I wish I had it to do over again."

His rheumy eyes watched her as he listened. "You sinned. You regret it. Now, ask God to forgive you. Which reminds me, have you gone to confession?"

"Not in years," she said with a wry grin.

"Maybe it's time," he said between bites.

"Maybe it is."

"While we're eating lunch, let me tell you a story."

"Okay."

"Sister Veronica was both a nun and neonatal doctor. She invited me to see a premie born at twenty-five weeks. Thea was so small, she fit in my hand." He grimaced, remembering. "Veronica would visit her every day after work. She'd hold her, sing to her." His voice drifted off as he recalled.

"What happened to Thea?"

"Her lungs never developed, and she died after five weeks."

"All that effort . . . and money." Judith sighed. "How did the family take it?"

"The family had abandoned her at birth."

Judith groaned. "Jeesch . . . ."

"Veronica asked me to help with the funeral expenses." He shook his head. "It was a cheap funeral, the most pathetic scene, a nun, a priest, the funeral director, and little Thea. The culture of death loomed over us like oily smoke. 'What's wrong with you?' Veronica asked. I said, 'Thea had nothing. She never breathed, never ate, never even saw her mother. Her life was meaningless.' Veronica looked at me as if I'd cursed. 'You forgot one thing,' she said. 'Thea was my gift from God. Thea had the power to evoke my love.'"

Judith kept her eyes down, pretending to be concentrating on her food, trying to hide the tears welling up.

"You see, Judith, that's the culture of life. It transforms even death. This is the message you need to share with your students."

ॐ

Ceren turned away when she saw lovers trysting in the *Zocalo*, re-senting their love, their happiness. She watched toddlers feed the pigeons as their doting mothers looked on. She envied a pregnant woman, walking arm-in-arm with her husband.

Everyone has a life but me. She wondered how she had gotten into such a mess.

The sun was shining. It was a beautiful, autumn day, but she felt as cold and wintry as a gray, January day in New Jersey.

She sighed as she walked home, lonely, jacket slung haphazardly over her shoulder. She turned on her cell phone and was surprised to see three messages.

"Ceren, it's me," said a familiar voice. "I need to talk."

"Ceren, it's Jarek. If you're there, please pick up. Call me when you get this, okay?"

"It's me. Please call me as soon as you can."

She deleted the messages, taking pleasure in each deletion. Yet she was curious about the sudden flurry of voice mail. The phone buzzed in her hands, and she answered automatically.

"Ceren?"

She inhaled sharply. Hearing Jarek's voice on the other end of the line made her feel an odd mixture of contempt and consolation. The pause lengthened as the two sides battled.

"Ceren, I know you're there. Please answer."

"What do you want?"

"We need to talk."

"About what?"

"About us, for starters."

Ceren wavered between hanging up and listening. "All right," she said finally, "I'll listen, but I don't believe anything you tell me, anymore."

"I can't blame you," he said drily, pausing.

"Go on . . . ."

The pause lengthened. "I don't know where to begin." Then the words began flowing faster. "Come back for the weekend, for the week," he said. "The school will pay for it. We'll call it a scheduled update or mid-semester report."

"Why not call it a mid-trimester report?"

"There's no need for sarcasm," he said, his voice rising.

"Who's being sarcastic?"

"I'm just saying, come back." He paused, adding, "I miss you."

"Hmm . . . ." Ceren was plainly unconvinced. "You do, huh?"

"Being away from you made me realize how much I . . . I need you."

"What brought this on?"

"The thought of losing you convinced me. I need to see you."

"Would your other wife be joining us?"

"There's no need to be nasty."

"Oh, excuse me . . . . Bye."

"I'm sorry," he said quickly. "Please don't hang up. I really do need to see you."

"You somehow manage to sound sincere. How do you do that?"

"Come back for a few days, a week, so we can be together, so we can renew our relationship."

"Wow, I'm honored. You've actually upgraded our 'affair' to a relationship. Lucky me . . . ."

"Okay, if you won't come here, let's meet somewhere. Mexico City? Cancun?"

"Why?"

"I want to see you."

"Yes, you've said that. Why really?"

"I have something for you."

Despite not trusting him, hope sprang eternal. Did he resize his grandmother's ring? Has the annulment come through, after all? She felt butterflies.

"What do you have for me?" She struggled to keep her tone noncommittal.

"A surprise."

"So far, I haven't liked your surprises. If this surprise is an object, mail it." She mentally patted herself on the back for not caving. "If it's a concept, tell me now."

"Like I said, it's a surprise."

She heard background noises and then muffled voices as his hand covered the speaker.

"Jarek?"

"I'll overnight it," he said finally. "Call me when you get it."

The line went dead. Again, he left her holding onto nothing but hope. Grunting, she looked at her bare ring finger, remembering the last time he had built her up for a letdown.

ॐ

As they stood outside the courthouse that hot, August afternoon, Jarek had reached into his pocket. "I have something for you."

"You do?" Hunching her shoulders at the prospect of yet another surprise, she grinned.

He handed her a small, purple, velvet box. "Open it."

Had he planned this all along? But then why hadn't he put it on my finger during the wedding? She hesitated, looking from his face to the jeweler's box and back. Finally, she peeked inside the box and gasped. An antique diamond wedding ring.

"It's beautiful, so dainty. Look at the intricate, gold filigree. When . . . where did you get this?"

"It was my grandmother's." Taking it from the box, he tried to place it on her finger, but it would not push past her fingernail. He tried slipping it on her little finger, but the ring was too narrow, too delicate.

"It didn't even clear the first knuckle." Her smile morphed into a grimace as she looked at her bare ring finger. Then she put on a brave facade. "Your grandmother must have been a tiny woman."

"Don't worry, we'll have it resized when we get back to Austin." Jarek replaced the ring in the jeweler's box, tucked it in his pocket, and gave her a hug.

Tucking her arm in his, they started back to the car. Along the way, they passed a gift shop specializing in handcrafted silver jewelry. The showcased silver flashing in the sun caught her eye, and she paused in front of the window.

"Want to go in?"

"You must have read my mind."

"Actually, it was your dead-stop halt that was the subtle clue." Chuckling, he opened the door for her.

She grinned as she reached for his hand and meandered past the display cases. When she saw the rings, her face lit up. "Why don't we ask if they can enlarge your grandmother's ring?" She looked at her bare finger. "I'd feel," she hesitated, choosing her words carefully, "more married."

"More married?" He laughed. "How can you be 'more married'?"

She squirmed. "I just don't feel married. A ring might make it more tangible."

The jeweler made eye contact with her. "Can I help you find something?"

"Yes, do you—"

"No need to bother," whispered Jarek. "I know a goldsmith in Austin."

Then turning to the jeweler, he said, "Could you point us toward your earring display?"

"Sure, right over here."

Jarek leaned over to whisper. "You'll have your wedding ring back in a week or two. In the meantime, how 'bout rings for your ears?"

She grinned at his play on words and impulsively reached up to kiss his cheek. Then, looking over the display, she pointed to a pair of lapis and opal earrings. "Can we see those?"

ॐ

The next morning, a box arrived. Too large for a ring, the box had no return label, but Ceren recognized the handwriting. She tore into it, praying the Jarek who sent it was the same man she had married—the same man she loved—not the person she had come to know recently. He may redeem himself yet. Taking a deep breath, she unwrapped it. Instead of jewelry or token promises, she found abortifacients.

Her shoulders drooping, Ceren clutched her breasts and, hyper-ventilating, gulped air. When her breathing returned to normal, she dialed Jarek, her eyes falling on her bare ring finger. *Everything about him's been an empty promise, a pretense. How stupid am I?*

"You didn't even have the courage to put a return address on the box. No paper trail, is that it? You coward. You bastard!"

"Look, this is a simple process." From his tone, he might have been reading a recipe. "All you do is take a pill or two, and nature takes its course."

"Nature doesn't kill babies. Mifeprex does."

"It's no big deal. No need to even see a doctor."

"No big deal . . . ." She repeated sarcastically, shaking her head.

"Meet me." His tone softening, he added, "We can make it a romantic getaway."

"So we're supposed to fool around while our baby is dying in—"

"Don't be so dramatic! It's nothing more than a late period."

"It's a baby," she said, "your baby," and she hung up.

ح

Judith knocked on the door. One look at Ceren's face, and she could see something was wrong.

"What happened?"

Ceren recounted the phone call and showed her the pills.

"The bastard," said Judith, reading the label.

"My words exactly."

"So what are you going to do?"

Ceren sighed, and then shrugged. "I'm not sure."

"Do you want to talk about it?"

"Not really, I have some thinking to do." Smiling wryly, she gave a snort. "Better late than never."

"Sure, I understand." Judith turned to go and then remembered her reason for coming. She held up the letter. "They delivered this to me by mistake."

Reading the envelope, Ceren said, "They probably saw it was from the university and assumed it was yours."

Judith turned to leave as she opened it.

"Wait a sec," said Ceren, reading the letterhead. "It's from the Grants Department. This may concern you."

Skimming the letter, Ceren's face paled.

"What's the matter?"

"This isn't about the Writing-Across-the-Curriculum grant, as I'd thought," Ceren said. Then she read aloud: "Due to unforeseen budget cuts, the funding for the position of the Art History Department Adjunct Professor has been eliminated, effective at the close of the semester. As a result, your contract will not be renewed."

"That son-of-a-bitch," said Judith, breathing heavily.

"I wonder if he—"

"Of course he did," Judith snapped.

Ceren slumped into the chair. "He just asked me on a 'romantic getaway.'"

"The man has no conscience." The set of Judith's mouth was grim. "C'mon, let's get a cup of coffee."

"No thanks." Ceren shook her head as she managed a tight smile. "I'd rather be alone awhile."

"You're sure?"

Ceren nodded as if in a daze. Judith started to leave but then turned back.

"You'll call me if you need anything?"

"Sure." Ceren shrugged, and then looked up, remembering her manners. "Thanks."

Again, Judith hesitated at the door. "I just had a thought. We weren't planning to go until tomorrow, but why don't we do our research at the basilica today?"

"What's the point?" Ceren Asked. "I'm out of a job, and—"

"Not yet, you're not! You're a member of this grant team until December. Do a good job on this book, and it will be your recommendation to your next position."

Ceren half smiled.

"Besides," she said, looking around, "it'll do you good to get out of this cubby hole."

Two hours later, they were at the Basilica of Our Lady of Guadalupe.

"Do you want me to go to the museum with you?" Judith asked. "I really should see it."

"Thanks," Ceren said, a smile coming through her voice, "of course, you're welcome to come, but I know art doesn't interest you. I'm fine."

"You're sure?"

"Yes," said Ceren, raising her eyebrows, "don't worry."

Judith waved and took off toward the basilica while Ceren walked to the museum. She tried to focus on the job at hand, but she passed pregnant woman after pregnant woman.

Everyone was either carrying a baby or pushing a baby carriage. She groaned inwardly. *What do I do?* She breathed deeply, trying to center herself. *I have to concentrate on my chapter's theme,* Flowers and Song, *the symbols* Nahuatl *poetry used to interpret life and express imagery.*

She stopped to jot down a thought in her notebook.

The Marian visions on Tepeyac were transformed into images: colors, content, and composition. It was the art, along with the oral traditions, that became the basis for the devotion.

How does the faith spread now? Through the reproduced image of Our Lady of Guadalupe.

How did the devotion to Guadalupe begin? Through divine art. It was the image of Our Lady on Juan Diego's tilma that began the religious zeal.

It was rare Castilian roses blooming in the New World in December that left their imprint on, or imbued the cloak with, their subtle hues. It was birds singing, specifically the Tzinitzcan bird's song, that Juan Diego first heard: flower and song.

As she walked into the museum, Ceren struggled to focus on the art, not her personal problems. She carefully avoided stepping on the blue tape that outlined the statues and areas in front of wall-hangings, not wanting the guards to scold her for stepping too close to the objects.

She noted that the paintings could be categorized into *al fresco* scenes of nature and interior scenes inside structures. In the outdoor vistas, roses and birds predominated: flowers and song. She found herself dwelling on the flowers' fleeting beauty.

Her thoughts began to drift back to her baby. Flowers bloom only a day or two. How fragile, how ephemeral is life.

Forcing herself to concentrate, she jotted down another note in her journal.

The Tzinitzcan birds' song was so sweet that the natives believed the birds held people's souls in a mystic trans-migration. The birds symbolized this incarnation, which made them divine: the embodiment of song.

She fingered the bottle of pills in her purse. *How easy it would be to take these.*

She took a deep breath and moved on to the next illustration, trying to focus on her work. Ceren stared at the sash at the Virgin's waist. She jotted into her journal:

This sash symbolized to the natives that Mary was pregnant.

Pregnant: I can't get away from pregnancy.

She forced herself to note the artist's name and the year, 1686. She moved onto the next series of wood carvings. She wrote:

Angelic musicians, songbirds, and flowers surrounded the Virgin.

Virgin. Her thoughts returned to the baby, but she forced herself to continue the research.

She stopped in front of a large reproduction of the Virgin's image with a sky map superimposed over it. She took notes of the stars' pattern on the cloak and mantle of Our Lady. Translating, she wrote:

The constellations were portrayed as if seen from Tepeyac, with East at the top, instead of at the traditional right side. The constellation of Leo covered the Virgin's womb, identifying Christ as the Lion of Judah. The constellation Gemini, the twins, positioned over her legs, signified the birth of Christ.

Womb, birth. Again, Ceren's thoughts returned to her own baby and her future. *What will I do? How can I support myself . . . us . . . after the semester ends?*

Tears started, and a sob escaped her lips. The sound echoed off the museum's hard surfaces, and a guard eyed her suspiciously. Swallowing hard, she brushed the tears off her cheeks and hurried outside.

Nearly blinded by tears and the bright sun after the dimly lit museum, she stumbled toward a stone retaining wall. She sat down beneath a flowering tree and listened to a bird's song.

It's so beautiful here. What a contrast: all this beauty, and I've made such an ugly mess of my life.

Tears dropped onto her notebook, and the ink ran. Oblivious to her notes, she fingered the bottle of pills in her purse.

Suddenly, she heard a voice with her inner ear: Visit the tilma. *I've seen all the artwork recreating the tilma, maybe it's time I saw the original. Besides, it might take my mind off the pills.*

Following the crowds, she located the moving walk beneath Juan Diego's cloak. She stared up at the painting, sensing she was in the presence of something unworldly. As she raised her eyes to it, she found it easy to accept that the artwork had not been created by human hands.

When she stepped off the moving walk, she leaned against the wall to jot a note in her journal. Referring to Lafaye's treatise, she wrote:

The most notable example of syncretism between the ancient Mexican divinities and Christian saints is Tepeyac. Originally a place of pilgrimage for Tonantzin-Cihuacoatl, it's now become the sanctuary of Our Lady of Guadalupe. The significance of Tepeyac pre-dates history.

History. Again Ceren's thoughts returned to her future, and it looked bleak. She made a decision. Finding the concession tents, she bought a bottle of water and took the container of pills from her purse.

ح

When Judith left Ceren, she went to the moving walk beneath the tilma. She stared up at the painting, feeling goose bumps. Compelled to see it again, she left the building and rejoined the queue of pilgrims.

A giggle rang out above the crowd's mumbling. Ears perked, Judith looked around at the moving throng of people. Suddenly, she spotted the child's head, roughly nine feet ahead of her. The girl's dark head peeked out from the crowd as if searching for her.

Then their eyes met. The child's eyes crinkled into a mischievous smile. Then, with a giggle, she ducked back in line, out of Judith's sight.

This time through the queue, Judith barely looked up at the Virgin's painting. All she could think about was finding this giggling child.

Judith searched the basilica but did not find the girl. She checked the gift shop, chapels, and alcoves. Disappointed, she finally left to visit the old basilica. As she entered, she saw the child dash out another exit. Judith followed the girl through the crowd of pilgrims to the concession stands.

The child stopped and met Judith's eyes, as if taunting her. With an impish giggle, she dashed around the corner.

Broken arm or not, Judith raced after her. As she rounded the corner, Judith bumped into Ceren, knocking a container to the ground.

"Oh, Ceren, I'm so sorry. I was following that girl and wasn't looking." Then Judith noticed Ceren's tear-streaked cheeks. "Are you all right?"

"Yes. I, uh . . . I'm fine," Ceren said, clearing her throat. She reached for the container and tossed it into her purse.

"What was that?"

"Nothing," she said, shrugging.

"That's what Jerk sent you, wasn't it?" She eyed Ceren suspiciously and noticed the open bottle of water. "You weren't going to take those pills, were you?"

Ceren started to cry. Judith led her to a less public area, where they could talk.

"What were you thinking?"

"I can't do it. I can't go through with this."

"What are you talking about?"

"I can't afford a baby. I won't even have a job soon. I can't do it." She took a deep breath. "This will solve everything. Like you said, no one will even know about it."

"Ceren, you don't realize what you're saying."

"Yes, I do." She took another deep breath. "I finally get it. You were right that first night."

"No," Judith shook her head. "I was so wrong to tell you that. Maybe this is my fault. Look, Ceren, don't do something you'll regret for the rest of your life."

"What was it you called it, a missed period, a worm, a clump of cells? You were right. That's all it is. I'm going to take your advice and take those pills." She reached into her purse for the container. Looking at it, she scoffed. "You know, this is the only thing Jerk ever gave me . . . besides the bun in the oven."

Judith's jaw fell open. "You sound like me. What happened?"

"What happened? I was deceived, impregnated, abandoned, humiliated, and fired. Is that concise enough?!"

The rage came through Ceren's voice, and Judith took a step back.

"Wow." Judith swallowed hard. "I understand, believe me. I've been there."

Judith took a deep breath, reliving her own hurt four decades past. Flashbacks rushed through her mind: Tim, his elopement, the abortion clinic, the tears. She tried to focus from her past onto Ceren's tear-stained face.

"No, don't do this," said Judith. "Don't ruin your life like I did."

"What are you talking about?" Ceren scoffed. "You're the most successful person I know . . . published, tenured, respected. You're at the height of your career."

"Uh-uh . . ." Judith shook her head. "In the Seventies, there was so much talk about equality of the sexes. I bought into the idea that motherhood was a symptom of a disease called failure. Pregnancy was the default for women who couldn't cut it in the job market.

"To an extent, that line of thinking's still around," said Ceren.

"Yet," said, Judith, her eyes far away, recalling the past, "I remember how happy I was when I first learned I was carrying life. 'You look like the cat that swallowed the canary,' someone told me. You see, the life I carried was also a secret I carried. Even though I couldn't tell anyone, the happiness showed through. But then . . . ."

When Judith paused, Ceren sighed and said, "You did what you had to."

"No, I did the dumbest thing I could. I was given this incredible gift, and I threw it away. I killed it. The day I had that abortion, more than the baby died. Call it my solar plexus, my third chakra, my heart, but a big part of me died that day, too."

"That's not what you said that first night." Ceren's eyes penetrated hers.

"No, it isn't," said Judith softly.

"You were all gung-ho, rah-rah about abortion. What changed your mind?"

Judith sighed, not knowing where to start. She had been unaware of a change, let alone a transformation. Looking around, her eyes took in the area.

"It all started here," she said, gesturing with outstretched hands.

"Mexico?"

She shook her head. "At the Basilica of Our Lady of Guadalupe, the last time we were here."

"What happened, besides breaking your arm?"

Ceren's sarcasm hung in the air, but Judith ignored it.

"Breaking my arm was part of it, but just a small part."

"What else happened?" asked Ceren.

"For lack of a better phrase, I experienced a conversion of the heart." Judith told her about the experience in front of the image of Our Lady. "And, yes, my broken arm, I've hated the way it's kept me from doing things, but, I feel it's taught me a lesson."

"What, not to chase giggling kids?"

"That's another story," Judith said lightly, "but the broken arm's taught me humility. It's taught me that it's all right to lean on others occasionally. It's shown me that Maryl, I mean, Pastora, truly cares for me."

"You're not making sense," said Ceren, rolling her eyes. She gave a deep, aggravated sigh.

Judith could see she was bored.

"You're right. I'm trying to squeeze too much into this conversation. Look, Sam will be here tomorrow."

"So?"

"So, if I remember correctly, you've got seven weeks to use Mifeprex, right?"

"Up to sixty-three days from the day of the last period, it says."

"Then you've still got time." She shrugged. "At least, wait until after you have the DNA tests done."

Judith watched while her words sank in. Ceren's jaw worked as she thought it over.

"Okay, I can wait a week or so."

"Thank you." *Thank God.* Judith sighed. Wishing she could conceive and carry a baby in her own womb, she prayed she could help save this one.

ॐ

"Good morning," said Ceren, addressing the graduate students through the auditorium's microphone. "Thank you for joining the Dark Virgin Art Lecture Series. Today's lecture features photos of painted panels, wood cuttings, book illustrations, textiles, and more recent reproductions of the tilma's image."

Dimming the lights, Ceren brought up the PowerPoint presentation on the overhead screen. As she clicked through the slides, each displaying a different image, she discussed the artwork's background and history.

"Some scholars find similarities between the images of Our Lady of Guadalupe in Extremadura, Spain, and Mexico City. Do you see the comparison?"

She projected both images onscreen, providing a side-by-side comparison. The students shook their heads.

"Visually, there's little in common between the doll-sized, dark-faced Madonna of Extremadura and the image of the Virgin on the tilma," said Ceren. "On the other hand, there are similarities between the images of Our Lady of Guadalupe in Mexico City and another statue in Extremadura, the Immaculate Conception."

She projected those images in a side-by-side comparison. This time, the room resounded with enthusiastic murmurs.

"As you can readily see," Ceren said, responding to their interest, "the two bear a striking resemblance. According to *A Handbook on Guadalupe by the Franciscan Friars of the Immaculate*, the friars had installed this image in the Shrine of the Immaculate Conception in Extremadura several decades before Juan Diego found the image of the Virgin of Guadalupe in Tepeyac. Besides visual likenesses, are there any other similarities between the Virgin and the Immaculate Conception?"

She pointed to one of the students raising their hands.

"Yes, she first appeared on the Feast Day of the Immaculate Conception."

"There's also reason to believe that the Franciscans in the New

World were familiar with the image of the Immaculate Conception in Extremadura," said Ceren. "Many of the conquistadors, including Cortes, came from that region. There's speculation that a reproduction may have been brought to Mexico, but there's no proof to support that theory. What about the name 'Guadalupe?' Is that a word from the native *Nahuatl* language?"

She called on another student.

"No, there were no 'g' or 'd' sounds in *Nahuatl*," said the student. "I've read that the Virgin called herself *Coatlaxopeuh*."

"Could you pronounce that name again, please?"

"QUAT-la-zhupe," he said, sounding it out.

"I can hear why the Spaniards may have misunderstood it as 'Guada-lupe,'" said Ceren, "There's definitely a similarity in sound: QUAT-la-zhupe versus GWOD-a-loop-A. What does *Coatlaxopeuh* mean?"

She pointed to another student raising her hand.

"The one who crushes the serpent."

Ceren clicked to the next slide.

"This artist's rendition of the image of Our Lady shows her standing on a serpent in addition to the crescent moon. Can anyone offer an interpretation?"

She pointed to a student waving his hand.

"Some say that the snake is a reference to *Quetzalcóatl*, the feathered serpent," he said. "That could represent Christ replacing the local god."

She nodded and pointed to another student with her hand in the air.

"I think she's standing on the devil, the snake from the Garden of Eden."

Ceren clicked to the next slide, which was similar to the previous, except it contained children in the image. "What do you think this version of the Virgin represents?" Ceren asked, pointing to another student.

"She's defending children."

"She defending the unborn," corrected another student.

Ceren inhaled sharply, reminded of her own unborn child, the baby she had wanted. *Will it be born? Am I able to carry it to term, or would it be better to abort it?* She felt the tears welling up. Glad for the darkened room, she cleared her throat, struggling to return her focus to the class.

"Of course, these are all interpretations, conjecture," said Ceren, clicking to the next image. "Besides her comparison to the image of the Immaculate Conception, Our Lady of Guadalupe has also been equated with the Woman of the Apocalypse. In 1648, Miguel Sanchez compared her to the New Testament's Revelation 12:1, saying she was 'clothed with the sun, and the moon under her feet, and upon her head a crown of twelve stars.' Speaking of crowns, do you see a crown on the image of Our Lady?"

The students shook their heads no. Ceren fast-forwarded through the slides, chronologically pointing out the similarities and differences among the images.

"Until 1895, nearly every reproduction showed the Virgin wearing a crown, conforming to the original artwork on the tilma. However, after the Basilica's renovation in 1895, the crown was gone from the image."

She showed a brown, tintype-color reproduction on the screen.

"Though it's hard to make out, the Codex 1548 portrayed her without a crown. This parchment, which only came to light in 1995, is thought to be the oldest reproduction of Juan Diego's meeting with Our Lady of Guadalupe. Some say the crown was painted over. Whatever the reason, it's not there now." Ceren turned from the screen to her students. "What material was used as the 'canvas' of the painting?"

"*Maguey*-fiber from the agave plant," answered a student, "woven into a cloak."

"What was the medium: ink, oil, charcoal?" Ceren pointed to another.

"Roses," she answered. "They left an imprint on the tilma."

"Who was the artist?"

"God," answered some students.

"The Virgin Mary," answered others.

"Has a human hand ever helped paint the image?" asked Ceren, clicking ahead to the next photo. "Trick question. Anyone?"

Half the students answered yes, and the other half said no.

"In 1666, Dr. Francisco de Siles and several other university professors examined the tilma. They described flaking paint, where apparently silver paint had been added to the moon, tarnished black, and then flaked off. They also mentioned that the rays surrounding her had been painted gold, which later discolored. For the most part, however, they confirmed that the original colors of the Virgin's face and hands appeared untouched by humans. They said it was as if the roses' colors had been pressed into the fibers."

"Have any other studies been done?" asked a student.

"In the nineteen thirties, a German chemist analyzed the tilma. He concluded that the color did not come from anything animal or mineral. Since synthetic dyes didn't appear until the nineteenth century, synthetics have been ruled out," said Ceren.

"Has any study been done more recently?" asked a student.

"In the seventies, scientists performed an infrared study. They were unable to explain the radiance of the pigments, especially after nearly five hundred years. It seemed to them as if the image's features were formed within the twisted fibers of the material itself, not painted on or added in any way."

"In the sixties, Dr. Wahlig compared the colors to a photo imprinted directly onto the fabric, as if the tilma itself were the negative." Ceren asked jokingly, "Were cameras around in 1531?"

The students chuckled.

"Photography, as we know it, didn't evolve until roughly three hundred years after the Virgin's image was impressed on Juan Diego's tilma, so that's ruled out, as well."

"What about the rumor that the eyes of the Virgin reflect Juan Diego?" asked a student.

"Shakespeare said it first: The eyes have it." She smiled and clicked ahead several slides. "Digital imagery was a natural progression from photography. Dr. Tonsmann studied the irises and pupils of the Virgin's image for over two decades."

Ceren clicked to the next slide. It showed a close-up of Dr. Tonsmann's enlarged photo of the iris.

"After magnifying her eyes 2,500 times, Tonsmann claimed to identify thirteen reflected images of people imprinted in them. He compared the Virgin's eyes to an ethereal photo, capturing the moment that Juan Diego first opened the tilma in front of the bishop."

"So is the image of Our Lady of Guadalupe real or fake?" asked a student. Assuming a confrontational pose, she folded her arms in front of her chest.

"That's a question for each of us to answer, not me." Ceren shook her head. "A devout person might respond that God speaks to us daily through images and events. How we interpret these visions or experiences depends on many factors . . . including the lenses of our life experiences." Ceren surveyed the assembly, her eyes resting on the questioning student. "Keep in mind, though, this is Art History, not Philosophy or Religion."

Arms still folded, the student said, "The story of the tilma sounds to me like an invention, a myth."

"Fabric or fabrication," Ceren said, her eyes twinkling as she addressed the class, "that's the question."

The students chuckled.

"Again, this is Art History, not Debate. As your professor, my role is to introduce you to these chronological works of art and encourage you to analyze them."

"I think this tilma story's nothing but religious propaganda," said the student.

Ceren met the girl's challenging gaze. "Your role in this class is to scrutinize these reproductions of the Virgin's image through your own filters. Then, based on evidence, draw your own conclusion." She turned her gaze to the class. "I'd planned a discussion following this lecture, but perhaps it would be more meaningful if you research the subject and write a paper regarding the authenticity of the tilma and the veracity of its artist."

Amid groans from the students, Ceren distributed copies of a handout.

"Remember, I'm your mentor, not your tormentor," said Ceren.

Even the defensive student chuckled.

"These handouts contain summaries of studies conducted on the tilma between 1751 and 1982. You'll find excerpts from the published findings of Miguel Cabrera, a prominent artist; José Antonio Flores Gómez, an art restorer; Philip Callahan, a biophysicist and entomologist; and José Sol Rosales, of the National Institute of Fine Arts in Mexico City. They focus on specific characteristics of the image: material, primer, under-drawing, surface layer, glaze, and binding medium."

"What's the topic of the paper?" asked a student.

"The title's *Fabric or Fabrication: Is the Image of Our Lady of Guadalupe a Forgery?*" Using the information from these technical analyses, make your case."

Ceren slumped into her chair after the students filed out. *It's hard enough to wrestle with my conscience on my own time, but double that when I'm lecturing.* The discussion of the Virgin as the Patroness of the Unborn had left her limp, and the authenticity debate with the student had drained her.

Not Feel, Love is Something You Do

"Love is a mutual self-giving which ends in self-recovery."

~ Bishop Fulton Sheen

When the phone rang Saturday morning, Pastora answered.

"Who may I say is calling?"

"This is Sam, Judith's ex-husband."

"Sam, I'm looking forward to meeting you. I'm Judith's sister, Pastora. Just a moment, while I get her." She started to call.

"I'm right here," Judith said, standing behind her, surprising her.

Pastora jumped and then handed her the phone. "It's Sam."

"I'm right here, too," he said, smiling to himself, having overheard.

"In Puebla? I thought you'd call from Mexico City," Judith said.

"I caught an early flight, didn't want to wake you until a decent hour. I'm at the *Zocalo*. Is that anywhere near you?"

"About five minutes away." The smile came through her voice.

"Why don't you and your sister meet me for breakfast?" he asked, the smile coming through his.

"We'll meet you by the fountain. Just be a minute."

"Will you recognize me, or do I need to describe what I'm wearing."

Judith laughed. "Who could forget a face like yours?"

When she hung up, Pastora said, "I haven't heard you laugh since," she paused, remembering, "since you were a girl."

"Sam always could make me laugh."

Pastora noted that the fine lines around Judith's eyes looked relaxed, smooth. Her lips curled in a gentle smile that brightened her face.

"Funny, you even look younger since you took his call," Pastora said with her trademark smile.

"Flatterer," said Judith, grinning. "Sam's at the *Zocalo* and wants to take us to breakfast. Hungry?"

"I definitely want to meet this man who brings a smile to your face."

Five minutes later, Judith pointed to a tall, trim man in a navy sports jacket, polo shirt, and tan pants. Broad-shouldered, he stood a head above everyone else.

"There he is!"

Judith's eyes locked onto Sam's. They hurried toward each other, with Pastora several feet behind, struggling to keep up. As they met, they hesitated briefly, opting to kiss each other's cheek instead of lips.

As Pastora caught up, she smiled, seeing their obvious affection for each other.

"You must be Sam," said Pastora, holding out her hand.

He took it, drawing her to him in a hug.

"And you must be Sister Pastora."

Looking past his graying temples, she saw the laugh lines around his eyes and his clear, steady gaze.

"You remind me of someone," Pastora said, scrutinizing him. Then she gasped.

"What?" asked Judith, alarmed.

Pastora chuckled. "He reminds me of our father, at about the time you were born, Judith. Of course, you couldn't remember Father as a young man. He aged so quickly after Mother passed away."

"Thank you for the compliment," said Sam. "It's been a while since anyone's called me a young man." He smiled warmly. "I hope you're hungry."

"Oh, heavens," said Pastora, making a show of looking at her watch. "Now that I've delivered Judith into safe hands, I have to get back to the convent."

"Please stay," said Judith. She grinned crookedly, surprised that she meant it.

Their eyes met, connecting. Smiling, but shaking her head no, Pastora turned toward Sam and held out her hand.

"It's been a pleasure meeting you, and I hope to see more of you."

This time, he kissed her hand. "I look forward to it."

As Pastora waved goodbye, Sam noticed Judith's cast.

"What happened to you?"

"Long story," she sighed. "Can I tell you over coffee?"

ॐ

Breakfast became brunch before Judith brought Sam up to date on the events.

"You've had quite a time here, haven't you?

She nodded. "It's been a growth experience, that's for sure." She turned toward the waiter, who was holding the coffee urn. "Just a half cup, please."

"And your arm in that cast," he asked, "hasn't it been frustrating for you?"

"Yes and no." She paused, thinking. "It's slowed me down drastically. I can't deny it . . . ."

"But . . . ."

"But it's made me aware of something, too." She held up her casted arm. "This handicap has limited my range of movement. I've had no choice but to rely on others help me dress, help me bathe."

"Your sister?"

Nodding, she said, "Pastora's been very generous with her time, staying over, helping me, and then doing her duties at the convent."

"As I recall, you were never that fond of her," he said.

"You're putting it mildly. I thoroughly resented her my entire adult life."

"And you credit this cast with that conversion?" he asked, lightly tapping it.

The sound was hollow.

"Do you hear that?" she asked. "That empty thud?"

"This?" He tapped it again.

She nodded. "That was me, hollow. A stiff shell surrounded me, protected me, but inside that emotional cast, I atrophied."

"What do you mean?"

"See my arms?" she asked, holding them side by side. "After three weeks in this cast, the muscles of my right arm have shrunk."

"You're right," he said, comparing her arms' size.

"I realize, when . . . when I was wounded all those years ago, I put a cast around me to protect me."

"And your spirit atrophied?" He nodded. "I think I understand. So when this cast on your arm made you dependent, you regained your vulnerability."

"Yes," she said, smiling, "that's it exactly." She pointed to it. "This has taught me to appreciate the people who try to help me . . . not resent them or drive them off."

Sam took her hand in his, and their eyes met.

"More coffee, *Señor*?" asked the waiter.

"What do you say?" Sam asked, raising his eyebrow quizzically.

"I'm coffeed out." Her hand still in his, she gave him a friendly squeeze. "Instead, let me show you around Puebla."

Five minutes later, they were walking through the *Zocalo*. It seemed only natural when she reached for his hand. At *Reforma* Street, she pointed out the lattice-work balconies.

"It reminds me of the French Quarters in New Orleans," he said, turning toward her. "Remember?"

"How could I forget where we honeymooned?" She smiled, sharing the memory. "The architecture of these homes was based on the Eiffel Tower." She pointed to a structure's brick, showing the date of construction: 1889.

"Check out all the street lights with dragons," he said, pointing.

"Puebla's nicknamed the City of Street Lights. I've heard there are nearly two thousand of these wrought-iron lamp posts."

"Why the dragon motif?"

She lifted her shoulders in a shrug. "I'm guessing it refers to the Book of Revelation, where St. Michael fought the dragon."

"Okay," said Sam, scratching his head, "so how does St. Michael enter into this?"

"St. Michael's the patron saint of Puebla," she said, recalling his statue at Tepeyac. "He's a popular theme in this area." She pointed back toward the *Zocalo*. "We met near his statue in the fountain."

Turning the corner, Judith led him onto *Ruta de Prueba* Street. They sampled herb-dipped apple slices as they window-shopped, peering into colorful store fronts until they saw a man on stilts, dressed as a skeleton.

"What is that?" Sam asked.

"Give him a few pesos, and he'll 'tell' you your fortune."

Sam handed the man a coin. A bony hand reached out from a black cape and pointed to a basket of rolled papers.

"Pick one," Judith said.

"Here, you translate," he said, handing it to her.

She unrolled the tiny fortune and read, "You and me and baby make three."

"If he's the grim reaper," said Sam, "the baby must be the New Year's baby."

"Maybe," she said, pausing as she recalled another New Year's baby. The mood now changed, she took a deep breath and reminded herself of Ceren and the reason for Sam's visit. "Are you up for meeting my friend?"

"Sure."

"I'll see if she's in," she said, dialing her cell number.

ح

"But I'm in Mexico, not Texas," Ceren said. "Won't that make a difference?"

"It shouldn't since residency isn't necessary to establish paternity."

"Can this be done during pregnancy?" Ceren asked. "We wouldn't have to wait until the baby's born, would we?"

Ceren felt a tightening in her chest at the thought of having to carry the baby to term just to prove paternity.

"If we were to involve the Texas OAG—"

"The OAG?" Ceren squinted, trying to translate the acronym.

"The Office of the Attorney General," he said, "if we involve the OAG, we'd have to wait until after parturition since they swab the mouths of the baby, mother, and alleged father to test for DNA."

"No, I can't wait that long," she said, "the sooner, the better. What can be done during pregnancy?"

"AFT is an option." Then responding to Ceren's quizzical squint, he added, "amniotic fluid test or amniocentesis."

She nodded. "When can we start?"

"After the DNA data's established, we can begin filing the Order to Show petition. Then we can file the paternity suit itself."

"How long does all that take?" she asked.

"Usually, about three months," he said.

"Three months!" Feeling a heaviness in her stomach, Ceren paled. "I can't wait that long." She looked pointedly at Judith. "I agreed to wait a week."

Judith shot Sam a look of concern.

Responding to her raised eyebrow, he continued, "Once the respondent receives the paternity lawsuit . . . ."

"The respondent, you mean Jarek?" Ceren asked.

"Yes, once he's served, he has thirty days to file a response with the court."

"And if he doesn't?"

"If he doesn't file or contest the baby's paternity, the court can enter a default judgment that day."

"What if he does contest the paternity?"

"In that case, the Attorney General orders genetic testing."

"Then what?" Ceren asked.

"If the test proves Jarek's the father, the court enters a paternity judgment: case closed."

"Time's the issue," said Ceren, catching Judith's eye.

"What do you mean?" Sam looked from one woman to the other.

When Ceren hesitated, Judith filled in. "She's considering ending the pregnancy."

"If your firm can file the petition today," said Ceren, her jaw line set firmly, "I'll make an appointment for the test."

ह

"Mail," said the grad student, dropping the letter in the department's mail-basket.

"Thank you," the assistant mumbled without looking up.

She waited until he left, then opened the envelope. As she scanned its contents, her eyes widened. With a sniff, she picked up the phone and dialed from memory.

"Hello, Mrs. Witunski, this is Peg at the Dean's office. Yes, I'm fine, thanks, although . . . concerned. A letter just arrived that may interest you . . . ."

ह

"Has Ceren gotten the results of the amniocentesis yet?" asked Sam.

"Her doctor's appointment is this morning," Judith said.

"Did your sister take her?"

"No, Ceren insisted on going alone."

"Sounds familiar," he said with a chuckle.

"What do you mean?"

"She reminds me of you, the old you," he said, correcting himself, "when we were married."

"No," she scoffed, "she's just exerting this show of independence, this blatant self-reliance because she feels so vulnerable now with the pregnancy and paternity issues. Whether naïve or not, she truly loved Jarek and wanted his baby. He turned her world upside down, and now she's struggling to land on her feet. This bravado is part bluster and part pluck, but mostly it's meant to bolster her self-confidence."

"What was your excuse?" He grinned at her.

"Hey." She gave him a playful jab with her elbow.

"Watch how you wield that sling," he said with a laugh. "Seriously, her pose of self-sufficiency reminds me of you."

"Now?"

She looked at him expectantly, her eyes widening. The effect was not so much curiosity as naïveté. A half-smile playing at his lips, Sam gazed at her as if seeing her for the first time.

"No, not now . . ." he said slowly, scrutinizing her. "You seem different now."

"How so?"

"Fewer barriers," he said with a wry chuckle. "Where you'd had a twelve-foot, chain-link fence, topped with razor wire, you now have a pruned, bayberry hedge."

"Oh, really?" She turned toward him, looking up into his face, seeing him through a new light. As opposed to when he had been her husband, this man seemed to understand her.

Gently pulling her closer, he lightly brushed her lips with his. She didn't pull away. Instead, she nuzzled his neck, recalling the warm relationship they had shared in the first years of their marriage.

ॐ

The doctor entered the examination room, carrying the full panel print-out. After closing the door, he frowned and pressed his fingers together, as if gathering his thoughts.

"The amniocentesis indicates there's a high probability of trisomy twenty-one," he said.

"Trisomy twenty-one, what's that?" Ceren asked, squinting.

"It's more commonly known as Down syndrome, a condition caused by an extra twenty-first chromosome."

"I thought that only occurred with older mothers," Ceren said. "I'm only twenty-six."

"How old is the father?"

"Forty-two, why?"

"Recent data suggests the paternal age can also increase the risk of DS."

"Are you sure the fetus has Down syndrome?"

"There's more than a fifty-percent probability." He shrugged. "I'd recommend terminating the pregnancy as a pre-emptive move."

ह

On her way home, Ceren spotted Judith in the *Zocalo*.

"Did Sam's office contact Jarek about the paternity suit?" she asked.

"Yes, he should have the letter by now," said Judith.

"Has he answered?" Ceren asked too quickly.

"Not to my knowledge," said Judith, shaking her head. "Remember, he's got thirty days to respond."

"That's right . . . ." Her voice dropped an octave.

"You don't . . . do you still have feelings for him?"

"Just hate," Ceren snapped, her lip curling scornfully. She sighed, adding, "And love . . . and loathing."

"Is anything wrong?" asked Judith.

"No, not a thing," said Ceren, throwing her arms up. "I'm pregnant, basically unmarried, and soon to be out of a job. I'm just on top of the world."

"Mmm-hmm . . . are you hormonal or what?"

"I got the DNA results at the doctor's." Ceren took a deep breath as her eyes bore into Judith's. "The fetus has Down syndrome."

Stunned, Judith remained silent, deep in thought.

"Did I miss something?" Sam asked, returning with two containers of coffee.

Both Judith and Ceren jumped, surprised by his voice.

"Here, Ceren, take mine," he said, offering her a cup. "I'll get another."

"No, that's all right. I . . . I can't stay," she said, walking off. Then she turned and called as an afterthought, "Thanks, anyway."

Sam handed Judith a container. When she didn't take it or seem to notice, he held up the cup for her to see.

"Didn't you want coffee?"

"Huh?" Then she noticed the cup. "Oh, thanks." She chuckled penitently, accepting the steaming brew.

"Okay, what did I miss in the five minutes I was gone?"

"Sam, the baby has Down syndrome." She sighed. "I was hoping Ceren would reconsider having the abortion and give the baby up for adoption." She shrugged, resigned. "But now . . . ."

"Who says the fetus has Down syndrome?"

"The doctor, I suppose . . . the lab tech . . . whoever gave her the results of the amniocentesis."

"Those results are often inaccurate," he said. "I wouldn't be so quick to accept that prognosis."

"Why do you say that?" She looked at him quizzically, warming her hands around the coffee cup.

"Lab tests can be wrong." Counting off on his fingers, he said, "Fetal blood in the amniotic fluid can cause false readings. The technicians can culture the mother's cells by mistake. Lab techs can misinterpret chromosomal patterns. The lab can ambiguously diagnose or completely misdiagnose results."

"Really?" Feeling vulnerable, she looked up at him for reassurance.

"Really," he said, a trace of a smile playing at his lips.

He put his coffee down, put his hands on her arms, and looked into her eyes.

"Any number of factors can influence the test and cause errors in lab results," he said. "I wouldn't accept this prognosis as absolute fact." He stared at her face as if trying to read her thoughts. "Why are you taking this so much to heart?"

"It's a serious issue," she said, not meeting his gaze. "Ceren wanted to get an abortion as it was, but now these lab results will clinch it."

"Yes, an abortion's very serious, but there's more here than meets the eye. You're taking this personally. Why?"

"As you know, I had an abortion forty years ago."

"Yes," he nodded, "but you've known other friends who've had abortions. That never seemed to faze you in the past. What's different?"

Looking into his eyes, she said, "I am."

Judith shared her experiences at the Basilica of Our Lady of Guadalupe, about the giggling girl by St. Michael's statue, about the shadows in the *Rosario* Chapel, about her conversion of the heart that began in front of the tilma.

When she finished, she looked at him shyly. "I've always relied on you for solid logic. What do you think of all this?"

He cocked his head and rubbed his chin. She could hear the sound of his whiskers beneath his fingertips and the wheels of his mind churning.

Finally, he said, "You've had quite a time in Mexico, haven't you?"

"You think I'm imagining this?" she asked, chin down, eyes tipped up at him.

"I don't think you're imagining it," he said slowly, scratching his head. "I believe you're convinced these things happened."

"But you don't believe they actually happened . . . the way I interpreted them . . . ."

He took a deep breath. "I believe you visited the basilica and saw a girl dressed in white, and I believe you saw shadows in the chapel . . . ."

"But you don't believe they were anything beyond that," she interrupted, forcing him beyond polite discussion.

"Look, I don't want to debate with you, but, in all honesty, no, I can't believe there was any spiritual significance to your experiences."

Silent, mouth pursed, she acknowledged his answer with a curt nod. The mood broken, an estranged silence followed. After a few minutes, Sam picked up his coffee cup.

"It's cold."

She knew him well enough to know he was talking about more than the coffee. She shrugged.

"Judith, let's not end the conversation this way, the way we always used to."

She read the plea in his eyes, nodded, and gave him a shy smile.

"I thought I'd changed," she said with a sigh and a self-deprecating chuckle. She set down her cup and threw her hands up in resignation. "I felt I'd undergone some kind of epiphany, but—"

"Who says you didn't?" he asked. "Just because you had a private revelation that isn't apparent to me or anyone else, doesn't make it any less real."

"Then you believe me?" Her face brightened.

"What have I been trying to tell you? Yes, of course, I believe you saw and felt and experienced these occurrences, but I personally don't feel there was any divine intervention."

"But—"

"You can believe anything you want," he quickly added. "I won't debate your interpretations of these encounters."

"Yes," she said gleefully, "that's the right word, encounters. You do understand! I truly feel I rubbed shoulders with something that can't be explained, something unearthly."

"Obviously."

Chuckling, he looked at her with an open smile, his dimple adding to his charm.

Reacting without thinking, Judith reached up and kissed him. Sam took her in his arms and tenderly returned her kiss. For a moment, she forgot the divorce, remembering only the love she felt for this man.

An icy, autumn wind blasted them with grit and leaves, instantly chilling Judith and waking her out of Sam's warm embrace.

"Brrrrrr . . . that was a cold slap in the face," she said with a self-conscious laugh. Still pressed against him, she was a bit embarrassed by her show of affection.

"To be continued," he said hoarsely.

Then he smiled his easy-going grin, putting her at ease again. She gave his arm a friendly squeeze and gently extricated herself. Almost immediately, she began shivering.

"Cold?" he asked, taking off his jacket and placing it around her shoulders.

"Mmm-hmm . . . Thanks. That wind really picked up."

As if to punctuate her words, another wintry gust blew through, whipping her hair. They watched a cap tumble toward them, fueled by the wind, a mother and young boy chasing after it. Sam caught the small, crocheted cap and handed it to the mother.

"*Gracias*," the woman said, trying to tie the flaps around the boy's head.

Judith looked at the boy, suddenly realizing he was a Down-syndrome child. She bit her lip, realizing the poignancy of the moment.

Then the boy looked up at her, smiling, eyes joyful. When he saw her hair blowing in the wind, he tried to take off his cap. At first, his mother struggled to keep his cap on, and then, realizing his plan, she helped him remove it.

"*Para usted*, for you," he said, emphatically placing his cap in Judith's hand.

Tears immediately formed in her eyes, though she hid them in a too-bright smile and bent down on one knee to hug him.

"*Gracias*, but you need this," she said softly, trying to place it on his head and tie the crocheted flaps under his chin with her one hand.

"No," he insisted, shaking his head, touching her windswept hair. His small hand brushed her hair away from her eyes.

His mother smiled at the boy. Words were unnecessary in any language. Judith could see the pride she had in her son.

"*Por favor*," the mother said, "he wants you to have it."

Judith noticed her trembling lips and the boy's beaming face.

"*Gracias*," she said, touching the cap to her heart, "*muchas gracias*."

"*No es nada*," the mother said, taking her son's hand.

The boy pulled from his mother's hand to hug Judith once more and then rejoined his mother. Judith couldn't take her eyes off him. Every few steps, he turned and waved. Still kneeling, still clasping his cap to her chest, she waved back.

By the time he was out of sight, tears were rolling down her cheeks. Judith finally stood up and faced Sam. He held out his arms, and she hugged him, crying against his chest.

When the tears subsided, Sam fished in his pocket for a tissue and handed it to her.

"Thanks," she said through a teary smile.

Still sniffling, she placed the cap in her sling, holding it next to her chest. She tucked her other hand in Sam's and began walking.

"This is what I mean. Ever since I got here, I've felt that someone is trying to tell me something." She turned to face him. "You'll notice that I didn't say anything about divine intervention, just that someone is trying to tell me something."

"Duly noted," he said, chuckling.

"And people think that little boy is handicapped or is a burden. Why . . . ." At a loss for words, she sighed deeply. "Handing me his cap had to be one of the kindest gestures I've ever experienced. What a little sweetie . . . ."

Hand-in-hand, they walked in silence while Judith processed the morning's events. Suddenly she stopped and turned to him. No more tears, she clearly saw what she had to do.

"I've made a decision."

"About what?" he asked, alarmed by the directness of her gaze.

"I'm going to adopt Ceren's baby, whether or not it has Down syndrome."

He sucked in his breath. "That's quite a decision."

"Now don't try to talk me out of it," she said, eyes widening to begin battle.

"I'm not," he said, holding up his hands, as if in self defense, "but I would like to walk you through a few scenarios."

"Fair enough." She nodded in agreement. Taking her hand in his, they resumed walking.

"First and foremost, what if Ceren's dead-set on having the abortion?"

"I don't know," she said slowly. Then, getting an idea, she smiled, adding, "I'll let you and your lawyer's silver tongue talk her out of it."

He grunted, feigning annoyance.

"All right, what if the father wants the baby?"

"Fat chance," she said, dismissing the idea with a disdainful sniff.

"What if the father wants to marry Ceren legally and keep the baby?"

"The odds aren't worth considering," she said, tossing her head.

"What if Ceren wants to keep the baby?"

"Ohhhh . . . ." Judith felt the wind had been knocked out of her. "That never occurred to me." She turned toward Sam, fear in her eyes. "Do you think it's possible?"

"Of course, it's possible," he said. "It happens all the time."

"But not if the baby has Down syndrome," she said, regaining some of her confidence.

"One lab test is no guarantee that there's anything wrong with that baby."

She took a deep breath, thinking it over.

"I hate to admit it," she said, eyes cast down. "But it's almost as if I wish the baby does have Down syndrome, so I'd have less competition in the adoption process."

He raised his eyebrow. "Why would you go out of your way to adopt a baby with Down syndrome?"

"Don't you see?" she asked, looking up into his eyes, pleading with him. "I threw away my baby. I killed it, and I've spent forty years suppressing the pain and regret. Saving this baby might be my last chance to make up for it . . . to pay for it." She covered her lips with her hand and swallowed hard.

He nodded slowly. "You realize the implications, yet you're sure you want to adopt this baby?"

"No matter what," she said, taking a deep breath, "I want to adopt her."

"Her?" he asked, eyes twinkling.

"Oh, yes, I'm sure it's a girl. No doubt in my mind."

"Would this be a girl that giggles and leads you on wild goose chases?"

"Stop teasing," she said, giving his hand a playful slap. "I should never have told you about those encounters at the basilica. Now, Sam, be serious."

His eyes searched her face. Then his demeanor changed.

"You're set on doing this, aren't you?" he asked, his tone solemn.

"Yes, I am," she said, nodding adamantly.

"I'm not being callous here, but, technically, you're too old to adopt."

"Sam, I know you," she said, dismissing the idea with a wave of her hand. "You'll find some loophole."

"True," he said with a self-deprecating shrug, "but you're not married."

"Well . . . I . . . that's not so awfully important in adoptions, is it?" she asked, suddenly confronted with an issue she hadn't considered.

Shaking his head, he said, "That, combined with age, is what they call a show-stopper."

"Ohhhh." Her depression was as palpable as a flat tire.

"Unless . . . ." He hesitated.

"Yes?" she asked impatiently.

He paused, thinking, chewing his lip.

"Unless what?!"

"Unless you marry me . . . ."

Stunned, she couldn't speak. Then she noticed a mischievous glint in his eye.

"Sam, how can you joke at a time like this?"

"I'm not joking," he said, going down on one knee in the middle of the busy sidewalk. "Marry me."

"Sam, get up," she said, embarrassed, pulling at his sleeve. "People are looking."

He shook his head. "I won't get up until you give me an answer."

"Sam, for heaven's sake," she said, eyeing the people who had gathered around them. "Get up!"

"Not until you say you'll marry me."

"*Diga sí, Señora*, say yes, Lady," someone called, and the crowd laughed.

Sam looked up at her expectantly, one eyebrow cocked. Unable to resist him, she began laughing.

"Say it," he said.

"Yes!"

ح

"Let's not announce our wedding right away," said Judith later that afternoon, nestling against Sam.

"Why?" he asked, nuzzling the nape of her neck. "Embarrassed to be seen with me already?"

She laughed, tickled by his breath.

"Never!"

Then turning to face him, she met him in a long kiss.

"I just don't want to flaunt our happiness." She sighed. "Not yet, not while Jarek's being such a jerk, and Ceren's dealing with the pregnancy and paternity issues . . . ."

ॡ

No sooner did Ceren leave Judith and Sam, than she heard her name. Looking around the *Zocalo*, she saw Pastora hurrying toward her.

"Looks like a storm's brewing," said Pastora with a nod toward the swaying trees.

"Yeah." Ceren responded mechanically, preoccupied.

"How did it go?" she asked, catching her breath.

"Not good." As Ceren shared the DNA results and doctor's prognosis, she watched Pastora's hopeful, little-girl smile shrivel into worried creases.

"What are you going to do?"

"What can I do?" Shrugging, Ceren threw up her hands, dropping the manila envelope.

Pastora reached for it. "What's this?" she asked before handing it to her.

Ceren sighed. "Ultrasound, a sonogram."

"Can I look?"

"Go ahead."

At Ceren's shrug, Pastora removed the photo and held it to the light. Something caught her eye, and, bringing the photo closer, she turned it slightly and stared. "What's this over here?" She pointed to a whitish area.

Without looking, Ceren said, "I don't know, just the womb or tissue, I suppose."

"You haven't seen this photo, have you?" asked Pastora.

Setting her jaw, Ceren said, "No, and I don't want to."

"Look at it." Pastora held out the sonogram.

Her awed tone made Ceren glance at her. Pastora's smile had returned, and she was pointing to something that looked like a second image, just above the picture of the fetus. Taking the photo in her hands, Ceren examined it.

"I'm sure it's just some anomaly."

"No anomaly," said Pastora, beaming. "It's the face of an angel."

Pursing her lips, Ceren shook her head. "This is a compressed, two-dimensional picture of a 3D object, a slice of the scanned image. Your brain recognizes that shape and tries to put it into some kind of context." She scowled. "You're anthropomorphizing."

"Your baby has a guardian angel looking out for it, Ceren."

"That is nothing but wishful thinking on your part." Her eyes narrowed. "If you go looking for signs, you'll find them . . . whether or not they're there." With an exasperated sigh, she pitched the sonogram in the garbage.

"Really?" Pastora's eyebrow lifted. "Then what do you make of that cloud?" She pointed to a formation rapidly gathering over the cathedral.

Ceren's eyes widened. "It looks like a heart." With a snort, she added, "A perfectly shaped heart that's broken. See the jagged split down the center as it's breaking apart?"

Pastora's smile returned as she shook her head. "Not two halves of a broken heart, Ceren, but a pair of angel's wings. Look, your baby has a guardian angel watching over you both."

द

Judith and Ceren visited the basilica again. This time, they both visited the art museum, but at their own paces. Judith scanned the artwork quickly, moving from one painting to another, while Ceren spent more time studying each work of art and jotting down notes.

"I'm going to view the statues downstairs," Judith whispered.

"Okay, I'll catch up in a minute." Nodding, Ceren looked up. "Just want to finish notating these woodcuts," she whispered.

As Judith began descending the steps, she could see between the columns and catch a partial view of the statue gallery. She squinted, letting her eyes adjust to the room's dimmer lighting compared to the sunlit stairs.

All of a sudden, the giggling girl darted out from behind one of the carved images. In an impromptu game of peek-a-boo, she peeped out, grinning. As if daring Judith to catch her, she ducked back behind and then peeked out from the other side.

Judith scurried down the steps, catching a glimpse of the girl's billowing, white gown as she jumped behind another statue. Determined to capture the girl, Judith approached from the left, not the more direct route on the right. She did a swift about-face and sidestepped in front of an immense, stone sculpture.

Suddenly face to face with her grinning quarry, she reached out to grab the girl's arm before she dashed behind the statue.

Instead of flesh, all she felt was humid air. The vision evaporated before her eyes. Blinking, Judith gasped and took a step back to regain her balance.

"Are you all right?" Ceren asked, concerned at her friend's wild-eyed expression.

"Did . . . did you see that?"

"See what?" Ceren asked suspiciously.

"The girl . . . the giggling girl," said Judith.

"As I was coming down the steps, I saw a girl near you," said Ceren. "She was wearing a lacy, white outfit."

"Yes, that's the giggling girl!" In her excitement, Judith grabbed Ceren's arm, glad to make contact with flesh and bone. "Did you see her disappear?!"

Ceren's eyes widened. "I saw you reach out to her . . . ."

"Did you see how she just vanished?!"

"I saw her, but, then, as I stepped down, the column blocked my view for a moment." Pointing at the wide columns, Ceren said, "A half-second later, I saw you standing here alone."

Judith took a deep breath. "I've got to sit down."

"Are you all right?"

"I don't know." Judith shook her head and chuckled ruefully. "I'm not sure what I just witnessed, but," she watched Ceren's reaction, "I think I saw a ghost."

"Well, I did see a girl, a solid, three-dimensional girl by you, so you didn't imagine that." Her forehead puckered. "You know, she looks familiar. I'd swear I've seen her face somewhere before, just wish I could remember where . . . ."

"She just 'wisped' away . . . like fog," said Judith. "One moment she was there, so real, I reached out to her, and the next she was gone."

"You're so pale." Ceren gave a nervous laugh. "You actually look as if you saw a ghost." Then noting Judith's trembling hands, she gasped. "You're shaking. Let's get you outside in the sunshine, warm you up."

Deep in thought, Judith nodded absentmindedly. "Ever since I touched that clammy mist, I've felt queasy, chilled to the marrow."

Ceren put her arm around Judith's quaking shoulders. "C'mon, let's get you out of here, and then I'm calling Juan to pick us up early."

Distracted, Judith allowed Ceren to lead her. Then she stopped abruptly. "Am I hallucinating?" She looked hard at Ceren. "Did I imagine it, or did I just connect with a spirit?"

ॡ

That night, Judith dreamt she was at Tepeyac. It was early morning, just before dawn. All she could see were the rocky outcrops and green fern tips peeking above the mist. The basilica was nowhere in sight. Then she realized it was before the basilica, Bell Tower, or Atrium of the Americas had been built.

She wandered along narrow deer paths, her feet breaking the mist into foggy wisps. Suddenly the girl appeared, her dazzling glow dispelling the mist. Instead of her usual impish grin, the girl wore a welcoming smile and held out her arm, as if beckoning Judith nearer. Trance-like, Judith slowly walked toward her. She reached out her hand and touched the girl's arm, this time connecting. Judith gasped. Before her eyes, the girl transformed into a young woman.

"Do you know who I am?" she asked.

Several ideas ran through Judith's mind. As if reading those thoughts, the woman smiled and nodded.

"Yes, all of those," she said, "I am the child you discarded. I am the young mother you could have been. I am your daughter, the child your friend carries. I am *Inninantzin in huelneli Teotl Dios.*"

With a flash, she was gone, and Judith awoke. Still trying to interpret the dream, she slipped back to sleep.

Song That Never Starts

"Sometimes the only way the good Lord can get into some hearts is to break them."

~ Bishop Fulton Sheen

Ceren tossed and turned all night, unable to sleep, thinking of the recent events. As the sun rose, she drifted into an uneasy slumber where she walked through mist-covered paths. Suddenly the girl she had seen with Judith appeared, her bright, white gown shimmering in the mist. It took a moment to recognize her.

Ceren gasped. "I know who you are," she said, pleased that she could identify her.

The girl transformed into a young woman and spoke, but her words were drowned out by the knocking, the incessant knocking.

"Who is it?" Ceren called, annoyed that she had been roused so rudely.

"It's Jarek."

For a moment, Ceren thought she was still dreaming and, closing her eyes, drifted back to sleep. The persistent knocking escalated to pounding.

"Ceren, it's Jarek. Open the door."

The hammering irritated her as her mind struggled to comprehend.

"Just a minute," she called, still groggy.

She pulled on a robe, tied back her hair, and cracked the door.

No dream, Jarek stood on her doorstep. He stepped toward her, and she tried to slam the door.

"Wait," he said, blocking it. "Ceren, the annulment came through."

"What?"

"I left my wife and resigned from the university."

"This is so surreal," she said. Rubbing her eyes, her brain not quite accepting what her eyes saw, she tried to wake up.

"All I want is to be with you."

"To be with me . . . with me . . . . All you want is to be with me." Galvanized now, she asked, "What about the baby, our baby?"

"To be with you and our baby," he said, correcting himself. Sighing, he looked down at the floor and then up into her eyes. "Ceren, thank God you didn't get the abortion. I'm so sorry for having put you through that." He shook his head and swallowed. "It was my w . . . my ex-wife's idea." Tears glistened in his eyes.

"Spare me your crocodile tears." Arms folded, eyes narrowed slits, and lips pursed, she surveyed him. "I don't believe a word you're saying. All you've ever told me is lies."

"I deserve that," he said humbly, head bowed. "Please tell me what I can do to make it all up to you."

"Admit you're the father."

"Done," he said, nodding.

"No, legally declare it," she said, arms akimbo. "Get a DNA test and prove it!"

"Name the time. Name the place," he said, nodding. "What else?"

She stopped to think.

When she hesitated, he asked, "Is that all you want from me?"

"I don't want anything from you, you pathetic liar. You've given me enough . . . enough lies, enough heartache, and enough humiliation to last a lifetime." She grabbed the doorknob to slam the door, but his body blocked it. "Get out of here before I call the police!"

"What can I do?" A tear trickled down his cheek.

She rolled her eyes and groaned.

"What can I do to prove I'm telling you the truth?"

"Out!" She pushed him out of the way.

"Where?"

"Where? Anywhere, just get . . . and stay . . . away from me!"

"I mean, where can I take the DNA test?"

His plaintive tone made her look at him. She tried to read the face she hated, the face she had loved. His eyes moist and pleading, his lashes were still wet. She drew in her breath.

Pointing, she said, "Go to *Calle de los Dulce* and turn right. Go three blocks, and . . . ." Her chest heaved. "Never mind," she said, closing the door. "I'll get dressed and show you where to get a cheek swab."

"Thank you, Ceren, I swear you'll . . . ."

"Save your breath. I just want to be sure you go through with your promise . . . for once."

She splashed water on her face, trying to wrap her mind around the morning's events. *Jarek here? Am I dreaming?* She snorted. *This is more likely a nightmare.*

Could the annulment have come through? These are the words I've been waiting to hear. Groaning, she shook her head. *That's probably all they are, words, more empty promises. I can't believe anything he says. Our months together have been nothing but a series of lies, a very sad joke.*

Still, he is here. Is it possible he actually has left his wife? She scratched her head. *If I could only trust him.*

Her hands rested on her belly. *But will he accept responsibility for our baby? It's not just how I feel about him. I have to think of the baby.*

Glancing at her bare ring finger, she heaved a sigh. Not one of his promises has panned out, not one.

Still, he is here . . . Pursing her lips, bobbing her head in a firm nod, she made her decision.

I'll walk him to the clinic. If he goes through with the DNA test, admits paternity, and proves he actually has left his wife, I'll . . . well, if he does that, I'll see . . . .

ह

Two days later, Jarek showed up at Ceren's door, carrying two letters.

"The DNA lab results came in," he said, his eyes dancing.

"And?" she said as nonchalantly as possible. Although her pulse was racing, she managed an aloof shrug.

"It proves I'm the father." He paused, adding, "As we both knew."

Arms folded, she looked him in the eye, challenging him. "What are you going to do about it?"

"Marry you legally . . . and in church."

Primed to do battle, she wasn't prepared for a proposal. Her jaw dropped as her arms fell to her sides.

"That is, if you'll have me." His eyes looked into hers.

"After all you've put me through? You nauseate me." She suddenly felt light-headed and leaned against the door frame. "What gives you the idea I'd want to spend the rest of my life with you now?"

"If nothing else, I'm the father of your child," he said, reaching his arm behind her, supporting her. "Please say yes to an idiot who finally realizes the gift you're giving him."

He tipped her chin toward him and tentatively brushed her lips with his. She closed her eyes, yielding in an uneasy truce, not trusting him, yet wanting to believe in happy-ever-after endings.

"Jarek?" said Judith. "Are my eyes playing tricks, or are pigs flying . . . to Mexico?" Before he could answer, she asked, "How's your wife? Or should I say your other wife?"

"Hello, Judith." He cleared his throat. "My ex-wife is adjusting to our separation."

"Separation?" questioned Ceren, her spine straightening. "I thought you said you'd left her. Which is it?"

"Both," he said smoothly. "When I left her, we separated."

"How's your divorce proceeding?" asked Sam.

Jarek turned to him. "I'm sorry, have we met?" The lines around Jarek's eyes crinkled in a smile, but his eyes remained stony.

"Sam Brannon," he said, holding out his hand, "Ms. Hernandez' attorney."

"Jarek Witunski," he said, limply shaking hands.

"And how's your divorce proceeding?" Sam repeated, firmly gripping Jarek's hand.

"The annulment is going well, thank you." Jarek tried to extricate his hand.

"At what stage are the proceedings?"

"Perhaps you should discuss that with my attorney," said Jarek, finally pulling his hand away.

"And who might that be?"

"I fail to see the reason for this cross examination." Jarek's eyes narrowed, though his smile remained.

"Professional curiosity," said Sam. "Apparently, you've received the letter from our office." He smiled blandly. "Once you supply me the contact information, I'll be happy to continue this dialogue with your attorney."

"There's no need," Jarek said, handing him one of the letters. "Here are the DNA results." He focused his attention on Ceren. "I'm proud to say I'm the father of this child."

Judith and Sam exchanged looks.

"Not only that," he said, putting his arm around Ceren's shoulders, "we're getting married."

Ceren gave a delayed, stiff smile as Jarek brusquely hugged her, shaking her in the process.

"This is a turn of events," said Judith. "What does your wife have to say about it?"

"My ex-wife has accepted it," he said, turning toward Ceren. "What does my present and future wife have to say about it?"

Ceren realized she had not given an answer. She thought of the dreams she had had when they first married. She bitterly recalled the hours of waiting by the phone, the rejection, the humiliation, the tears. She considered their baby and the specter of abortion.

"Well?" Jarek said, sounding more like an authoritative patriarch than a fiancé.

Without enough time to deliberate, she responded automatically to his demanding tone. "I need to think about it."

"I'll take that as a yes," said Jarek.

"What about the baby?" Judith asked quickly, catching Sam's eye.

"Our baby will have a name, a father, and a home," said Jarek.

Judith caught Ceren's eye and mouthed the words, Did you tell him? Ceren shook her head no, mouthing, Not yet.

"What?" asked Jarek.

"Nothing," said Ceren, "I'll tell you later."

"Ah, that reminds me," said Jarek, handing Ceren the second letter. "Consider this an early wedding gift."

A curious smile playing at her lips, she tore into the envelope and began reading.

"Since your grant-funded position at the university came to an abrupt end," said Jarek, "I thought it only fitting that I find you another."

Skimming the letter, Ceren said, "Jarek's gotten me a position at this university!"

"Not just any position," said Jarek. "Read on."

"Ohmigosh, Assistant Professor," she said, beaming, grabbing his hand. "You did this for me?"

"It took a little persuasion, but . . . ."

"I'd given up hope in you, but you came through in the end!" She hugged him. Then a thought occurred. "But, if I work here, where would we—"

"We'll start fresh in Mexico," Jarek said quickly.

Narrowing her eyes skeptically, Judith scowled, clearly distrusting him.

Ceren gazed at Jarek, reappraising him. Feelings stirred that she had not felt in weeks. Could he be telling the truth?

I want to believe him. After all, he is my husband. She rolled her eyes. *Whether or not the State recognizes our marriage, I made a sworn promise to cherish him 'in good times and in bad.'*

Lips pressed together tightly, she mentally groaned. *Have to admit, I still have feelings for the man I married, at least, the person I thought he was.*

Then she recalled her conditions for reconciliation. *He did go through with the DNA test and admit paternity. Getting me the university position proves he's actually trying to make amends.*

If I could only be sure he's left his wife . . . . She chewed her lip. *I need to talk to him about our baby, and I need to see his annulment decree.*

ॐ

"Good morning," Judith said, addressing the assembly. "Welcome to today's lecture about Our Lady of Guadalupe. Let's start with a question. Is there anything to suggest that Our Lady of Guadalupe could be a modern-day counterpart of an ancient Aztec deity?"

A girl in front raised her hand, and Judith called on her.

"Some say she's *Tonantzin.*"

Playing devil's advocate, Judith asked, "Why?"

"In the *Nahuatl* language, *Tonantzin* means Our Mother," said another student, "like *Nuestra Madre María.*"

Nodding, Judith asked, "Anything else?"

"Tepeyac Hill had been holy ground to *Tonantzin* long before Juan Diego met Our Lady of Guadalupe there," said another.

"Tepeyac Hill is definitely sacred geography," said Judith. She paused as a memory of the dream flit through her mind. "Does *Tonantzin* have any other names?" When several hands went up, she said, "Just call them out."

"*Toci.*"

"As *Toci*, she was known as Our Grandmother. As *Tonantzin*, she was known as Our Mother," said Judith. "Were any other names associated with her various aspects in regard to age?"

"*Ilamatecuhtli.*"

"Yes," said Judith, "Father Sahagun, a Franciscan missionary, iden-tified *Tonantzin* as both old and young since he associated her with

Ilamatecuhtli, which translates to a noble old woman, and *Cozcamiauh*, which means a necklace of . . . ."

"Corn flowers," filled in a student.

"Suggesting youth," said Judith. "Any others?"

"*Xochiquetzal*," called a student.

"The Flower Queen," said Judith, "the Goddess of Spring, again suggesting youth."

"*Tlazolteotl*."

"Was *Tlazolteotl* a young or old aspect of *Tonantzin*?" asked Judith.

"Young," said a student. "She was the Lust Goddess."

"Old," said another. "*Tlazolteotl* was the Filth Eater."

Judith waited for the giggles and groans to subside.

"You're both right," she said. "*Tlazolteotl* had four aspects that corresponded to the phases of the moon. She was the young temptress, correlating to the new moon; the bold, sensual woman, the waxing half-moon; the High Priestess who ate filth or consumed sin, the full moon; and the old hag, who destroyed youth, the waning half-moon. Can you think of any literary archetype today that has similar forms?"

No one raised their hand.

"Anyone?" asked Judith, viewing the blank faces. "This is similar to the three forms of our legendary witches: maiden, matron, and crone. Who was the Goddess of the Witches?"

"*Tlazolteotl?*"

"Yes, and, as the Earth Mother, she was also viewed as a fertility goddess. Did *Tonantzin* have any other name?"

"*La Llorona*."

"As *La Llorona*, she was the Weeping Woman who haunted crossroads, stole children, and warned of impending danger. *Tonantzin* was known by over a dozen names that corresponded to her different aspects. Would you say this was an important Aztec deity?"

Their heads nodded in agreement.

Judith said, "You notice, I chose the word deity instead of goddess. Why?"

"They could be both gods and goddesses."

"Yes, Aztec divinities were not only called by different names for each facet of their personas, but they could be dual gender, female and male. Trick question: did *Tonantzin* have a male or dualistic aspect?"

To their nodding heads, she asked, "Which god?"

"*Ometeotl?*"

"Yes, she was the feminine side of *Ometeotl*, the supreme creator. An amalgam of many aspects, *Tonantzin* was a fusion of opposites and contradictions. Male, female, young, old, she was also portrayed as a goddess of life and death," Judith said. "Often called mother, was she ever called the Mother of the Gods?"

To their nodding heads, she asked, "What was her name in that role?"

"*Teteo Innan.*"

"In her life-giving role, *Tonantzin* was the mother of both humans and gods. What was her name when she appeared as death?"

"*Coatlicue.*"

"Was there anything unusual about *Coatlicue's* appearance?"

"She wore a skirt of serpents."

"Anything else?"

"She wore a necklace made of human skulls and hearts."

"You might say she wore her hearts on her sleeve," said a boy in the back, basking in the giggles that followed.

"As *Coatlicue*, she was called the Mother of the Southern Stars and the Goddess of Fire and Fertility. In this aspect, *Tonantzin* was believed to be both mother and virgin, underscoring the Aztecs' concept of duality. Can you think of another name for *Tonantzin* when she represented death?" asked Judith.

"*Cihuacoatl?*"

"Yes," said Judith, waving her hand in a so-so motion, "and no."

The class chuckled.

"As *Cihuacoatl*, she was the Goddess of Motherhood, Fertility, and Midwives: life. She was also the patron of women who died in childbirth: death. As the Goddess of Life, Death, and Rebirth, she could give and take away life. Would you say *Cihuacoatl* shared any similarities with Our Lady of Guadalupe?"

"Our Lady of Guadalupe is the Patroness of the Unborn," said a student.

Patroness of the Unborn: Judith's ears perked at the title. "In the tilma's portrait, Our Lady wears a sash, which indicated to the Aztecs that she was pregnant. That sash signifies she's the protector of life."

Judith recalled her flashbacks in front of the tilma. Suddenly, memories of her abortion began washing over her. With a shudder, she shook them off, struggling to regain her composure.

"What about Our Lady's role in regard to death? Is there any parallel with *Cihuacoatl?* You," she said, pointing to a student raising her hand.

"When we pray the Rosary," said the student, fingering the crucifix she wore at her neck, "we petition Our Lady to 'pray for us sinners now and at the hour of our death.'"

"Good point," said Judith, nodding, "besides being the Patroness of the Unborn, her intercession's petitioned throughout life, as well as at death." She turned to the class. "How did Our Lady of Guadalupe identify herself to Juan Diego?"

"*Inninantzin in huelneli Teotl Dios*," said a student.

"*Inninantzin in huelneli Teotl Dios*," Judith repeated in a whisper, remembering her dream. "Which means what?"

"Mother of the Great Truth," he said.

"Mother of the True God," said another, correcting him.

"The True God," said Judith, realizing the implications. *So who visited me in my dream?* Suddenly aware she had been daydreaming, she turned her attention to the class. "Mother of the True God," she repeated, "which would have been interpreted differently by the Aztecs and Spanish." She stared at her students, looking from face to face. "From our vantage point in time, can you grasp the consequences of those two interpretations? Can you see why some relativists say Mesoamerican Catholicism is an example of syncretism, a mingling of pre-Columbian religion and Christianity?"

They nodded, murmuring.

"Some ethnographers say the Aztecs transferred their beliefs from *Tonantzin*, which means 'Our Mother' in the *Nahuatl* language, and who was a virgin in her *Coatlicue* aspect, to the Virgin of Guadalupe, Our Blessed Mother. And that, ladies and gentlemen, is the topic of today's discussion . . . . Was *Tonantzin* a forgotten Aztec deity, or was she a syncretized predecessor of Our Lady of Guadalupe?"

ह

"Was this the first time you've sat in on one of my lectures?" asked Judith, gathering up her lecture notes.

Nodding, Sam said, "You brought up some interesting contrasts and comparisons between the Virgin of Guadalupe and *Tonantzin*."

"But did I make you think?" She met his eyes.

"Definitely," he said, his dimple deepening as he smiled, "but, then, you've always been thought provoking, if not downright provocative."

"You're fast becoming teacher's pet," she said, leaning across the podium to kiss him.

"Can I carry your books, Teach?" he asked, picking up her briefcase.

"You can do anything you like." She linked arms with him, snuggling.

"Were you able to talk with the university's department head this morning?"

"Only briefly," she said, "but long enough to know Jarek's full of hot air."

"What'd she say?"

"Ceren's been doing a bang-up job here, and they'd like her to stay on. They contacted Jarek, asking if there'd be any conflict of interest if they offered Ceren the position."

"They contacted him . . . hmmm . . . not exactly his version."

"There's more," she said. "Apparently, Jarek made up some cockamamie story about university protocol. He said they couldn't offer her the position directly, that he'd have to approach her on their behalf."

"So he had nothing to do with getting Ceren's new position."

"That man is such a phony." She shook her head and sighed. "Why can't Ceren see that?"

"Love's blind," he said, shrugging.

"*El amor es ciego*." They shared a wry smile.

"Are you going to tell her?"

"If I have to," she said. "I just hope she discovers it for herself."

"Don't wait too long," he said, his mouth set in a tight, grim line.

"I won't," she said, "but there is one bright ray in Jarek's turning up."

"What's that?"

"Ceren hasn't mentioned the word abortion lately."

"True," he said. "The longer she waits, hopefully, the less likely she'll be to abort the baby."

"On the other hand, she hasn't told Jarek about the possibility of Down syndrome," she said.

"I wonder how that will impact events."

"Who knows?" she said, grimacing. "Why did he have to show up now?"

"And why would he suddenly want the baby after all he's done to destroy it?"

"It's so frustrating," she said. "Just when we thought we had a chance to adopt this baby, he shows up."

"I hate to say this," Sam said gently, "but, if Jarek actually has had a change of heart, wouldn't the baby be better off with her birth parents?"

Judith stopped and stared at his face. "You said her birth parents."

"So?"

"*Her* birth parents," she repeated. "Let me tell you about a dream I had."

ॐ

Ceren threw off the covers, plumped the pillow, tried lying on her back, covered up again, and finally looked at the clock. Great, four-thirty. She sighed and turned over, expecting to feel anxious again, but, instead, this time, she felt a lulled sense of well-being.

Within moments, she was walking the misty paths of Tepeyac, following the mystical, white snake. Again it disappeared around a corner, and the beautiful, little girl materialized. Suddenly, the two-year-old grew into the girl she had seen with Judith, her bright, white gown shimmering in the mist. Then the girl transformed into a young woman.

"Do you know who I am?"

This time, Ceren recognized her immediately. "Yes," she said, gasping, pressing her hands to her mouth in wonder. "I've seen your face in so many paintings of Our Lady of Guadalupe."

"It wouldn't be the first time Christianity has used local traditions to spread the gospel," said the vision, "but you and I have a special bond. I'm the daughter you carry."

With a flash, she was gone, and Ceren awoke, this time, aware and alert. By the time she showered and dressed, Jarek was knocking at her door.

"Ceren," he called as he pounded, "are you up?"

"Even if I weren't, I would be now," she called through gritted teeth. Trying to mask her annoyance, she put on a smile as she unlocked the latch.

"What would you like to do today?" he asked, apparently unaware either of the early hour or Ceren's aggravation.

"Jarek, we really need to talk."

She closed the door behind him and sat at the far edge of the bed. Taking her cue, he joined her, but kept a respectable distance between them.

"Talk about what?"

"Several things," she said, as if talking to a student, "to begin with, the baby . . . our baby."

He touched her stomach, and she jumped as if goosed.

"Don't do that!" she said, eyes widening irritably.

"Sorry, just trying to make this . . . less confrontational," he said.

She drew in her breath, gathering her thoughts, grounding herself.

"There's something you need to know about the baby," she said.

"He's mine," he said, his eyes relaxed and self-satisfied. "That's all I need to know."

"There may be a lot more to know." Taking a deep breath, she said, "First of all, what makes you think it's a boy?"

"I just presumed," he said, shrugging.

"Don't be so sure," she said.

"It's a boy," he said, nodding his head in confirmation, "the son I've waited for all my life."

Her eyes narrowed, scrutinizing him. "Why is a son so important?"

"He's someone to carry on my name, of course." His tone implied he was stating the obvious.

"What if it's a daughter?"

"Why are you bringing this up?" he asked, turning toward her. "Did the amniocentesis indicate the gender?"

"If it did," she said, shrugging, "I haven't asked."

"Well, what then?"

She turned to look him in the eye. "Forget about the gender a minute. What if the fetus has trisomy twenty-one and an extra chromosome?"

He recoiled. "Why do you ask?"

Noting his reaction, she inquired, "What do you know about it?"

He sighed and began slowly, seeming reluctant to share. "Two of my cousins had children with translocations involving chromosome twenty-one," he said.

"Translocations . . . what? Sorry, this is unfamiliar territory." She shook her head, trying to clear her thoughts and grasp the medical terminology.

He looked her in the eyes. "It runs in the family," he said somberly, making his point.

"So you've known about this possibility?" She stood up and whacked him on the shoulder. "Why didn't you tell me? Why didn't you at least warn me?"

"I wanted our son to carry on the family name," he said.

"Family name," she sniffed. "I'm talking about something much more important than traditions."

"My w . . . my ex-wife . . . got pregnant and aborted twice."

"Did I hear you correctly? Did you say your wife had two abortions?"

"Ex-wife," he corrected. Wearing a complacent smile, he nodded, as if pleased with himself for distinguishing the difference.

Blinking, she asked, "Why did she abort?"

"The amniocenteses indicated trisomy twenty-one. We didn't want to be burdened with Mongoloids."

She stiffened. "I believe it's called Down syndrome these days."

"Whatever." He shrugged.

"What if this baby, our baby, has Down syndrome?" she asked. "You've certainly pressed me to get an abortion recently. Would you want this baby aborted now?"

He paused, rubbing his chin, considering the options. Finally he asked, "What did the doctor recommend?"

"He said the amniocentesis indicated a high probability."

"And?"

"And . . . that he'd recommend terminating the pregnancy." When Jarek remained silent, she repeated sternly, "Would you want our baby aborted?"

"Ceren, let's not waste our time together quibbling." Taking her by the arm, he turned her toward him. "Don't drive a wedge between us." He looked at the close surroundings. "It's this tiny room. It's depressing. Let's get out of here. Let's go to breakfast."

"Fine," she muttered under her breath, "whatever's best for you." Mentally exhausted, she lacked the energy to grapple with him. Still, in the elevator, she felt compelled to ask once more. "If this baby has DS, would you want it?"

"This isn't the time or place to discuss it," he said, waving off the matter as if it were a gnat.

"Then when is?" she snapped, a scowl creasing her brow.

He remained silent through the rest of the ride, ignoring her. As they left the elevator, a man approached them in the lobby.

"Dr. Witunski?" he asked politely.

"Yes," said Jarek, "do I know you?"

"No, but you'll remember me." He sneered as he placed a letter in Jarek's hands. "Consider yourself served." With a parting snicker, he turned and walked away.

Jarek looked from him to the letter in his hands, suddenly comprehending. With a curse, he tore open the envelope and began reading it silently.

"Jarek, what is it?" asked Ceren.

In his own world, he did not hear her. He ran his fingers through his hair, dropping the letter in the process.

"I can't let her do this to me," he muttered.

"Can't let who do what?" she asked, alarmed by his actions. "Jarek, what's wrong?"

"What?" He looked at her, wild-eyed. "Oh, nothing," he said, reaching for his cell phone. "I, uh, I need to call my, uh . . . make a call."

As he dashed off, she noticed the letter on the floor.

"Wait," she called, retrieving it, "you dropped this."

She followed him for a step or two but saw he was nearly out of sight. With a frustrated sigh, she decided to wait rather than chase him. She sat on one of the lobby's overstuffed chairs, propping a pillow behind her back, and began reading the letter. With each paragraph, her breathing became more labored. By the time Jarek returned, her chest has heaving.

"I've got to, uh, I have to attend to, uh, university business," he said, stammering, "that is, I have to make a short . . . business trip."

"At least, make the alibi plausible," she said, struggling to control her voice. "Go, and don't come back."

"What . . . what did you just say?"

As Ceren's words penetrated his thoughts, he became of aware of her appearance. Her cheeks were flushed, and her pale lips were clenched tightly. Her bloodshot eyes glared at him.

"Ceren . . . what's wrong?"

She snickered "You mean, what's right? Time and again, you've told me you were divorced, had the marriage annulled, and that you'd left your wife."

"I have," he said, "when I . . . ."

He stopped speaking as she held up the letter.

"If you left her, why were you served with divorce papers?"

"This is all legal mumbo-jumbo," he said, dismissing it with a wave of his hand. "You don't understand these things."

"Don't patronize me." She shook her head slowly and took a deep breath."Are you so used to lies, you're incapable of the truth?"

His jaw worked as he struggled for a retort.

"You were served, and it serves you right! You deserve whatever you get!" She took a deep breath, counted to ten, and began again in a calm voice. "Why did you come to Mexico? It obviously wasn't because of me, and it certainly wasn't because of the baby."

He shrugged. "I needed somewhere to stay until this all dies down."

"Excuse me!" She put her fingers to her forehead, trying to quell the sudden pain that shot between her eyes. "Until all what dies down?"

"You, the paternity issue—"

"Me!"

What am I to him? Did he ever take me seriously, take me for his wife? She shook her head. *Unbelievable. This Writing-Across-the-Curriculum assignment's been nothing but a ruse to keep me under the radar.*

"Not you, necessarily," he said, shrugging, "our marriage, the paternity issue, my dismissal . . . ."

Each response brought her new clarity. *He's never given a thought to raising this child. He had no intention of leaving his wife. Did he think I'd fade away quietly, that he'd have no repercussions for his actions?* The thoughts staggered her.

"Dismissal, so you didn't 'leave' the university any more than you 'left' your wife. No wonder you didn't want to 'quibble' over whether or not to abort the baby." She looked him in the eye. "You had no intention of staying to find out, did you?"

Opening his mouth as if to answer, he shut it instead and shrugged, not meeting her eyes.

She stared at him with loathing. "You disgust me."

"If I want to be insulted, I'll go back to my wife."

"Good luck." She waved the letter under his nose. "From the sound of this, you don't have a wife or a job." She snickered, adding, "Or anyone else who gives a . . . plug nickel about you." She shoved the letter in his face. "Here, take the last thing you'll ever get from me, and get out of my sight!"

She turned and strode toward the elevator.

"Ceren," he called, "Ceren!" He stuck the letter inside his jacket, rubbed his chin thoughtfully, as if debating whether or not to follow, but caught up with her as the elevator door opened. "Ceren, be reasonable. I have to take care of this . . . this little matter, and then . . . then I'll be back, and we . . . ."

"Little matter . . . ." She drew in her breath sharply and did an about-face. Pointing to her womb, she said, "The future of my baby and my marital status are not 'little matters.' And, another thing, you and I are not a 'we.' Now, get out of here. Get out of my sight. Get out of my life, and, this time, stay out!"

Glaring at him, she turned and entered the elevator.

"Ceren, don't," he said softly, his eyes solemn, "please . . . ."

As the gated doors closed behind her and the elevator began to rise, she watched him through its bars, growing smaller and smaller in her sight.

ॐ

When the doors opened, Judith and Sam were waiting for the down elevator.

Judith's eyes flew open when she saw Ceren's face. "What's happened? Are you all right?" Her jaw went slack. "Is the baby—"

"Don't worry," Ceren said, shaking her head, "the baby's fine." She took a deep breath. "I just discovered what a liar Jarek is."

"Good, I'm glad you found out," Judith said with a sigh. "Don't let him take the credit for you landing this Assistant Professor position. You've earned it all by yourself."

"What do you mean?" asked Ceren, the crease between her eyes deepening. "Don't tell me he lied about that, too?!"

"All he did was hand you the offer letter," said Judith, beginning to realize Ceren was referring to another issue. "Why? What else has the jerk been lying about?"

"Sorry to interrupt," said Sam, looking from one woman to the other, "but, before you two start comparing notes, I have to leave for a conference call." He leaned over and kissed Judith. "See you for lunch?" When she nodded, he turned toward Ceren. "If what I think has happened, has, I say good riddance."

"Thanks," she said, managing a wry smile.

Judith caught Sam's eye, mentally relaying her message. He nodded.

Before the door closed, he added, "Judith and I want you to know we're here for you. You're not alone in this."

Alone. The word choked her. Bobbing her head, Ceren swallowed hard, trying to squeeze back the tears. *I gave Jarek everything I had to give: my love, my body, a baby. He's taken both hands, and thrown it all away. I'm left with nothing, alone.*

"So what did you discover?" asked Judith. Ceren began sobbing. "C'mon," Judith said, putting her arm around her shoulders, guiding her. "Let's go to my room. I even have some of that sweet-potato candy you've become so fond of lately."

Ceren laughed through her tears.

ॐ

"All this happened this morning?" asked Judith, shaking her head, after hearing Ceren's story.

"Just before I met you at the elevator," said Ceren.

"Sam was right. Good riddance," Judith said, passing the bowl of candy with her casted hand.

"When's the cast coming off?"

"Today, thank God."

"Bet you're glad," Ceren said, unwrapping her third piece of candy.

"Absolutely," said Judith, "but I'm not altogether sorry I had to wear it."

"Why's that?"

"It's forced me to depend on my sister and Sam." She smiled. "Because of that, I've seen what good people they are."

"And now they're both back in your life."

"To stay," said Judith. "It's as if, when the cast went on, the blinders came off."

"What you're saying is, good can come from bad," said Ceren, the crease deepening between her eyes again.

"Something like that," said Judith, wondering if this were the right time to mention it. "There's something Sam and I have been waiting to share . . . ."

"You're getting married."

"Re-married," said Judith. "How did you know?"

"Who wouldn't have guessed, watching you two these past weeks." Ceren chuckled. "You act like moonstruck teenagers in puppy love."

"So it wasn't a secret, after all?"

Smiling, Ceren shook her head. Judith took a deep breath, unsure where to start.

"Well, what I'm about to say may surprise you, and I hope you don't take it the wrong way."

"Okay," said Ceren slowly, looking uneasy.

"As you know, I had an abortion forty years ago."

Ceren nodded.

"Lately, I've compared it to Moses' wandering to find the Promised Land," said Judith. "It's been a passage through a . . . a desert of denial. For decades I denied any wrong-doing, any grief for killing my baby. What was done, was done. I moved on, wandering. I simply hardened myself to it, expecting to get pregnant some day and make it up to that child."

"The atonement child," said Ceren. "I've read of that."

"When the subject of abortion came up, I either didn't speak up, afraid of being a hypocrite, or I promoted the Right of Choice."

"I can attest to that," said Ceren, arching her eyebrow. "I'll never forget our conversation that first night."

"It's embarrassing," said Judith, smiling wryly as she recalled her earlier tirades. "But now that you're at the same decisive point I was, I feel compelled . . . ." She stopped and looked at Ceren's eyes, watching her reaction. "I don't know how else to say it, so I'll just blurt it out. Sam and I want to adopt your baby." She took a deep breath. "There, I've said it."

Stunned, Ceren inhaled sharply. "You weren't kidding about surprising me." As she paused, the silence became awkward.

"You haven't said anything," said Judith, disappointed.

"I don't know what to say," Ceren recounted the changes as they came to mind. "Initially, I was thrilled to be pregnant. I'd wanted this baby with all my heart." Her eyes lit up momentarily and then clouded as quickly. "Later, as Jarek's lies became too evident to ignore, I began feeling abortion was the only alternative. Now, that Jarek's out of my life . . . ." She looked Judith in the eye. "And I can't forget the results of the amniocentesis or the doctor's recommendation."

"It doesn't matter to Sam or me whether or not the baby has Down syndrome," Judith said quickly.

Ceren hesitated before speaking. "Jarek admitted this morning that DS runs in his family."

"Please don't let that be a consideration," said Judith. "We'd welcome this child, either way."

Ceren nodded, internalizing. "I appreciate that, but I'm not sure I could deal with seven more months of being a human incubator. Thinking of labor pains and risking my life scares me. People tell me, 'you'll forget the pain once you hold your baby.'"

Judith nodded at the old adage.

"That's just it. All the discomfort, pain, and risk would be for a baby that wouldn't be mine." Ceren's jaw worked as she struggled to verbalize the thoughts passing through her mind. "It sounds selfish, but I'm not sure I could deal with the consequences of carrying a baby to term, delivering it, and then . . . ."

"Handing it off," said Judith, finishing for her. "I know. The choices aren't easy."

"There's more. I want no reminder of Jarek, of us, of the mistake I made," Ceren said, taking a deep breath. "I don't want to preserve his presence in me. Do you hear what I'm saying?"

"Loud and clear," said Judith, her face strained, pale. "I understand all too well. You think if the baby weren't physically inside you, you'd be done with it, am I right?"

Ceren nodded.

"I have news for you. Even if the abortion clinic takes the fetus out of you, a part of the baby will always remain."

"You're talking about a memory." Ceren sniffed, dismissing it with a shrug.

"No, I mean the part of that baby that attached itself to your womb is now permanently a part of your body, physically inseparable from you."

Ceren gave her a quizzical look. "What?"

"Over the years, I've studied it," said Judith. "The blastocyst, that cluster of cells that becomes the embryo, attaches itself to the wall of your uterus. A small piece of it remains after birth . . . or after an abortion. Basically, that child will always be a part of you."

"You have to admit," Ceren said, wearing a skeptical scowl, "that sounds a tad far-fetched."

"It's true," said Judith, nodding in confirmation. "Research proves that a teaspoon of a pregnant woman's blood contains hundreds of cells from the baby. These fetal cells are gifts from the baby to the mother. They'll stay inside you and defend you from diseases for the rest of your life."

"Are you telling me," Ceren paused, taking a deep breath, "that this baby is protecting me, even while I'm considering ending its life?"

"Yes," said Judith, drawing a deep breath as the image sank in, "and not just during pregnancy, but for decades, basically throughout your whole life."

"Wow . . . ."

"There was a study done on a mother of five children, who contracted and recovered from hepatitis. They discovered that fetal cells repaired her liver."

"If that's true," said Ceren, her eyes widening, "it's spooky."

"I know," said Judith. "You want to be done with every reminder of Jarek, once and for all. You think that if the baby weren't inside you, all this would be over."

"Yes," said Ceren, nodding emphatically. "An abortion would end it. A few painful minutes, and it'd be done, finished."

"No, that's where you're wrong," said Judith. "The abortion's only the beginning." She groaned. "Ceren, I listen to you, and I hear myself talking forty years ago. Please don't make the same mistake I made. Don't have the same regrets."

"You're not me."

"When I was a child, Pastora would scold me for not cleaning my room," said Judith. "After I pointed out that my room was no worse than the rest of the house, she'd say, 'Do as I say, not as I do.' Or, in this case, listen to the voice of experience. Learn from my mistakes."

"Haven't we had this conversation before?"

Judith tried again. "Let me describe what I've experienced each year after the abortion, what you can expect if you go through with this. I had my abortion in January, so each New Year, instead of the symbol of the new baby, I see the specter of death, like the skeleton man on *Calle de los Dulce* . . . ."

"The one holding the scythe and telling fortunes," said Ceren, nodding in recognition.

"New Year's isn't a new beginning for me," she said. "It's the anniversary of my child's death, a painful reminder of killing my baby. When I look back over the past year, I don't review what I've accomplished. Instead, I think how old my child would have been this year. I can't tell you how many New Years I've gotten drunk to forget."

"Is that when you began drinking?"

The question took Judith off-guard. She looked at Ceren for any glimmer of malice but saw it was an innocent question.

"Ouch," she said, coming to a revelation. "Actually, it started after my abortion."

"Sorry . . . ."

"Apparently, my forty years of wandering still aren't over," Judith said wryly. "But, to continue with the calendar parallel, on Easter, instead of coloring Easter eggs and buying him or her a new outfit for church, I'd come home to a silent, empty house, with no sound of childish laughter, no magic of the Easter bunny."

Judith watched Ceren's face for a flicker of understanding.

"On Mother's Day," she said, "oh, how I despise and detest Mother's Day! The priest would have all the mothers stand up at the end of Mass. As people applauded them, each mother received a rose. I was one of a handful of women still seated. People around me would urge me to stand or try to give me a rose, only adding to my humiliation. It was a reverse form of public shaming. I felt I was wearing a scarlet letter 'A' across my chest, 'A' for abortion . . . ."

"Instead of adultery," said Ceren, nodding, "Hester's punishment in *The Scarlet Letter*." She smiled drolly. "I get the picture."

"That's when I stopped going to church. I didn't need to be reminded so vividly. And I stopped going to family gatherings when well-meaning people kept asking when I was going to start a family. I isolated myself, so I wouldn't be reminded of the abortion, the child I longed for, the baby I couldn't publicly grieve, the baby I killed. The abortion didn't end anything. It was only the beginning. Can you understand what I'm trying to say?"

"Yes," said Ceren slowly, "but that was you. It doesn't necessarily mean that I'd react the same way."

With a sigh, Judith tried once more. "To end the calendar analogy with December, Christmas decorations were minimal. There was no reason to decorate. There was no Advent, no anticipation, no Santa Claus, no hiding gifts, no joy that only a child can bring."

Ceren grunted at the imagery, thinking.

"Christmas mornings were quiet, reflective. There were no excited kids jumping on the bed, anxious to open gifts. Instead, the ghost of Christmas Past icily crept into the bedroom, reminding me of what could have been. Christmas dinners were formal and short, no highchairs, no sippy cups." Judith cleared her throat and swallowed. "There was just spilled milk, and, trust me, that was cried over."

Judith paused, watching for a response from Ceren, but she appeared miles away, deep in thought.

"Do you see where I'm going with this?" Judith finally asked.

"Yes," said Ceren slowly, mentally returning to the present. "I can see how the abortion and the childless years that followed have burdened you. I'm truly sorry for that." She touched her hand to her heart. "I appreciate what you're trying to do for me, both in sharing your story and offering to adopt my baby, but this is something I have to decide for myself."

She saw the disappointment in Judith's moist, glassy eyes as the older woman struggled to contain her tears and put on a brave smile, but Ceren continued.

"I understand how your adopting a baby, this baby, could change your life, could even partly right the wrong you feel you've committed, but . . . ." Ceren took a deep breath, gathering her thoughts. "The last thing I'd want to do is mislead you. I don't want to tell you one thing, then change my mind and let you down. Let me think this through. I promise you by the end of the week, you'll have my decision."

ح

That night, Judith slept fitfully, thinking of her abortion and the possibility of Ceren's. She finally got up and walked to the *Zocalo*. Watching the dark, pre-dawn sky, she thought about what life might have been. The black night gave way to a deep cobalt blue, and then to a crystal-clear, sapphire blue sky, gradually paling to a powder blue as the first rays of dawn crept overhead. Warmed by the sunrise, wispy cirrus clouds took on sky-blue-pink hues, contrasting against the baby-blue sky.

Watching the sky's pageantry, it occurred to her that in the clouds, in the heavens, were the blues and pinks used in baby blankets and bassinets. *Would I have decorated in pink or blue? Would my baby have been a girl or a boy?*

More people began passing through the park on their way to Mass or work. Deep in thought, Judith barely noticed them until a sound woke her from her musings.

"Faith . . . Faith!"

She looked up to see her sister standing over her.

"Were you asleep?" asked Pastora, concern clouding her usual smile.

Stretching and blinking, Judith looked at the sun high in sky. "I must have dozed off."

"Probably not the safest thing to do," said Pastora, wearing a worried frown.

"I couldn't sleep, so I came here."

"What's wrong?" Pastora sat down beside her on the bench.

Judith told her about the previous day's events, ending with her forty-year analogy to Moses.

"Did you know Moses and his people were once eleven days from the Promised Land? It should have taken them only three weeks to make the journey from Egypt, but, because of their stiff necks and backsliding, it took them forty years to reach their destination."

"No," said Judith, "I didn't know that."

"Think of it as an image," said Pastora, "a pilgrimage. Those forty years represent a pilgrimage in your life, in all our lives. We move ahead; we slide back. Good thing God puts up with us and forgives us seventy times seven. It takes time to get to heaven, but it's not just the passing of time. It's what we learn along the way, how we live."

"The journey, not the destination," said Judith, nodding.

"You may be the doctor, but I'm prescribing something for you," said Pastora.

"What?" Judith asked, mid-yawn. "Bed rest?"

"Love," said Pastora, "it's both a prescription and condition of life."

ॡ

Ceren could not sleep. All night, she tossed and turned, soul-searching, debating the pros and cons of ending the pregnancy. Just before dawn, she made her decision. Opening a bottle of water, she took the container of abortifacients from the medicine chest and sat on the edge of the bed, determined but scared.

"It's just a pill that will bring on my period," she told herself, trying to relax. Still, she hesitated, breathing deeply. Mentally stalling, she read the instructions one last time.

"What!" Hyperventilating, she reread the bottle's label a third time, hoping her tired eyes were playing tricks: effective up to ninth week of pregnancy.

It can't be! She checked the calendar on her desktop, calculating the weeks: eleven, plus who knew how many days between her last period and conception. *How could I be so stupid?*

She counted back to when Judith had asked her to postpone her decision. First there was Sam's arrival and sending the letter to Jarek, then the amniocentesis and two-day wait for the results. Then the Jerk had appeared . . . and disappeared. Somehow two weeks had flown by.

She groaned. *How could I be such an imbecile?*

She considered taking the initial pill, anyway, but, after checking online, learned that miscarriage after nine weeks was unlikely. All she could expect were bleeding and pain but no abortion. She took a deep breath and gathered her thoughts.

Now my only option's a surgical abortion.

She searched online and found fourteen public hospitals offering abortions in the Federal District of Mexico City, *gratis*. One problem: in Mexico, abortions are legal only up to the twelfth week, this week.

I've got to move fast on this. I'll have to take a bus. They run regularly between Puebla and Mexico City.

Furious with herself for delaying so long, she pulled up an online schedule and printed out a map. Ceren dressed, and, at the first glimmer of light, walked to the bus stop. Cutting through the *Zocalo*, she stopped. *Is that Judith?* Blinking, she decided her tired eyes were only playing tricks.

Within minutes, she caught the first bus of the day into Mexico City. As she boarded, she noticed the passengers looked particularly festive for such an early hour. What were they dressed for? Some of them carried marigolds. She frowned, thinking the golden-orange, and blood-red petals grotesquely cheerful in the morning's gloom, but she had too much on her mind to give it more thought.

Ceren chose a seat in the back, hoping to sleep on the way, but she had no more success on the bus than in her bed. *I simply can't come to terms with ending my pregnancy.* Then she recalled what Judith had said that first night. "I took a bus to Manhattan . . . alone."

She dropped her head into her hands. *Who am I becoming?*

Día de los Muertos

"Send in your skeletons. Sing as their bones go marching in . . . ."
~ Foo Fighters

Alighting in Mexico City, she understood the reason for the festive passengers. It was November first: Día de los Muertos—Day of the Dead. The city was vibrant in multi-color paper cutouts. Crimson, fuchsia, canary yellow, cerise, and chartreuse papers fluttered from every shop, cart, and street. Even at the early hour, the *Zocalo* was filling with people in costume, waiting for the Day of the Dead parades. More and more people began arriving, their faces painted to resemble skulls.

Rapt in her own world, Ceren had forgotten about the holiday. Fear caught her breath. What if the clinic wasn't open or closed early? The urgency spurred her on, but the gathering crowds and ghoulish spectacle of the city slowed her stride.

At every corner, she saw sugar skulls and *pan de muerto*, bread of the dead, for sale. Rows of painted ceramic skulls lined the stalls around the

Zocalo. Macabre skeleton dolls, carvings, caps, shoes, earrings, necklaces, and assorted kitsch vied for her attention.

For those not artistically inclined themselves, *Calavera-Catrina* and *Catrine* face painters had set up shop in front of the cathedral. Ceren paused, momentarily joining the onlookers. The artists created black hollows around their subjects' eyes, painting black over the lids, eye sockets, and areas beneath the eyes. Whitewashing the rest of their faces clown white, the artists added a black triangle at the tips of their noses, and drew black 'stitches' over their lips. Some finished with black blusher under the cheekbones for a hauntingly hollow effect.

Everywhere, I see the face of death.

A few faces sported colorful flower shapes around their eyes with hearts and curlicues on their foreheads and cheeks. But it was the half-decorated faces that caught her eye, grins that began on natural features and crossed the face to become painted skull smiles.

Ceren stared at the half-skull makeup, the faces caught between life and death. She sniffed, twisting her mouth into a grimace. *I can relate.*

Smelling the fresh-baked *pan de muerto*, she realized she had left before sunrise without eating. She bought a loaf and hungrily tore off a bite, but, as it touched her lips, she shivered. Still shaking, beads of perspiration broke out on her forehead. *What am I doing, partaking in some kind of unholy communion with the dead?* As she struggled to swallow the bread, she suddenly felt nauseous.

"Are you all right, miss?" asked the shopkeeper.

Ceren smiled wanly. "Just a little dizzy."

The shopkeeper nodded knowingly. "I also get emotional on *Día de los Inocentes.*"

"Day to celebrate the lives of the innocents?" Ceren asked, unfamiliar with the phrase.

"*Sí, los niños* who died."

"The children who died," Ceren repeated softly. *Now I understand.* Her body sagged, and she leaned against a lamppost for support.

The entire country's remembering the lives of their deceased children, and today, of all days, I'm having an abortion . . . .

A wave of nausea quickly grounded her in the present. She took a deep breath to bolster her determination, referred to her map, and started off toward the nearest hospital. Surges of people wearing *Catrina* and *Catrine* faces passed her on the sidewalk, watching her with their blank, black eyes. As absurd as it seemed, she had the unreasonable feeling that the grinning skull faces knew her intentions and were jeering at her.

Within minutes, she arrived at the hospital and learned the abortion wing was operating despite the city-wide celebration. Both relieved and disturbed that it was business as usual, she took a seat in the waiting room. She stole glances at the other young women's faces, wondering their reasons for being there. A sinking feeling in the pit of her stomach told her she wasn't alone in her mission. Death doesn't take a holiday.

ॐ

"Good morning," Judith said, addressing the graduate class. "Welcome to today's lecture about the culture of death, specifically *Dia de los Muertos*, the Day-of-the-Dead celebration. Why is it called Day of the Dead when it takes place over two days?" She called on the first student to raise his hand.

"The first day celebrates the lives of children who died, and the second day celebrates dead adults who had lived full lives."

Celebrate the lives of children who died. Judith's ears perked at the oxymoron. *It's a hard concept to accept: celebrating the death of children.* She swallowed the lump in her throat, thinking of her own baby's death and worrying about the life of Ceren's.

Clearing her throat, she asked, "Are these solely indigenous holidays, or do these correspond with any Christian holy days?"

"Yes," said a student up front, drawing chuckles.

"Would you care to elaborate?" asked Judith, smiling good-naturedly.

"It's a combination of the two, but originally it was an Aztec celebration."

"It can trace its roots back farther than that," said Judith. "Based on a three-thousand-year-old Olmec tradition, *Dia de los Muertos* later became part of the Toltec, Maya, Zapotec, Mixtec, and Aztec cultures. They held the celebration in the ninth month of the Aztec Solar Calendar, roughly corresponding to August, and it lasted all month," said Judith. "How does this tie in with the Christian religion?"

"The Spanish moved the celebration from August to November first and second," said a student.

"As part of the Christian-conversion process after the Spanish conquest," said Judith, "they merged it with All Saints' and All Souls' Days. Occasionally, the line between ancient folklore and Christian custom blurs." She raised her eyebrows. "How did the tradition begin?"

"The Aztecs believed death was a door to another existence," said a student, "an open door."

"To remember their dead, they kept their skulls," said another.

"Considered symbols of death and rebirth," said Judith, "skulls were used to honor the dead. How do skulls play a role in today's celebration?"

"We eat them," said a girl, chuckling. "We buy sugar skulls with the names of dead friends or relatives written on their foreheads with icing."

"You can eat them," said another, turning up her nose, "but those are made to decorate altars and graves, not eat."

"White-chocolate skulls taste so much better than the pure sugar," said a third, as the students vied to voice their preference.

"Let's see a show of hands for chocolate," said Judith, grinning, counting. "Okay, chocolate skulls beat sugar skulls fourteen-to-two. Now, returning to our topic, the Aztecs believed the dead visited the living during these celebrations. Did the Spaniards share this belief?"

The class murmured no and shook their heads as Judith called on a student.

"Definitely not," he said. "The Spaniards viewed death as the end of life."

"That's true, while the Aztecs viewed death as the continuation of life. Instead of fearing it or mocking it, the Aztecs embraced it," said Judith. "They believed they lived in a perpetual dream, only truly awaking in death. What about today? Does anyone believe the dead visit the living in this day and age?"

"Some say the gates of heaven open at midnight on Halloween. They believe that, during *Día de los Angelitos*, the *angelitos*, the spirits of dead children, reunite with their families on November first."

Judith caught her breath, not having heard it phrased that way before. Suddenly a flashback reminded her of the child she had aborted. She wished its spirit could visit her. She thought of Ceren's baby and wondered about her decision. A student's voice interrupted her musings, recalling her to the present.

"It's also called *Día de los Inocentes* or *Día de Muertos Chiquitos*, the Day of the Little Dead."

"Is this a time of mourning or celebration?" Judith asked, stalling to regain her composure.

"Celebration."

"It's a joyful occasion where the continuity of life is celebrated," said Judith. "It's not a time for mourning. Why?"

"The elders tell us the trail back to the living world must not be made slippery by tears," said a student, shrugging.

"Give an example of celebrating life with the dead," said Judith, pointing to a student.

"Some families build *ofrenda* altars in the cemeteries on October thirty-first and then stay up all night, singing, telling stories, waiting for their children's spirits to visit."

She pointed to another student, raising his hand.

"Others buy toys for the children's spirits, such as molded sugar coffins." Demonstrating, he added, "Pull the coffin's string, and a smiling *calavera* skeleton jumps out."

"A lot of people put out tiny sugar skulls for the *angelitos* on November first," said a student in the back, "and then replace them with full-sized sugar skulls on November second for the adult spirits."

"Along with tequila, mescal, pulque, and beer," added a student up front, grinning.

"Spirits for the adult spirits," said Judith, chuckling, "combined with music, food, and vibrant colors. Instead of the grief shown in other parts of the world when families visit relatives' graves, here, it's a festive family reunion with ancestors. This, ladies and gentlemen, is the topic of our discussion today: comparing and contrasting the pre- and post-Hispanic attitudes regarding the culture of death."

ॐ

"It's a good thing you didn't take the Mifeprex this morning," said the abortion counselor. "After nine weeks, it would harm the fetus but not kill it."

"Are they sure I'm eleven weeks along?" asked Ceren, still uncertain. "Maybe I'm only nine weeks."

"You're definitely eleven weeks pregnant, plus," said the counselor. "Your examination proved that."

Ceren started to ask a question, but then sighed in resignation.

As if reading her mind, the counselor said, "Your only option now is a surgical abortion."

She nodded. "Can they do it today?"

She checked her records. "Yes, you're in luck. We've had a cancellation. Are you ready?"

Ceren's eyes widened and she flushed. "Yes," she said as calmly as she could muster.

"Let me check your blood pressure," said the counselor, affixing the band to her arm. Moments later, she said, "You're fine. Have you had anything to eat within the past two hours?"

Ceren remembered the *pan de muerto* that had made her queasy. "Just a bite about an hour ago."

"You shouldn't risk it," said the counselor, frowning.

"But I'm from out of town," said Ceren, now worried that her venture would end in failure. *I don't know if I could go through this again, and, if I wait, it'll be too late.* "I have to do this today. Please . . . ."

Checking her schedule again, the counselor gave her a reassuring smile. "Come back in two hours. Don't worry, I'll fit you in then."

"Thanks." Relieved, Ceren took a deep breath, but the words reminded her of Jarek's invitation to a romantic weekend getaway. Her nostrils flared at the memory. Only then, instead of fitting me in for an abortion, the doctor would have squeezed me in for a D&C. She rubbed her forehead. *Why did I wait? Why did I prolong this pregnancy when the result's going to be the same? Either way, my baby's heart will stop.*

The woman finished with a reminder. "A sip of water's all right, but be sure not to eat anything!"

ॐ

Ceren wondered where to wait. If the clinic was depressing, the *Día de los Inocentes* festivities in the street were morbid, especially as the afternoon's appointment loomed ahead of her. Remembering the park at the basilica, she hailed a cab.

"*Nuestra Señora de la Basílica de Guadalupe, por favor,*" she told the driver.

Though not a civic holiday, the traffic was heavy. Once she arrived at the basilica, she found that it, too, was crowded with people celebrating *Día de los Inocentes*. She climbed the hill's steps, hoping to escape the hordes. Thirsty and out of breath, she stopped to buy water at a vendor's stand one level below the Saint Michael Chapel. The woman in line ahead of her turned to her and began a conversation while they waited their turns.

"I come here every *Día de los Angelitos* to remember my little angel," she said, fingering a necklace of tiny skulls resting on her chest. "The *Basílica de Guadalupe* is a sacred space."

Ceren grunted politely, dismissing the macabre necklace as costume jewelry for the occasion. Disinterested, she started to look away, but the sun reflected off the woman's metal belt and arm band, catching her eye.

Fashioned like a snake, the flexible belt coiled around the woman. The belt's two ends looked like a snake's head swallowing its tail, clasping her waist. A golden armband, also in a serpentine shape, wrapped itself around her withered bicep.

"She would have been forty this year," she said, heaving a great sigh.

The woman looked up to the heavens, shook her gray head, and brought her wrinkled hands to her heart. Wishing she could escape, Ceren murmured absentmindedly and looked away, but the woman pressed on, seeming to enjoy her captive audience.

"Me, I'm too old to have another angel." She gestured futilely and shrugged. "But you, you have motherhood ahead of you." Looking at

Ceren's womb, she leaned toward her and lowered her voice, speaking confidentially. "The womb is a sacred space." She nodded knowingly and winked.

Am I showing? Ceren glanced at her waistline and saw a small bulge.

The woman noticed. Her expression changed, and she looked from Ceren's face to her womb and back again. "*Mi madre*, are you . . . you're pregnant, aren't you?"

Before Ceren could answer, the shopkeeper called, "*Siguiente*, next." The woman moved ahead.

Saved from answering the uncomfortable question, Ceren breathed a sigh of relief, wanting only to get her water and get away.

"*Siguiente*," called the shopkeeper.

Ceren moved to the front of the line. As they passed, the old woman paused, her purchased water in hand.

"Enjoy it while you're young," she whispered hoarsely. "The womb is a sacred space."

ॐ

The old woman's words distressed Ceren, and she walked to a shady place near the angel statues. Remembering the counselor's words, she took only a sip of water. Then she pressed the cool bottle to her forehead and temples, trying to relieve her headache, as she collected her thoughts.

She chose a bench beneath a flowering tree and listened to a bird trill its melody. She looked up to see the bird perched above her with spectacular plumage of green, red, and white feathers. The bird flew to another branch, its long tail brushing a flower loose from the branch overhead. Fuchsia and pink petals floated down onto her lap.

The old woman's words haunted her. "The *Basílica de Guadalupe* is sacred space."

Listening to the bird's song, she watched it flit from branch to branch, its magnificent feathers reflecting the sun.

"The womb is a sacred space," the old woman had also said.

Sacred spaces, she thought, glancing at the flowering trees, flower and song. *These are the last experiences I'll share with my baby.*

She got up from the bench and leaned against the angel statue, looking out over the railing. Absorbing the beauty around her, Ceren had to admit, there was something special about Tepeyac. She breathed deeply, filling her lungs, catching the unmistakable scent of ozone.

A breeze blew through her hair, and then another, causing her to look up. From a sunny, sky-blue morning, it had turned angry gray with tumultuous clouds obscuring the sun. She watched the rapidly moving squall line overtake the azure blue, the clouds' gun-metal-gray line as clearly delineated as the task that lay in front of her.

A drop of rain splashed her face, and then another. *How long have I been here?* She checked her watch, wishing she could stay but all too clearly recalling her appointment.

Another drop splashed in her eye, and she blinked.

"The weather's unpredictable on Mt. Tepeyac," said the old woman, standing beside her.

Where did she come from? Ceren looked around. The chapel's court-yard had been empty.

"You never know what to expect." The old woman stretched her lips into a coy smile.

Standing so close, Ceren could not help but notice the woman's features. Her mouth was so wizened, its wrinkles resembled the stitches others had painted on their lips for *Día de los Muertos.*

"Yes, this certainly blew up quickly." The woman had no sooner said that than the wind began howling through the tree tops below them, shrieking upward, past them, and rising off the angels' wings.

"What's that hissing sound?" Ceren shouted against the wind.

The old woman shook her head as if she could not hear.

"What's that sound?" she repeated, shouting at the top of her lungs.

The woman shrugged as the air emitted a crackling or frying sound that seemed to run up and down the musical scales.

"It . . . it almost sounds like singing." Ceren looked around, wondering who would be singing at a time like this. Following the contours of the angel's wing, her eyes were drawn upward. At the wing's crest, violet-blue tufts of flame flashed and arced to the crown of the angel's head and gradually dropped, tracing along the blade of its sword.

"What is that?" Ceren stepped back, partially to get a better view, and partly to move away.

The high-pitched, musical hissing crackled louder as the short, tufted flames followed the sword's edge down through the serpent's stony profile. Then the violet-blue tufts leapt to the angel's leg, and began a slow descent along its periphery, gradually creeping closer. Frozen now with fascination, Ceren stood riveted, unable to recoil or retreat. Only her eyes moved as they tracked the flames' descent. Nearer and nearer they edged toward the statue's feet until the violet flames blazed inches from her and the old woman.

Bound in wonder, Ceren watched the impossible happen. The flames jumped from the statue's toe tips to the old woman's metal armband, seeming to shoot out from her jewelry's serpentine head and tail. Ceren blinked. The armband seemed to wriggle around the old woman's withered bicep as the flames inched down her arm to her fingertips. Her nails began glowing violet-blue like tiny jets of flame.

The old woman looked at her fingers, looked at Ceren, and then cackled as if she had thought of something amusing. Never taking her eyes from Ceren's, she reached over, and touched Ceren's hand, igniting her fingertips.

"Passing the torch," she hissed against the wind.

Ceren watched in horror and fascination. Her fingertips sparked and flickered with violet-blue flames. Other than a slight shock when the old woman had touched her, she felt nothing. No pain, it wasn't consuming her. It wasn't fire, at least as she knew it. She watched the tiny hairs rise on her arms and shuddered as the hair rose on the back of her neck.

Tickled, laughing with relief, she said, "It's static electricity on steroids."

Again she felt a drop of rain, but this time it gave off a mild shock as it touched her. It reminded her of the time she had visited a farm as a child. She had held onto the electric fence, almost enjoying the tingling sensation of the slowly pulsating, electric current.

Another drop and then another sprinkled them, each drop generating milder and milder shocks, diminishing the flames' intensity, until their fingertip flames went out. Ceren checked her hands, but the flames had left no trace, other than their memory. She looked at the sky and watched the squall line move on, leaving only cirrus clouds in its wake. As quickly as the storm had blown up, it blew away, leaving the air refreshed.

Ceren breathed deeply. The peculiar experience left her feeling like a child who had gone out to play in the rain. She felt cleansed, carefree, cheered, until she remembered her appointment.

Again, she checked her watch. Thanks to the traffic and crowds, it had taken longer than expected to reach the chapel. It would take at least as long to return. She sighed, hating to leave Tepeyac, loathing her next destination.

She turned to say goodbye to the old woman, but she was gone. Ceren looked in all directions, checked the chapel's courtyard, but, except for a couple standing on the steps, she was alone.

Weird.

She peered over the railing, seeing all the way down the steps to the next level, but the old woman was nowhere in sight. Closing her eyes, Ceren placed her hand on the base of the angel and said a silent prayer to help her through the next few hours.

I've got to do it. I've got to do it. It became her mantra, propelling her steps and driving her to find a cab.

When she arrived outside the hospital, throngs of *Catrina* and *Catrine* faces again seemed to jeer at her through their death masks. She kept her eyes focused on the sidewalk, unable to meet their blank, black eyes.

Near the hospital door, she brushed against a tree's low-hanging branch. A mockingbird suddenly flew out from the foliage and, cheeping loudly, attacked her, kamikaze style. A second bird flew at her, swooping down, brushing against her hair, forcing her to duck. The first bird came directly at her again, this time aiming for her eyes, changing course only at the last possible moment.

This is bizarre. It's like they're trying to chase me away.

"Mockingbirds," said the custodian standing inside the door, watching.

"They have a nest nearby." He grinned, showing a gap where a tooth had been. "They're only protecting their young."

Ceren's heart sank nearly as low as her self-esteem. Managing a wan smile, she said, "Thanks."

As she pressed the elevator button, she shook her head. *Mockingbirds mocking me. Even the birds are better parents than I am.* Instantly, she replaced that thought with her mental mantra: *I've got to do it. I've got to do it. I've got to do it.*

The elevator door opened. Ceren took a deep breath and got onboard.

ॡ

When the elevator door opened at her floor, Ceren stood transfixed. Her pulse was racing. Her breathing came shallow and fast. She recalled the last time she had felt that way.

As a teenager, she had climbed the pool's high-dive. Standing poised on the tip, she had looked down. Suddenly breathless and anxious, she had nearly fallen off the board. Had it not been for the long line of jeering divers behind her, she would have gladly climbed down. That time, she had filled her lungs with air and taken the plunge.

She tried to catch her breath. The person behind her squeezed past to exit the elevator. Another person jostled her getting on. Her mantra 'I've got to do it' became 'I can't do it.'

Ceren got off at the next floor and found a restroom. She washed her hands and face and then caught sight of herself in the mirror.

Just do it, said a tiny voice in her brain. *Jump. Take the plunge. You'll go to sleep, and, when you wake up, all your troubles will be over.*

No, said another tiny voice. *This is something you'd regret, something that would haunt you for the rest of your life. Find another way.*

"How could I have gotten to this point? How can I be so close to killing my baby?" she asked her reflection. "Abortion's against my beliefs, against my religion." She took a deep breath and stared at her image. "I've redefined my religion. That's how."

ॡ

By the time Ceren returned to Puebla, it was dusk. Judith was waiting for her in the lobby.

"Where have you been?" The lines in Judith's forehead were deeper, more pronounced than usual. "You missed your afternoon class. You can thank me later for covering for you. The department was worried. I was worried. Pastora's been a nervous wreck. Where have you been?"

"I took the bus to Mexico City," Ceren said, her voice hoarse, raspy, barely above a whisper.

It was then that Judith looked at her. Ceren's face was ashen gray. Her eyes were red from weeping. Sounding familiar, the words finally penetrated Judith's mind. Her eyes flew open as she recognized them, and she gasped.

"You took a bus alone?" Judith asked, her eyes darting, searching the girl's face for answers.

Ceren nodded, choked up, unable to speak.

"Tell me you didn't have an abortion."

With a quick bob, Ceren walked away, sobbing. Judith roughly grabbed her by the shoulders and shook her.

"Was that a nod? Did you have an abortion?"

As Ceren began to cry, they attracted the desk clerk's attention. Judith let go her shoulders.

"Answer me! Did you?" she whispered loudly.

The girl shook her head but continued to sob.

"I can't tell if you're nodding yes or shaking your head no. Ceren . . . ." Judith hissed, "I swear, if you don't answer me, I'll . . . ."

"No," Ceren managed to get out between sobs, her voice breaking.

"You didn't have an abortion?"

The girl shook her head.

"Really?" Judith asked, relief flooding through her. She took a deep breath as the atmosphere lightened. Then the skepticism returned. "No, tell me directly! Don't make me guess. Did you, or did you not, have an abortion?"

"No, I didn't!" Ceren shouted hoarsely, frustrated. "Now, leave me alone!"

"Excuse me," said the desk clerk. "Is there a problem?"

"No!" shouted both women simultaneously.

They stared him down until he held up his hands in resignation and walked away. Then, as they caught each other's eye, they went from glowering to chuckling, finally ending up in a hug.

"Just to double-check," said Judith, becoming serious. "Do you still have your baby?"

Nodding, meeting her eyes, Ceren said evenly, "We still have our baby."

Now it was Judith's turn to cry. She wiped her eyes and cleared her throat, trying to speak, but she was overwhelmed. She took a deep breath and tried again.

"Are you saying what I think you are?" Judith finally asked.

Ceren nodded. "The baby's fine," she said, patting her tummy. "He or she's yours if you and Sam still—"

"Oh, yes, we want her!" Judith interjected, her eyes brimming. Then she grabbed Ceren by the shoulders again, but, this time, holding her out to see her response better. "You're sure?"

Nodding, tearing up, Ceren swallowed hard. "Absolutely."

ะ

Pastora walked into the lobby wearing a worried frown that melted into a smile when she saw Ceren.

"You're all right," she said, a sigh punctuating her relief. "Where were you? We were worried about you."

"I . . ." Ceren stopped sheepishly, swallowed, and took a deep breath. "I went to Mexico City to have an abortion."

Pastora's eyes flew open, and her jaw went slack.

"I didn't have it," Ceren said quickly. "I changed," she paused, shaking her head. "Something changed my mind."

"What was it?" asked Judith.

"God," said Pastora.

"Maybe," said Ceren, shrugging her shoulders. She told them about the storm that blew up out of a blue sky and the violet-blue tufts that danced like candle flames on her fingertips.

Pastora quoted in a hushed voice. "His appearance was like lightning."

"St. Elmo's Fire," said Judith, nodding. "I've heard of it. Friction causes an electrical buildup."

"St. Elmo, the patron saint of sailors since they saw that fiery light at sea," said Pastora. "I've read Columbus' accounts of ship sails and masts glowing during storms."

"Now pilots see it on their windshields and aircraft wings," said Judith.

"All I can say is that it was eerie. I can't help but believe someone or something was trying to get through to me." Then Ceren told them of her experiences with the mockingbirds and the old woman with the skull and snake accessories.

Judith stared at her, wide-eyed. "Was she wearing a skull necklace?" she asked.

"Now that you mention it," said Ceren, recalling the woman. "Why?"

"You said she appeared before you decided to keep the baby?" Judith asked.

Ceren nodded. "She was partly . . . in fact, largely responsible for changing my mind."

"What did she say?"

"That she'd been going there every *Día de los Angelitos* for forty years, and . . . ."

Judith went pale.

"What?" asked Ceren. "What's wrong?"

"Nothing." Judith shook her head. "Go on. What did she say?"

"She said she went to Tepeyac to remember her little angel."

"Her angel," said Pastora, beaming, clasping her hands. "That's it, don't you see? She was an angel of the Lord."

"I wouldn't be so sure," said Judith slowly, working her jaw. "Little angel, *angelito*, could have meant the child she lost . . . forty years ago."

At her words, Ceren and Pastora both looked at Judith but kept their thoughts to themselves.

Her eyebrow raised, Judith asked, "The woman was wearing skulls and serpents?"

"Yes," Ceren said, shrugging noncommittally, "she was probably dressed for the Day of the Dead. A lot of people were wearing skull necklaces and earrings and skull-painted faces."

Judith glanced apologetically at her sister, took a deep breath, and said, "I realize how far-fetched this sounds, but it could have been *Tonantzin*."

"Why do you say that?" asked Ceren.

"Tepeyac was her home. When *Tonantzin* appeared as death, she was called *Coatlicue*, and she wore a necklace of human skulls and a skirt of serpents. The snakes would be her totem."

Pastora rolled her eyes. "Tepeyac is the home of Our Lady of Guadalupe. No doubt, Our Lady interceded, asking God to send an angel to counsel you. Ceren, where were you when this happened?"

"I was near the Saint Michael Chapel, just beneath the angel statues."

"Mmm-hmm," said Pastora, nodding knowingly, "under the protection of the angels. It wasn't *Tonantzin* or *Coatlicue*. It was an angel that spoke with you." She straightened up, as if a thought struck her. "There are two angel statues guarding the chapel. Which one did you say blazed with flames?"

"The one with the sword."

"That was St. Michael, the archangel. Don't you see? He holds the flaming sword."

"That would explain the violet-blue flames of St. Elmo's Fire," said Judith, musing.

"St. Michael was protecting your baby the way he protects Our Lady of Guadalupe."

"That's true," said Ceren, raising her head, recalling her art history. "In the tilma, the angel upholding Our Lady is often depicted as St. Michael."

Pastora crossed herself.

"What about the giggling girl in white?" Judith asked, arching an eyebrow.

"Where were you the first time you saw her?" asked Pastora.

Grimacing, fidgeting, Judith paused, as if reluctant to divulge it. "By the angel statues," quickly adding, "but, in a dream, she identified herself as *Tonantzin*."

"It was just that, a dream," said Pastora, dismissing it with a beatific smile. "You've both been touched by angels."

While the three women silently contemplated the interpretations, Judith and Pastora eyed each other warily, old antagonisms reawakening. Ceren stared into space, looking inward, mentally replaying her encounters with the snake lady.

Her words about the womb being a sacred space struck a chord, really affected me. She seemed to sense I was pregnant. And the way she appeared out of nowhere in the empty courtyard just moments before the storm, saying, 'You never know what to expect.' Ceren sucked in her breath. *It was uncanny.*

And bold. The flames didn't faze her. I was petrified. I couldn't move, but she was fearless. Eyes widening, Ceren raised her eyebrows as a thought came to mind. *When she passed that St. Elmo fire to me, it was as if she conveyed some of her courage along with it. I wonder how large a part she's played in saving my baby's life . . . .*

"So which is it?" Ceren finally asked, emerging from her reverie. "Aztec goddess or angel?"

"Actually, that's a microcosm of our book's thesis," said Judith. She smiled wryly. "Is it *Tonantzin* or Our Lady of Guadalupe that people have worshipped at Tepeyac for the past five hundred years?"

"Or," asked Pastora, head tipped to the side, as if thinking aloud, "was she simply a woman in the right place, at the right time, put there by God?"

Love and Remarriage

"Every person carries in his heart the blueprint of the one he loves."
~ Bishop Fulton Sheen

On Valentine's Day, the wedding party met at the *Rosario* Chapel.

"Before you get into your wedding gown," said Pastora, looking from Judith to Ceren. "Why don't we take a moment in the chapel to thank God for His blessings?"

Agreeing, the women filed into a pew. Pastora crossed herself and knelt, while Judith and Ceren sat a few feet apart.

Again, shadows swept and swirled in front of Judith, so close that she ducked. She looked over her shoulder, but no one was there. Ceren looked up but then looked away.

A moment later, Judith felt a presence, as if someone had sat down beside her, between her and Ceren. By coincidence, the pew creaked, and the younger woman moved slightly. Wearing a crooked smile, she looked at Judith questioningly.

Could it be? Judith strongly felt a presence. She prayed for her aborted baby, for Sam, for their lost time together, for Pastora, for the time she had squandered with her sister, for Ceren, and for her baby.

When a nun called Pastora away, Judith and Ceren moved to the bride's dressing room.

On the way, Ceren whispered, "I had the most peculiar feeling in the chapel."

"Really?" asked Judith, trying to sound noncommittal.

"Maybe I'm hallucinating, but I'd swear I saw shadows so close, so palpable, that I bobbed my head to avoid them." She laughed at herself. "It was as if they were trying to get my attention."

Judith grunted.

"I felt," Ceren stopped and looked at Judith, "I mean, I physically felt somebody sit between us."

"You did?"

"Yes," she nodded emphatically, "and it wasn't just my imagination. My stomach fluttered as if the baby sensed it, too."

Judith turned toward her, dropping all pretense. "Yes, I felt it, too." She sighed deeply. "In fact, it's the second time here that I felt it."

"What was it?"

"I can't say for sure, but I believe it's the spirit of my baby, the child I aborted." She paused and swallowed. "You also mentioned shadows."

"Yes, I saw and sensed something," said Ceren slowly. "It reminded me of the mockingbirds flying at my face and head. It was almost as tangible as the flutter of their wings." Her eyes widening, she gasped. "Angels?"

"Pastora said it could be the shadows of souls."

"Why not?" Ceren shrugged. "God works in mysterious ways."

"Funny," said Judith, "that's what she said."

ॐ

Judith wore the blue topaz earrings Sam had given her and a vintage Mexican wedding dress. The off-white dress had a full-sweep skirt, sheer fitted bodice, sweetheart neckline, and long sleeves with slightly puffed shoulders. Appliquéd lace trimmed the bodice, sleeves, and flounced ruffle.

The moment she had seen the dress, she knew it was right. Everything about it reminded her of the giggling girl at the basilica.

Earlier that morning, Sam had asked, "Now you have something old, something new, and something blue, but what's borrowed?"

"This," said Judith, holding up her bouquet. "The florist twined the little boy's crocheted cap into the silk flowers. See?"

"Sure enough," he had said, studying it closely. "That's quite a work of art. Wound into those overlapping circles, the cap looks like a white rose."

"It blends right in," she said, meeting his eyes, "the way our baby will, even if she has Down syndrome."

As Judith walked down the aisle, she smiled, happier than she had been since she had married Sam the first time. Taking her eyes off him only for a moment, she took in the scene. The *Rosario* Chapel had never looked lovelier. The onyx altar was nearly hidden by flowers, which added another fragrant level of beauty to the golden chapel.

At Sam's right, his junior partner, Justin, stood as his best man, having flown in for the wedding. As matron of honor, Pastora waited for Judith at the altar, her mouth trembling, tears in her eyes. Large now, nearly in her seventh month, Ceren sat in the front pew, grinning broadly. Faculty and students from the university filled the chapel's pews, all smiling, watching her. Wearing a white chausable, alb, and surplice, Father O'Riley officiated.

He's beaming as proudly as if he were my own father.

Judith smiled at each and then focused on Sam. *He's my heart and center of life. Why did it take me so long to realize it?* Then gratitude replaced the thought, and she smiled the wider, knowing how lucky she was.

"No, blessed," Pastora had corrected, when she had voiced that earlier. Judith agreed. She was blessed, and it had all started that day at the Basilica of Our Lady of Guadalupe.

ॐ

At the wedding reception, Pastora asked, "Have you given any thought to what you'll name the baby?"

Ceren, Judith, and Sam looked at each other.

"We think it'll be a girl, but we really don't know," said Judith. Then, smiling at her new husband, she added, "If it's a boy, we'll name him Sam."

"And if it's a girl?" asked Pastora.

"In honor of the day when Ceren decided to keep the baby, *Día de los Angelitos*, we thought we'd name her Angela," said Judith. She put her arm around Ceren's large waist and hugged her.

"Angela, in honor of the angels," said Pastora, nodding.

Ceren started to correct her, but Judith subtly shook her head.

Unaware, Pastora continued, "Isn't the baby due in May?"

"Yes," said Ceren, "May first."

"May is Mary's month. You might want to name her Maria. After all, it was at the basilica that the angel appeared to Ceren."

"Maria," said Judith, rolling it over her tongue. "Angela Maria, it has a certain ring to it, don't you think?" she asked Sam.

Wearing an indulgent smile, he nodded. "I do." He winked as his words reflected their recent vows.

"What about the baptism?" asked Pastora. "Will you hold that here, too?"

"We thought we'd have it at the *bautisterio* at the basilica," Judith said. "After all . . . ."

"The Basilica of Our Lady of Guadalupe has played such a large role in this baby's life," said Pastora, finishing her sentence. "Have you chosen the baptismal sponsors?"

"We've been meaning to talk to you about that," said Judith, grinning. "Besides being matron of honor, would you consider being the baby's godmother?"

"I'd be honored," said Pastora, her plain face lighting up with a beatific smile.

As she spoke, a tall, young Latino approached their group. Moving gracefully, he exuded an air of unassuming self-assurance.

"Justin," Sam said, putting his arm around the newcomer's wide shoulders, "I'd like to introduce you to my sister-in-law, Sister Pastora."

"Pleased to meet you," he said, taking her hand and kissing her cheek.

"I'd like you to meet Ceren. After Judith, this woman is making me the happiest man in Mexico." They laughed. "Ceren," said Sam, "I'd like you to meet the newest partner to my firm, Justin Garcia."

"It's a pleasure to meet you," said Justin, brushing his dark hair from his flashing eyes.

His eyes met Ceren's as he held out his hand. When their hands touched, Ceren gasped, sucking in her breath as she sucked in her baby bulge. Justin leaned down to brush his lips against her cheek in a formal kiss. Her nostrils flared as she caught a whiff of his cologne.

"Justin's heading up the firm's new Mexico-City branch," Sam said. Looking from one to the other, he added, "Ceren's lecturing at the university here in Puebla. Maybe she can find an afternoon to introduce you to the local sights."

"I'd enjoy that," Justin said, piercing her with his dark eyes.

"Happy to," Ceren murmured as a smile crept across her face.

Judith exchanged a sly smile with Sam.

Great Expectations

"The riddles of God are more satisfying than the solutions of man."
~ G.K. Chesterton

The phone woke them.

"Hello," said Sam, yawning. "What?!" He flipped on the light. "We'll be right there."

"The baby?" asked Judith, throwing off the covers.

He nodded. "Pastora's taking Ceren to the hospital." Checking the time, he added, "It's just past midnight."

"May first," said Judith. "She's right on time."

"May Day, May Day," said Sam, winking.

Ten minutes later, they met Pastora in the waiting room.

"She's already in labor," she said, holding her rosary, mid-decade.

Despite being half asleep, Judith's eyes were wide open as she looked at Sam. "This is it," she said simply, implying a world of change.

For months, they had planned this moment, making legal arrangements and providing for Ceren's and the baby's needs. Still, with the clock ticking the final minutes, Judith felt unprepared for the life-changes that were about to begin.

As Pastora continued her rosary, Judith whispered to Sam, "What if the baby has Down syndrome?"

"What if it doesn't?" he said.

"Are we too old to care for a child that would need special care his or her entire life?"

He smiled gently. "It's a little late to think of that now."

"I know," she said, "we've talked this through, but here we are. I mean, this is it. What if Ceren wants . . . ."

"What if this? What if that?" he said. "It doesn't matter. We'll deal with it." He kissed her. "Now relax."

"Yeah, right . . . ." She took a deep breath.

An hour and a half later, the nurse called them in.

Judith asked, "Is Ceren . . . ."

"Mother and child are doing fine," said the nurse.

Judith looked to Sam and took another deep breath before they stepped into Ceren's room.

"How are you feeling?" Pastora asked. Ceren's dark hair was still damp from labor.

"I'm fine," she said, her eyelids heavy, "tired but fine."

"Thank God!" said Pastora.

"How's the baby?" Judith asked, her voice barely above a whisper.

"She's a healthy girl," the doctor said, "eight pounds, one ounce."

"You mean she doesn't have Down syndrome?"

"She appears to be perfectly normal," the doctor said.

"Thank God," Judith said, eyes tearing. She ducked her head as she wiped her eyes, hoping no one had seen. Then she noticed the bundle in Ceren's arms. Eyes sparkling, she asked, "Is that . . . . ?"

Ceren nodded, smiling proudly. Judith automatically reached out for the baby, and Ceren flinched. For an instant, she pulled back, clutching the baby to her breast. Then she took a deep breath and held the baby out to Judith.

Lovingly but awkwardly, Judith took the baby from Ceren.

"Little girl," said Judith, overwhelmed at seeing the miniature person. She held the baby in the crook of her arm and marveled at the gesturing, expressive miracle in her hands. Her voice filled with quiet wonder, she said, "Look at the tiny fingers."

The baby stretched and flexed her minute hands. When Judith gently placed her finger on the baby's palm, she clasped the finger with her entire hand and held on. Judith was hooked. The bond was complete. Cuddling the baby, she pressed against Sam, feeling they were finally a family.

"And the baby's all right?" Judith asked the doctor again. "She doesn't have Down syndrome?"

"We'll run tests, of course, but, to all appearances, she's just fine."

Pastora peeked at the baby's red, wrinkled face, and laughed. "She looks like our great-uncle Henry."

The baby's antics provided comic relief after the months of worry. The baby yawned, stuck out her tiny tongue, pursed her little lips, and made chewing motions. Her miniature mouth in constant motion, each gesture brought another round of chatter and joy.

Judith fell in love with the little girl, wondering and laughing at her every move, her every expression. It came as a surprise when she heard Ceren crying.

"What's wrong?" asked Judith, her smile fading.

"What's wrong?" Ceren blew her nose. "After carrying this baby for nine months, feeling her kick, feeling her heart beat, I now lay here sore and alone, completely alone, while you . . . ." She broke off, sobbing.

Judith looked from Sam to Pastora and then back. "Ceren, I'm so sorry. I wasn't thinking." She leaned over and held out the baby. "Here, would you like to hold her?"

Her mouth set in a grim line, she snatched the baby from Judith's arms. "Hold the baby?" she asked shrilly. "I want to keep my baby." She clutched the baby tightly to her breast and began rocking back and forth. As she looked at their shocked expressions, Ceren added, "Actually, I want to be alone with my baby. Now, if you'll all please leave, I'm very tired."

"Ceren," Sam began gruffly, "let me remind you of your agreement . . . ."

The doctor interrupted. "Obviously, this delivery has exhausted the mother. Perhaps, it's best to come back in the morning." He showed them to the door. "Everything will seem better in the light of day."

Judith felt she had been punched in the stomach. Gasping, she could not catch her breath. She looked at Ceren, who seemed oblivious to them. Eyes on the baby, she had undone her gown and was beginning to breastfeed her.

As he escorted them down the hall, the doctor advised Judith, "Breathe slowly." When she began breathing steadily again, he asked, "You're familiar with the baby blues?"

Nodding, she asked, "It happens with most new mothers, doesn't it?"

"Roughly half," he said with a shrug. "And you've heard of postpartum depression?"

Again she nodded.

"For one in every ten new mothers, it can last for weeks . . . even months."

Judith glanced at Sam's long face. "Is that what you think this may be?" Sam asked.

"Possibly," said the doctor, "but, with this sudden onset, I'm concerned that this may be something else altogether."

"What?" asked Judith.

"I suspect this may be a temporary psychosis that can appear after childbirth."

"Is it common?" asked Judith.

"No, it occurs in only one out of five hundred women."

"It sounds serious," said Sam.

Nodding, the doctor agreed. "If untreated, it can be."

"What is it?" asked Pastora.

"It's a rare response to rapidly changing hormonal levels that triggers anxiety, confusion, hallucinations, and delusions."

"In other words, temporary insanity," said Judith, forcing herself to breath slowly. "Is the baby safe?"

"A nurse will monitor the mother whenever she has the child," he said, "and we'll begin administering paroxetine this evening."

"Is that safe if she's breastfeeding?" asked Sam.

"Yes, SSRIs are safe for the baby but will improve the mother's mood by increasing her serotonin level."

"So how 'temporary' is this?" asked Judith.

"With immediate treatment, hopefully, the mother will respond within the first week."

"What if she still refuses to let us adopt the baby?" asked Sam.

"It's best if you don't force the issue," said the doctor, his mouth set into a grim line. "As I mentioned, this condition could continue for months. The mother's already anxious, so I don't recommend aggravating her condition."

"You're prescribing patience," said Pastora, nodding.

"Patience and prayer, Sister."

ॐ

The next morning, when Judith and Sam arrived, Pastora was already with Ceren, quietly speaking with her. Ceren appeared relaxed until she saw Judith. Then her eyes widened and she clutched the baby to her tightly.

Afraid the baby might suffocate, the nurse tried to extricate the baby from her arms. "Time for the baby's nap."

"No," said Ceren, sobbing, clutching harder. "You'll give the baby to them. You'll give her to them!"

The baby began screaming. No amount of talking helped. Finally, the nurse gave Ceren a sedative, and Pastora was able to gently remove the baby from her grip. Pastora waved them out of the room while she stayed with Ceren, praying.

Judith and Sam followed the nurse to another room and held the baby, taking turns quieting the baby's cries.

Rocking the baby, Judith looked up at Sam. "What are we going to do if Ceren's condition continues?" He rolled his eyes. "I'm worried for the baby's safety."

"I am, too," he said, taking a deep breath.

"The good news," said the doctor, stopping in to check on them, "is that the baby's normal. Tests prove there's no indication of Down syndrome."

"Thank God," Judith sighed more than said. "After the amniocentesis, this baby came so close to being aborted . . . ." Her eyes met Sam's in a private, grateful smile.

ॐ

The following morning, Sam peeked into Ceren's room. Again Pastora was there, quietly talking with her. This time, the baby was not present.

"Hello," Sam said, "there's someone here to see you."

Holding Sam's hand, Judith took a deep breath and tiptoed into Ceren's room. She felt she was walking on egg shells.

"Hi,' she whispered, her body tense, "are you feeling better?"

Ceren nodded, but her eyes welled up with tears, and she began sobbing. Again, Pastora waved them out of the room while she stayed with Ceren, engaging her in quiet conversation. Judith and Sam were able to see the baby, but they had to hide in the nurse's station.

While holding the baby, Judith turned to Sam. "I'm afraid to get attached. What if Ceren decides to keep our little girl?"

"Let's cross that bridge if we come to it," he said. "Until the baby was born, we believed she had Down syndrome. As it turns out, she's perfectly healthy. Let's be happy with that for now and let tomorrow take care of itself."

ॐ

When Ceren woke up, Pastora was sitting beside her, quietly reciting her rosary.

"Why are you doing this?" asked Ceren.

"Praying is what I do," said Pastora, pausing in her decade.

"No, I mean, why are you being so kind to me when I'm . . . I've . . . ." She sighed. "I know how I'm behaving. I'm aware, just unable to stop myself."

221

"As human beings, we're called to be a gift, to be in the service of others."

Ceren began to cry softly. Pastora got up from her chair and sat on the edge of her bed.

"What's troubling you?"

"I've made such a mess of my life," Ceren sobbed through her tears.

"There's nothing God can't fix."

"Not this time." Ceren shook her head. "Jarek . . . this whole episode of my life started when I got involved with Jarek."

"So you made a mistake," said Pastora. "Who hasn't?"

"To be honest, I can't blame him for everything. I'm the one that nearly aborted my baby. I'm the one that doesn't want to give her up now, although . . . ." She wiped the tears from her face. "I don't know how I could care for her. I don't know if I could handle being a single mom."

"God calls each of us to different vocations." Pastora shrugged. "Maybe motherhood isn't your vocation, at least not at this time."

"I want to be a mother. I want to raise this baby, but . . . ."

"But you don't know how you'd manage it alone. That's not to say you wouldn't be capable of it, but . . . ." She grimaced. "It would be difficult."

"Why did I have to meet Jarek first? Why couldn't I have met someone with . . . ."

"Integrity?"

"Yes," Ceren said, "among other things, like honesty and loyalty."

"You're yearning for love," said Pastora."I can hear it in your voice." She sighed and smiled crookedly. "I don't have the experience to answer lonely hearts, but here goes. Some say we take earthly love where we find it because we're longing for God."

"Maybe." Ceren shrugged.

"When Judith was a little girl, she was naughty one day, and Father sent her to her room. She cried until she had no more tears. Finally, she started playing with her doll. After an hour, Father visited her. The moment she saw him, she dropped the doll and ran into his arms." Pastora studied Ceren's face. "Do you see what I'm saying?"

"I think so," said Ceren. "She wanted her daddy, not her dolly."

"The toy was a poor substitute for her father," said Pastora, nodding. "It's the same with us and our Heavenly Father."

"You're saying everything, everyone else is a diversion," said Ceren. "I understand, but I need to be loved. I want to be married. I want a family so badly." Hanging her head, she murmured into her chest. "I thought Jarek would give me that, but all he gave me . . . ."

"A piece is not the whole," said Pastora, shaking her head. "Flesh alone can't connect a man and woman. A loving marriage requires the body and soul of both partners."

"For someone who lives in a convent, you seem to know a lot about love and marriage." Smiling wryly, Ceren snickered.

"I've listened to Bishop Sheen a lot," said Pastora, laughing. "Let me paraphrase his advice. 'The flesh of the husband and wife may be a means to unity, but it's the spirit that unites them.' Be patient, and wait for the Holy Spirit to bring you the love you seek."

"But what do I do now?" Frustrated, Ceren sighed. "And what do I do about the baby?"

"We're called to be in the service of others." Pastora's eyes searched her face. "You're questioning your ability to raise this baby alone. Your instincts are right. It does take two. A loving couple could give this child the attention she needs. You know how Faith regrets her abortion. She considers this baby her atonement child. Think what a gift this little girl would be to her and Sam."

Her smile becoming a pout, Ceren narrowed her eyes, scrutinizing Pastora. *Now I see. I can't trust her. She's here for them. She's on their side.*

"In the service of 'others,'" Ceren repeated mockingly. "You mean Judith and Sam."

"Partly," said Pastora, "but I'm really talking about what's right for your baby. You might better serve her by giving her a privileged life.

"You mean, by giving her away," snapped Ceren, scowling.

"If you have to divide your time between your child and work, to fill two roles, you're not able to give her your best. If you raise this child as a single mother, you deny her a father."

"Part-time mother and absentee father," said Ceren distractedly, as if thinking aloud.

"On the other hand, by placing your own wants after your baby's needs, you'd be in her service."

"I do want what's best for her," murmured Ceren, eyebrows knitted, staring into space, perplexed.

"Then consider making a gift to Faith and Sam of the joys of raising this child. Consider making a gift to your daughter of your personal sacrifice."

"Give up so that I'll get." Glaring at the messenger, Ceren spat out the words. "Sacrifice now for some karmic reward in the future. Delayed gratification, isn't that what you're saying?"

"No. I'm saying, do what's right!"

ૐ

Pastora stayed with Ceren every minute during visiting hours. By the end of the week, Ceren appeared to be back to her usual self, even as Judith held the baby in her presence.

"Do you have something to say to Faith and Sam?" Pastora prompted.

Nodding, Ceren whispered, "I'm ready to sign the adoption papers."

"You are?" asked Judith, her ears perking. Tears came to her eyes, but she controlled herself, not wanting to upset Ceren.

"I'm all right now." Ceren looked from her to Pastora and back. She took a deep breath. "I'm sorry I put you through this wait. I . . . I just . . . the idea of giving up my baby . . . ." She stopped, bit her lip, swallowed, and continued. "It's all right. I'll sign the adoption papers whenever you're ready."

Afraid she could not control her tears, Judith could not look at Ceren. Instead, she looked at the miracle child in her arms, still not quite accepting the idea that now, after all these years, she was a mother. Not only that, but the mother of this particular baby. This little girl was Sam's and hers to love and guide.

Finally, God's forgiven me. The baby is proof. I'm a mom. Closing her eyes, Judith gave a deep, contented sigh and gave thanks in a silent prayer. Then she gently passed the baby to Sam, sat on the edge of the bed, and took Ceren's hands in hers.

"You know how much this baby means to Sam and me, but only do what your heart tells you." She took a deep breath. "Are you sure you want us to adopt this little girl?"

Ceren chewed her lip and then nodded. "Yes, I'm sure."

"In that case, you have an option," said Judith. "Sam and I've talked this over, and the choice is yours. If seeing the baby would be too painful, we understand, and we'll respect your wishes. On the other hand, if you'd like to be a part of the baby's life, we want you to be a regular visitor, an auntie."

Ceren looked to Pastora for an explanation.

"Don't look at me. This is the first I've heard of it," Pastora held up her hands and shook head.

"We'd also like you to come to our daughter's baptism," said Judith.

Ceren's eyes lit up. Looking to Pastora for moral support and then back to Judith, Ceren nodded.

"I'd be honored," Ceren's voice dropped to a whisper, "to be a part of her life."

Now Appearing

"The future comes one day at a time."   ~ Dean Acheson

Sister Pastora pulled in a few favors, but they were able to have the baptism in the basilica's baptistery on May 31.

"It's the feast of the Visitation of the Blessed Virgin Mary," said Pastora. "It celebrates the visit of Mary, pregnant with Jesus, to her cousin, Elizabeth, pregnant with St. John the Baptist. It's the perfect day for Angela Maria's baptism, and the baptistery is the perfect place."

The convent nuns had sewn an ornate baptismal gown from yards and yards of white satin, organdy, and ribbon for the occasion. Wearing a tiny white headband over her curling wisps of dark hair, the baby was nearly lost amidst the frothy, white fabric.

Standing tall, Sam beamed as he carried Angela into the round baptistery, her long gown flowing over his arms.

Teetering on losing her self-control, Ceren looked away quickly, focusing instead on the building's tile and stained glass windows. She dug her nails into her clenched fists, hoping the physical pain would overpower the emotional ache and keep her composed. Stealing only occasional glances at the baby, Judith, and Sam, Ceren tried to keep her eyes on the artwork and architecture.

"It reminds me of the Guggenheim Museum," she whispered, staying close to Pastora.

"What does?"

"This baptistery, it's built like a nautilus spiral. Doesn't it look like a cutaway mollusk shell?"

When she saw all the flowers gracing the baptistery, row upon row, bouquet upon bouquet, Ceren gasped. Then she heard the hymns.

"Flower and song," she said, with a wry laugh.

Pastora smiled at the phrase and then noticed a newcomer. "Look who's here."

Ceren turned toward the entrance as Justin Garcia entered the chamber. His eyes tracked the crowd until he saw her. Then, as their gaze met, his eyes lit up. Ceren politely nodded hello to him, suddenly feeling butterflies in her stomach, reminding her of the early days of her pregnancy. She groaned inwardly. Why did she have to think of that now? But, as he crossed toward her, everything fled from her mind except his intent stare.

"Glad you could join us today," said Pastora, taking his hand in hers. She called to Judith, Sam, and Father O'Riley. "Justin's here."

Before they could greet him, the priest called them to the baptismal font. Father O'Riley, Sister Pastora, Judith, carrying the baby, and Sam stepped forward. Of their party, only Ceren and Justin remained.

Gesturing toward the nearest pew, Justin said, "After you."

As she crossed in front of him, Ceren's arm brushed against his. The physical attraction was galvanizing. The hairs on her arms stood on end, reminding her of her episode with St. Elmo's fire. The kinetic energy made the hairs on the back of her neck stand on end. Ceren shuddered and then felt her cheeks redden. She looked at him and, as quickly, looked away. *How can this be happening . . . now of all times?* Justin slid in beside her, apparently unaware of her dilemma.

In deference to the group, the priest spoke in English. He gave a homily that clearly explained the scriptural reason for the baptism of babies, as well as the responsibilities of the parents and baptismal sponsors. He went on, speaking about the roles of the adoptive and natural mothers.

Ceren swallowed hard. *I'm giving Angela away a second time, first in the hospital, and now here in the presence of God.*

"Despite who gives birth, both mothers are impregnated with the Spirit," he said. "Together, they're the child's mother."

Judith and Ceren caught each other's eye. For a moment, both were one: Angela's mother. Ceren absorbed that knowledge, carrying it into her marrow. When a small sob escaped her lips, Justin moved closer and took her hand is his.

She glanced at him from the corner of her eye, meaning to smile her gratitude. All she could manage was a grimace before she felt tears starting. Blinking, she turned away quickly and cleared her throat, trying to swallow the lump.

Justin squeezed her hand. This time, Ceren squeezed back, but she could not meet his eyes. She stared straight ahead, biting her lip, trying to keep her tears in check.

Then the priest asked the parents what they wanted to name the baby.

Judith and Sam replied, "We want to call her Angela Maria Brannon."

"What do you ask of the Church?"

"We ask baptism," they answered.

The priest traced the sign of the cross over Angela Maria's forehead. She began smiling and waving and clapping her hands as if applauding.

Then Angela Maria began laughing and kicking and trying to wriggle away as if being tickled. Judith noticed first since she was holding the baby.

The priest applied two oils to Angela Maria's forehead. Then he called the sponsors to take the baptismal vows.

The priest began pouring holy water over the baby's head at the baptismal font, saying, "I baptize you in the name of the Father."

Instead of crying, the baby began smiling and then laughing out loud. From her reactions, she seemed to be responding to someone.

Sam and the priest began to smile at the baby's antics. Then Father O'Riley and Sister Pastora began chuckling, wondering what was so amusing to the baby.

The priest poured more water over the baby, saying, "I baptize you in the name of the Son."

Angela Maria literally shrieked for joy and then began a laughing spree. She seemed to be communicating with someone out of sight. Ceren, Justin, and the congregation could not help but join in the baby's joy, chuckling and murmuring amongst themselves.

The priest poured more water over the baby, saying, "I baptize you in the name of the Holy Spirit."

The baby's peals of laughter filled the baptistery. It appeared to all that she was looking at something behind the priest that made her laugh and kick her tiny feet for joy. Judith had her hands full holding onto the wriggling, giggling baby and passed her to Sam. Everyone looked behind the priest's shoulder but saw nothing except the window.

Then, for a moment, the sunlight streamed through the stained-glass window and backlit a figure. Only three people saw anything except the light.

Jaw slack, Judith saw the giggling girl in her bright, white, Mexican wedding gown, laughing and making faces to amuse the baby.

Eyes wide with amazement, Ceren saw the wrinkled woman in her skull necklace. As she moved, her snake belt and snake armband seemed to undulate, mesmerizing the baby.

Ceren flinched and drew in her breath. Justin turned toward her, his eyebrows raised quizzically. With a half-smile and subtle shake of her head, Ceren indicated nothing was wrong. Justin splayed his fingers to link with hers as he gave her hand a reassuring squeeze.

Apparently unaware of anything except Angela Maria's gleeful laughter, the priest continued with the ceremony, wrapping the shawl around the baby, signifying she put on Christ in baptism. Finally, Father O'Riley handed the baptismal candle to the parents, representing the one true light of Christ.

The priest addressed the congregation. "Please welcome Angela Maria Brannon."

Tears streamed down Ceren's cheeks as the people applauded and cheered at the joy-filled baby, who laughed at the cold, baptismal water poured over her head.

Instead of clapping, Pastora crossed herself in the presence of what she saw: an angel with immense wings so white, they appeared nearly transparent. Standing guard, captivating the baby's attention, quietly keeping watch, the image lingered in the streaming light.

Pastora blinked, gazing into the window's bright glare, and the angel vanished like a shadow. A dove fluttered in its place. White feathers gleaming in the bright sunlight, it spread its wings wide, gracefully soaring toward the baby.

As if given a signal, the congregation stopped clapping and went into suspended animation. No one moved. Other than the echoing resonance of the applause, the baptistery went silent. Mouths parted in wonder, all eyes watched as the dove descended, swooping toward the baptismal font. Alighting on its rim, the dove folded its wings and dipped its beak in the holy water.

"Friends, if I could have your attention," said the priest, holding up his arms as if giving a benediction. A chuckle escaped his lips. "My sisters and brothers, what you witnessed may not be all it appears."

He lowered his arms and smiled. "Yesterday, a bird flew into the baptistery but couldn't find its way out. Trapped inside overnight without water, it must have perched in the rafters. My guess is the applause woke it, and, when it saw the baptismal font uncovered, instinct guided it to water."

He chuckled. "Rather than a miracle, what you witnessed was a bird getting a drink." As if on cue, the bird lifted off the font and took flight. "Ushers, please open the doors. Let God's creature find its way out."

The congregation erupted with relieved chatter and muffled laughter, ignoring the bird's passage, while each person interpreted the event to their neighbor. Only three remained awed. Ceren swiveled in her seat, craning her neck to watch the dove, while Judith and Pastora stood transfixed, staring until it disappeared from sight.

Judith turned to Pastora, her jaw slack, her eyebrow raised quizzically.

In answer, Pastora quoted in a hushed voice. "His appearance was like lightning and his clothing was white as snow."

Epilogue: High Ten, Amen, and Yes

"A woman uses her intelligence to find reasons to support her intuition."

~ G.K. Chesterton

"Can I please wear your wedding dress for First Communion?" begged Angela, hands folded dramatically. "Puh-leeeeze?"

The missing baby tooth caused a slight lisp, so it sounded more like *Puh-leeeeth*. Amused by her daughter's histrionics, Judith chuckled and shook her head, wondering where seven years had gone.

Angela's dark eyes snapped and sparkled with excitement as she looked from the wedding photograph to her mother. Her luxuriant, dark hair, swaying with every movement, hung to the middle of her back. Her face animated, she tried again.

"Please, Mom? Puh-leeeeze?" Angela grinned impishly, showing a gap where her front tooth was missing.

"I guess we could have the dress resized to fit you," Judith sighed in resignation. It was difficult to say no when her daughter turned on the charm.

"Really? Thanks, Mom!" Angela wrapped her small arms around Judith's legs. "I love you!" She turned to look back at the wedding picture. "I love this dress." Then hugging tighter, she said, "But I love you more!"

"I love you, too," Judith said, kneeling to match Angela's height. She gave her a bear hug and then stood up. "Let's get the dress out of the back closet and then get you measured."

ॐ

On First-Communion Sunday, the front pews were reserved for the new communicants, with their families and friends seated in the pews behind them. Sam and Judith sat with Pastora.

"Where are they?" Pastora asked, looking behind to check the entrance.

"The Mass doesn't start for another five minutes." Sam inconspicuously glanced at his watch. "They'll make it," he said with forced assurance.

"After all, they are driving from Houston with two small children," said Judith.

"And Ceren's pregnant again," said Pastora.

"She is?!" Sam and Judith asked simultaneously.

"Rats," said Pastora, wincing, snapping her fingers. "That was supposed to be a secret."

"There she is," said Judith, waving to Ceren and her family to join them.

"Don't let on I told you," whispered Pastora.

"Mum's the word," said Sam, his eyes twinkling.

"You," said Judith, playfully tapping his shoulder.

The three moved over to make room in the pew. As Ceren, Justin, and their boys sat down, the organ music began.

Two-by-two, the long line of new communicants processed in, singing. The girls looked like miniature brides in white gowns and veils. The boys in white shirts and dark ties looked like little grooms, nervous faces, tight collars, and all. Though hands were folded demurely, each child's eyes danced in anticipation.

"There's Angela," said Sam, pointing her out. Seated on the aisle, he spotted her first.

Judith gasped. Eyes widening as Angela approached, Judith went pale.

"What?" asked Sam, his tone alarmed.

"That's . . . that's the girl," said Judith. She turned toward Ceren, and her startled nod confirmed it.

"What girl?" whispered Sam.

"The giggling girl I told you about in Mexico, the one at the basilica seven years ago." Judith slowly shook her head. "I never noticed until now. In my cut-down, Mexican wedding gown, Angela's the spitting image of *Tonantzin* or whoever that girl was."

Angela's eyes flashed as she passed them, and she grinned impishly. When she saw Ceren, her hands left their prayerful pose for an instant as she waved. Then she dutifully refolded them.

The children marched into the front pews, and the Mass began. All went smoothly until they filed to the altar after communion. The boys lined up on the top step. The shorter girls filed onto the next step, and the priest stood in front of them, his face level with theirs.

Quietly capturing the event on his camcorder, Sam focused on Angela, who stood obliquely off-center of the priest.

"Let us pray," said the priest, raising his arms for the prayer after communion.

Angela watched eagerly, caught up in the ceremony. As the prayer ended, while the priest's arms were still raised, she leapt up and slapped his hands in a spontaneous high ten.

"A-men!" she exclaimed, eyes dancing.

Her voice rang out over the parishioners' mumbled response. Heads turned. The congregants said their "Amen's" amid smiles and subdued laughter.

The priest stifled a chuckle as the youth leaders hurried the children off the altar and into their pews.

Judith laughed into Sam's jacket, trying to muffle it, while Angela beamed with sheer joy at her participation in First Communion.

Ceren and Justin couldn't stop chuckling, while their boys had a giggling fit.

"Caught the whole thing on video," Sam whispered, chortling.

They glanced sheepishly at Pastora, expecting a stern glare or reprimand. Instead, she was wiping tears from her eyes, struggling not to break into laughter.

ॐ

After Mass, the priest invited the congregation to a First-Communion reception in the church hall. As Sam took pictures of Angela and Pastora, Judith and Ceren found time to chat over coffee and cake.

"Angela Maria could be the giggling girl's twin," said Ceren.

"The resemblance is startling," said Judith. "Funny I never noticed it until this morning when she walked down the aisle in that white dress."

"I only saw the giggling girl once, briefly, that time in the museum," said Ceren, glancing at Justin eating with the boys. "But she appeared twice in my dreams, three times, if you count my pregnancy dream of a much younger girl."

"Really?" asked Judith. "Did she speak to you?"

"In the pregnancy dream, she only said, 'Hi,' as if seeing me for the first time," said Ceren. "I always felt she was a little messenger, announcing my pregnancy. The second dream was interrupted, but the third time she told me she was the daughter I carried."

"Wow!" Judith digested that, remembering her own dreams. "She also told me she was the daughter you carried, our little minx, Angela."

They smiled as they watched her race toward them, with Pastora several steps behind, panting.

"She's unique, all right," said Ceren, chuckling. "Did the giggling girl say anything else in your dream?"

"Yes," said Judith, "but I didn't interpret it correctly until later. She said she was *Inninantzin in huelneli Teotl Dios.*"

"Which means?"

"At first, I thought it meant Mother of the Great Truth, but a student brought it to my attention. Since *Teotl* means God in *Nahuatl* and *Dios* means God in Spanish, I researched it further. It means Mother of the True God."

"The True God," echoed Ceren thoughtfully. "Then her identity would depend on the interpretation."

"Or the interpreter," said Judith, warming to her favorite topic. "It's the title Our Lady of Guadalupe used to identify herself to Juan Diego."

"Given that introduction, the Aztecs would have thought the vision at Tepeyac was *Tonantzin*, while the Spanish thought it was Our Lady of Guadalupe," said Ceren. Raising her eyebrows, she inhaled. "My turn to say 'Wow'!"

"Her title's nuances summarize the book we published seven years ago," said Judith. "It's the basis for our original thesis question."

"That's right." Nodding, smiling wryly, Ceren asked rhetorically, "Is it *Tonantzin* or Our Lady of Guadalupe?"

Angela Maria ran up to them, hair and veil flying. Just inches from crashing into them, her rubber-soled shoes screeched to a halt on the tile floor.

"Yes!" she lisped, jutting out her chin, nodding emphatically.

Staring them straight in the eye, she looked from one woman to the other and back again. Then, apparently satisfied she had delivered her message, she giggled and bounded off, nearly bumping into Pastora, who was just approaching.

Astounded, the two women looked at each other, wondering if Angela had been making a point or making a joke. Since Pastora had not heard the question to Angela's answer, Judith rephrased it.

"So who have people been worshipping at Tepeyac for the past five hundred years?" she asked.

"No, not worshipping," said Pastora, shaking her head. "Venerating, people have been venerating the Mother of God. That's who." Then Pastora motioned to her purse hanging on Ceren's chair. "Hand me my bag, would you? I have something for you."

Ceren looked perplexed. "For me . . . why?"

Smiling mischievously, Pastora reached into her bag, pulled out a wrapped gift, and presented it. "On the occasion of your third pregnancy, I'd like you to have this."

Ceren tried to give her a reproving scowl, but it turned into an exasperated smile. "It's too early to make any announcement . . . anything could happen at this stage . . . and you really shouldn't have. This was supposed to have been our little secret."

Eyes twinkling, Pastora gave her little-girl grin. "Open it."

Ceren undid the wrappings, smiled, and turned the framed photo toward Judith.

"What is it?"

"I'd forgotten about this," Ceren said to Pastora. Then turning to Judith, she added, "This is Angela's sonogram, taken the day I got the results of the DNA test."

"I've never seen this before," said Judith.

"That's because she threw it in the trash," said Pastora. "I salvaged it and framed it."

Judith turned toward Ceren. "Why would you throw that away?"

"Aside from what was happening in my life then?" Ceren counted off the reasons on her fingers. "The doctor had just told me the fetus had Down syndrome. Jarek had deserted me, and I'd been fired. I had no husband, no job, and no way to support myself, let alone a baby. Besides that?" She sighed. "It's a flawed picture. Look at that white distortion in it."

"That's no distortion," said Pastora, catching Ceren's eye. "Judith, what does that white image in the corner look like to you?"

"I don't know, maybe the back of the uterine wall."

"See?" Ceren said to Pastora. "That's what I said the first time we looked at it."

"Look more closely. Doesn't it look like—"

"Judith," said Sam, fast approaching with a camera in his hands. "Oops, sorry, didn't mean to interrupt."

"No problem, what's up?"

"It's this new camera. I swear there's something wrong with the lenses. It's as if light's bouncing between them, creating artifacts. See these streaks?" He held out the camera and played back the last picture.

"I don't see anything," she said.

With an annoyed shake of his head, he clicked his teeth. "I didn't scroll back far enough. Here, here's one."

Judith looked in the camera's display and stiffened. "Are these light streaks in all the pictures?"

"No, only some."

"Can you play them back, one by one?" she asked.

"Sure, here's another one," he said, pausing for her to look "and another."

"Sam, do those light streaks only show up in pictures of Angela?"

"I hadn't thought about it. Let's see." He scrolled through the pictures slowly, scrutinizing them. His dark eyebrows nearly meeting, he nodded. "But only in pictures taken today. They don't show up in the pictures we took last night."

"Look at this photo Pastora just had framed for Ceren." Ceren handed it to him, while Judith turned the camera's display around for Ceren and Pastora to see. "Do you notice anything odd about the pictures Sam took today?"

Pastora crossed herself, while Ceren gasped.

"What is this photo," asked Sam, "a sonogram?"

Pastora nodded, a doting smile playing at the corner of her mouth. "That's the first picture ever taken of Angela."

"This is Angela?" Sam took another, longer look. He smiled, fondling the picture. Then, his puckered brow returned. "Let me see that camera again, would you?" He scrolled through the pictures once more, comparing the light streaks to the sonogram's anomaly. Finally, he turned toward the women, pointing at the irregularity. "What is this?"

"That's what we were just discussing. Ceren and I think it's uterine tissue or simply a distortion."

"As I recall, Pastora, you had another interpretation," said Ceren.

She smiled her little-girl grin. "Doesn't it look like an angel?"

"I have to admit there's a strong resemblance between the artifacts on the pictures I shot today and this ultrasound scan," said Sam, scratching his chin. "But let's keep this in perspective."

"Angela," called Judith, picking up the camera, "smile!" She snapped the shutter and waved. "Thank you." Finger still resting on the button, she turned to Ceren and Pastora. "Say cheese." They posed, and Judith captured it. Then they gathered around the display to compare the pictures.

"Ohmigosh," said Ceren, looking from one picture to the other. "It's the same image in every single picture of Angela."

"But not in photos of us or anyone else." Turning toward Sam, Judith shook her head. "I don't think there's anything wrong with the camera."

"There's got to be a logical explanation," said Sam, pressing different menu buttons, zooming in on the camera display's image.

"Now that you've enlarged it, the artifact *could* resemble a face," said Ceren, "but that's not possible, is it?"

"All things are possible with God," said Pastora, pointing. "Look, there are the eyes."

"And that could be a mouth," said Judith, indicating a dark area with her fingertip.

"It sounds farfetched, but . . . ." Leaving the thought unfinished, Ceren hunched her shoulders and shrugged.

Arching her eyebrow, Pastora said, "There are more things in Heaven and Earth . . . ."

"Than are dreamt of in your philosophy," finished Judith, nodding in agreement.

Angela's giggle rang out, and Judith's ears perked as she recognized the sound. Turning toward it, she gasped, and the others spun around to see. A shaft of sunlight shone through the window, drenching Angela in a bright, white light. Jaw slack, Judith's eyes widened as she recognized her as the giggling girl. Not a likeness, the original.

Ceren gasped in surprise and then, flinching, noticed a figure near Angela, an old woman wearing a snakeskin dress that rippled in the light.

As if she felt eyes watching her, the woman turned toward Ceren and greeted her with a wizened smile.

Ceren locked eyes with hers, recalling the first time she had heard of *Coatlicue*. On their drive to Puebla, Judith had described *Tonantzin* when she appeared as death, mentioning *Coatlicue's* skirt of writhing snakes. Ceren gave a nervous laugh. This is absurd.

She thought back to the first time she had met the old woman on Day of the Dead. *The woman had said the womb's a sacred space. Her words convinced me not to abort Angela. If anything, she was an advocate for life, not death.*

Yet the old woman's unwavering stare unnerved Ceren. *What's she doing here? And why now?*

Then Ceren's eyes lit up. "Sam, while the light's good, would you take a picture of Angela, capture the moment for us?"

With a nod, Sam pointed the camera, focused, and, with the old woman posing in the background, snapped the picture.

"Could I see that?"

"Sure." He held out the camera and played back the last picture, sharing the image.

"There's that same artifact again," he said, frowning, fingering the recurrent image.

Ceren smiled. The light streaked the photo in exactly the spot where the old woman stood, grinning. Ceren looked up and met the woman's eyes.

Angel?

As if reading her mind, the old woman waved as the light from the window shimmered and shifted, casting reflected shadows. Ceren waved back, but the woman had vanished.

End

About the Author

Born to rolling-stone parents who moved annually, Karen Hulene Bartell found her earliest companions as fictional friends in books. Paperbacks became her portable pals. Ghost stories kept her up at night . . . reading feverishly. The paranormal was her passion.

Wanderlust inherent, she enjoyed traveling, although loathed changing schools. Novels offered an imaginative escape.

An only child, she began writing her first novel at the age of nine, learning the joys of creating her own happy endings—usually including large families.

Professor emeritus from the University of Texas, Bartell and her husband live in the Texas Hill Country with four rescued cats she calls her "mews."

Connect with Me Online

Web site: KarenHuleneBartell.com

Facebook.com/KarenHuleneBartell

Twitter.com/KarenHuleneBart

LinkedIn.com/in/KarenHuleneBartell

Reading Group Guide for Sacred Choices

• Why is the title, *Sacred Choices*, significant? Why do/don't you like it? What would you have named *Sacred Choices?* Is the title a clue to the theme(s)?

• Did you enjoy *Sacred Choices?* Why/why not?

• What do you think *Sacred Choices* is essentially about? What's the main idea/theme?

• What other themes or subplots did *Sacred Choices* explore? Were they effectively explored? Were they plausible? Were the plot/subplots animated by using clichés or were they lifelike?

• Were any symbols used to reinforce the main ideas?

• Did the main plot pull you in, engage you immediately, or did it take a chapter or two for you to 'get into it'?

• Was *Sacred Choices* a 'page-turner,' that you couldn't put down, or did you take your time as you read it?

• What emotions did *Sacred Choices* elicit as you read it? Did you feel engrossed, distracted, entertained, disturbed, or a combination of emotions?

• What did you think of the structure and style of the writing? Was it one continuous story or was it a series of vignettes within a story's framework?

• What about the timeline? Was it chronological, or did flashbacks move from the present to the past and back again? Did that choice of timeline help/hinder the storyline?

• Was there a single point of view or did it shift between several characters? Why would Bartell have chosen this structure?

• Did the plot's complications surprise you? Or could you predict the twists/turns?

• What scene was the most pivotal for *Sacred Choices?* How do you think *Sacred Choices* would have changed had that scene not taken place?

• What scene resounded most with you personally . . . either positively or negatively? Why?

• Did any passage(s) seem insightful, even powerful?

• Did you find the dialog humorous . . . did it make you laugh? Was the dialog thought-provoking or poignant . . . did it make you cry? Was there a particular passage that stated *Sacred Choices'* theme?

• Did any of the characters' dialog 'speak' to you or provide any insight?

• Did the quotes at the beginning of the chapters 'set the tone' for the subsequent action? Which ones? How so?

• Have you ever experienced anything that was comparable to what occurred in *Sacred Choices?* How did you respond to it? How were you changed by it? Did you grow from the experience? Since it didn't kill you, how did it make you stronger?

• What caught you off-guard? What shocked, surprised, or startled you about *Sacred Choices?*

• Did you notice any cultural, traditional, gender, sexual, ethnic, or socioeconomic factors at play in *Sacred Choices?* If you did, how did it/they affect the characters?

• How realistic were the characterizations?

• Did any of the characters remind you of yourself or someone you know? How so?

• Did the characters' actions seem plausible? Why/why not?

• What motivated the characters' actions in *Sacred Choices?* What did the sub-characters want from the main character and what did the main character want with them?

• What were the dynamics between the characters? How did that affect their interactions?

• How did the way the characters envisioned themselves differ from the way others saw them? How did you see the various characters?

• How did the 'roles' of the various characters influence their interactions as sister, coworker, wife, mother, daughter, lover, and professional?

• Who was your favorite character? Why? Would you want to meet any of the characters? Which one(s)?

• If you had a least-favorite character you loved to hate, who was it and why?

• Was there a scene(s) or moment(s) where you disagreed with the choice(s) of any of the characters? What would you have done differently?

• If one of the characters made a decision with moral connotations, would you have made the same choice? Why/why not?

• Were the characters' actions justified? Did you admire or disapprove of their actions? Why?

• Ceren and Judith both had moments where they struggled with their faith. When was the last time your faith faltered? What helped you get through that time?

• What previous influence(s) in the characters' lives triggered their actions/reactions in *Sacred Choices?*

• Did *Sacred Choices* end the way you had anticipated? Was the ending appropriate? Was it satisfying? If so, why? If not, why and what would you change?

• Did the ending tie up any loose threads? If so, how?

• Did the characters develop or mature by the end of the book? If so, how? If not, what would have helped them grow? Did you relate to any one (or more) of the characters?

• Have you changed/reconsidered any views or broadened your perspective after reading *Sacred Choices?*

• What do you think will happen next to the main characters? If you had a crystal ball, would you foresee a sequel to *Sacred Choices?*

• Have you read any books that share similarities with this one? How does *Sacred Choices* hold up to them?

• What did you take away from *Sacred Choices?* Have you learned anything new or been exposed to different ideas about people or a certain part of the world?

• Did your opinion of *Sacred Choices* change as you read it? How? If you could ask Bartell a question, what would you ask?

• Would you recommend *Sacred Choices* to a friend?

Chocolate and Chilies Mexican Recipes

"God gave the angels wings, and He gave humans chocolate."

~ Anonymous

Molé Poblano (Meat Dish from Puebla)

Ingredients

    2 lb. fire-roasted Poblano chilies, purchased or roasted
    ½ lb. sesame seeds
    4 tbsp. olive oil, divided
    ½ lb. almonds
    ½ lb. peanuts
    6 plantains (or bananas)
    2 lb. raisins
    ½ lb. plum tomatoes
    ½ tsp. ground cinnamon
    ½ tsp. aniseeds
    2 oz. unsweetened Mexican chocolate, coarsely chopped
    4 turkey legs, pre-cooked

Directions

Purchase the chilies or roast on a grill or under the broiler until blackened, 5-6 minutes per side. Place in a plastic, food-storage bag. Seal and let steam for 15 to 20 minutes. Remove the chilies from the bag and rub off the skins. Then plump the Poblano chilies in water to cover. Reserve the water for later use.

Toast the sesame seeds in a dry sauté pan until golden brown and add to the food processor. In the same sauté pan, add half the olive oil and stir fry the almonds. Remove the almonds and add to the food processor. Sauté the peanuts. Remove the peanuts and add to the food processor. Sauté the plantains/bananas. Remove them and add to the food processor. Sauté the raisins in the remaining olive oil. Remove the raisins and add to the food processor. Sauté the tomatoes. Remove them and add to the food processor.

Process the sesame seeds, almonds, peanuts, bananas, raisins, tomatoes, Poblano chilies, and spices in the food processor. Thin the mixture to desired consistency with the left-over chili water. In a large saucepan, add the molé and simmer slowly for ten minutes to marry the flavors. Add the chocolate. When melted, add the pre-cooked turkey legs and simmer five minutes or until the turkey is heated through. Serves 4.

Chiles en Nogada (Stuffed Chili Peppers in Walnut Sauce)

Ingredients for Chilies

4 fire-roasted Poblano chilies, purchased or roasted

1 tbsp. vegetable oil

½ lb. beef, chopped (or ground)

½ medium yellow onion, coarsely chopped

3 cloves garlic, finely chopped

½ tsp. ground cinnamon

½ tsp. ground allspice

¼ tsp. dried thyme

¼ tsp. dried oregano

1 plum tomato, cored and coarsely chopped

1 medium green apple, peeled, cored, and chopped

¼ cup pecans, coarsely chopped

¼ cup dried apricots, coarsely chopped

¼ cup raisins, coarsely chopped

Salt and black pepper, to taste

Ingredients for Walnut Sauce

½ cup roasted walnuts, coarsely chopped

½ cup (4 ounces) cream cheese

½ cup sour cream

¼ cup milk, or to taste

¼ tsp. cinnamon

¼ tsp. salt, or to taste

Ingredients for Garnishes

Seeds from 1 ripe pomegranate

Cilantro, coarsely chopped

Directions

Purchase the chilies or roast on a grill or under the broiler until blackened, 5-6 minutes per side. Place in a plastic, food-storage bag. Seal and let steam for 15 to 20 minutes.

While the chilies are steaming, heat the oil and add the chopped beef. Sauté until lightly browned. Add the chopped onion and sauté until translucent, 3-5 minutes, and then stir in the garlic, cinnamon, allspice, thyme, and oregano. Add the chopped tomato, apple, pecans, apricots, and raisins. Season to taste. Stirring occasionally, sauté until blended and warmed through.

Remove the chilies from the bag and rub off the skins. Slice each chili lengthwise and remove the seeds and membranes. Divide the picadillo filling, and stuff each chili with one-quarter of the filling.

For the sauce, combine the walnuts in a blender with the cream cheese, sour cream, and milk. Blend until smooth. Add the cinnamon and salt. To thin the sauce, add more milk.

To serve, arrange one stuffed chili on each plate. Spoon walnut sauce over all. Garnish with pomegranate seeds and cilantro leaves. Serve warm or at room temperature. Serves 4.

Special Bonus!

Here's a free sample of Karen's companion novel, *Sacred Gift*, available at Pen-L.com, and in online and walk-in bookstores.

Everyone is gifted, but some never open their package.

HAPPY READERS:

Another grand slam for Karen Bartell. This story, set years later, gives us a glimpse into the life of the child from the first book, but also more back story on the three women from the first book. The story was woven like the strands of a tapestry. A tapestry I am anxious to know more about. Highly recommend.

~ MICHELE BREAUX-ROWLEY

This is a beautiful story of survival – rich with redemption, forgiveness, and love! It visits two of the choices women have when faced with unexpected pregnancies. Abortions can leave the mothers with feelings of guilt, anger, and bitterness. Choosing adoption can leave the mother with a different sense of heartbreak and loss. Characters alternate in the spotlight, but Angela is the hub, with her spiritual connections playing key roles in the story. At times the story drags, feeling more like a history lesson touching on Religion, Art, Architecture, and Solar Geometry in connection to Franciscan friars and their design of Mission churches in Texas hill country . . . it's informative and entertaining, with a positive ending. Hats off to Karen Bartell for a job well done!

~ LORI LEGER AT *IND'TALE MAGAZINE*

Sacred Gift crosses generations of choices, history, and religions, bringing to light a special message: We all make mistakes. Some can be fixed and some can't, but life goes on after death – here on earth and in heaven – and the choices we make in life may stay with us forever.

Judith and Ceren, who had made some choices of eternal significance, take the reader on an emotional roller coaster. Their choices brought grief and sorrows in their own lives and the lives of those close, and not so close to them, but ultimately they were the ones to carry the heavy burden. Pastora, a woman of faith, and Angela, a daughter who all her life has been in touch with spirits–help Judith and Ceren find peace with what they've done, and put the broken pieces of themselves back together. They also help those affected by Judith and Ceren's decisions to find their way around the debris through faith and trust that God has a plan for everyone.

~ ICA IOVA, AWARD-WINNING AUTHOR OF *UNSUNG VICTIMS*

EXCERPT FROM *SACRED GIFT*

Develyn's black-outlined eyes opened wide. Then she looked down, hiding what-ever slid through her mind. "I had a grandmother."

Angela smiled politely, thinking she was joking. "You mean your mother was older when she had you?" Nodding her head, she snickered. "I can relate."

"No, I mean I never knew my mother, never had a mother. My grand-parents raised me." She sipped from her straw.

"Why's that?"

She grimaced. "My grandparents only gave me a sketchy summary, no details. Basically, they said she died giving birth to me." She grunted. "It was like this forbidden topic. Every time I brought it up, my grandmother got teary-eyed and left the room."

"Did your grandfather ever talk to you about it?"

Develyn scoffed. "He'd just shake his head, sigh, and mumble things like, 'maybe when you're older.'"

Angela raised her eyebrows. "And I thought I had it rough."

"Why?"

Angela sighed, and then licked her lips. "I knew I was adopted. It was an open adoption, for heaven's sake. I grew up with two...*three*...mothers, but recently my birth mother told me she almost aborted me."

"No." Stopping, Develyn grabbed Angela by the shoulder and turned her so they faced. "You're serious?"

"Yeah." Angela grimaced. "Talk about wondering if you were wanted—"

Her eyes big, Develyn said, "I'm a survivor."

"A survivor of what?" Angela snickered, again thinking she was joking. "The Titanic?"

"No," she started slowly, keeping her eyes on her cup. "Abortion."

"What do you mean?"

She looked Angela in the eye. "My mother tried to abort me. The abortion failed. She died, and I survived."

Angela's jaw dropped. "Ohmigosh." She blinked. "Are you sure? I mean, how could you know—"

Develyn's lip curled. "My darling cousin told me one day, laid it right between my eyes in no uncertain terms." She caught Angela's eye.

Grimacing, Angela shook her head slowly. "Sorry."

Develyn tried to shrug it off. "To quote the tee-shirts, it is what it is." She looked away.

In step, they turned and walked in silence, each sipping her coke, each lost in her thoughts. People passed them. Tour boats floated by.

Finally, Angela asked, "Have you ever . . . communicated with your mother?"

"Like in séances or Ouija boards?" Develyn held up her hands, shaking them as if she were scared, then abruptly dropped them and made a sour face. "What do you think?"

Angela heard the sarcasm. It was hard to misinterpret. She raised her eyebrows and was ready to back off. Then shoulders slumping, she groaned. Taking Develyn by the elbow, she stopped her.

"Look, whether you want to believe me or not, there's someone here who'd like to speak to you."

Develyn's left eyebrow and lip curled. "Yeah, right." She started off, but Angela again caught her elbow.

"I'm serious."

"And I'm Cleopatra." Develyn smirked.

"Fine, you don't want to listen, that's your business." Angela sighed. "I tried. I'm done," she said to the night.

"Who are you talking to?"

"Nobody." She sullenly sipped her coke. Then she threw back her head and groaned. "Okay, but this is the last try."

"Who the hell are you talking to?" asked Develyn.

"Ginny." Angela grimaced. "She's asking if the name Ginny means anything to you." When she was met with silence, she peered at Develyn. "Does it?"

Develyn's eyes reminded Angela of an owl's. "You're not kidding, are you?"

"Who's Ginny?"

Develyn shook her head. "Ginny only to her family, Virginia was her name."

"All right, who is she?"

"My mother."

FIND SACRED GIFT AT YOUR FAVORITE BOOKSELLER OR AT
www.Pen-L.com/SacredGift.html